I0705567

DISTANT LANDS

BURDEN OF TRUTH

By KAREN T. LOCKRIDGE

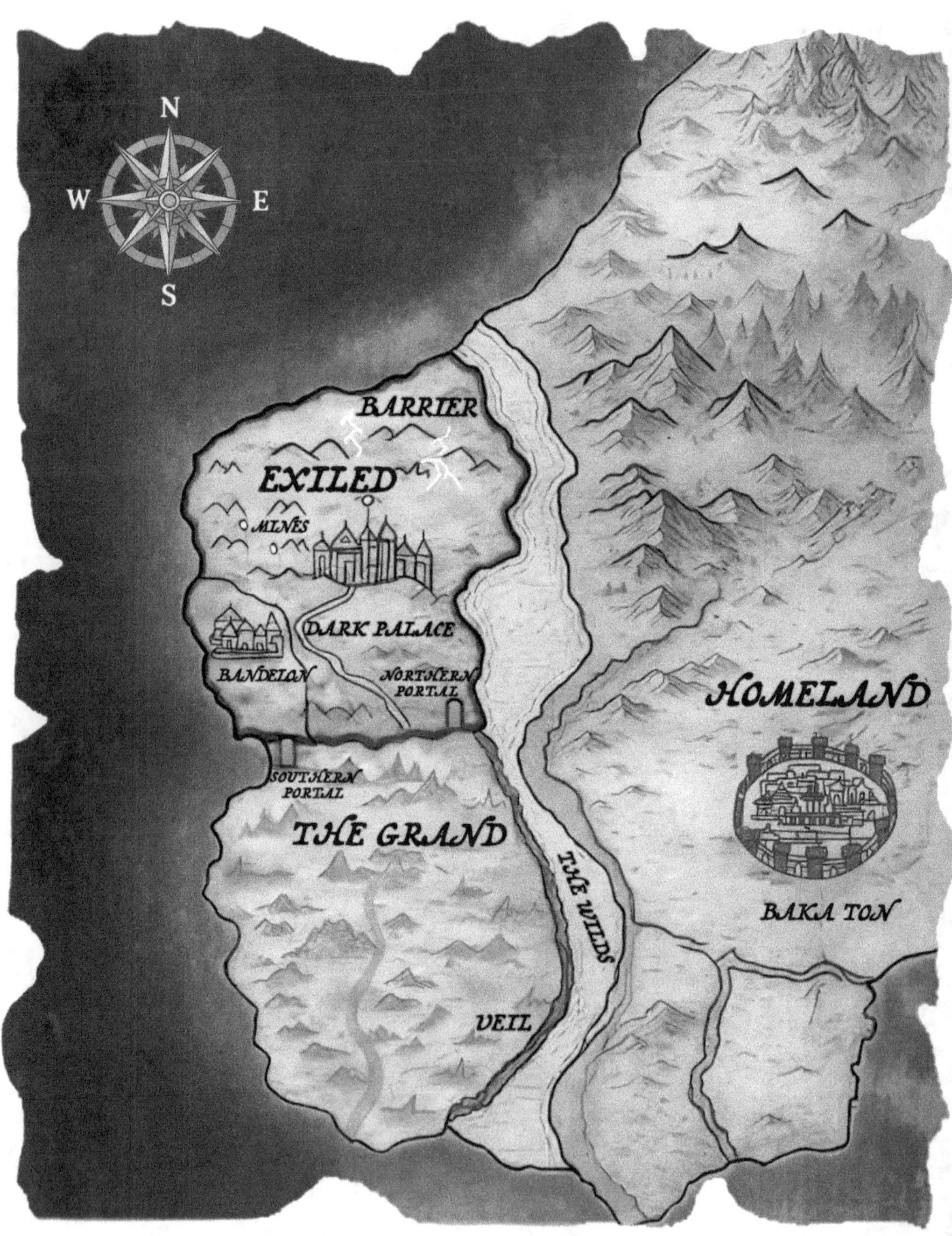

N
W
E
S
BARRIER
EXILED
MINES
DARK PALACE
BANDELON
NORTHERN PORTAL
SOUTHERN PORTAL
THE GRAND
THE WILDS
VEIL
HOMELAND
BAKA TON

Copyright © 2025 Karen T. Lockridge
All rights reserved.
ISBN: 979-8-89324-858-6
Printed in the United States of America.

No part of this publication shall be reproduced, transmitted, or sold in whole or in part in any form without the prior written consent of the author, except as provided by the United States of America copyright law. Any unauthorized usage of the text without express written permission of the publisher is a violation of the author's copyright and is illegal and punishable by law. All trademarks and registered trademarks appearing in this guide are the property of their respective owners.

The opinions expressed by the Author are not necessarily those held by the Publishers.

The information contained within this book is strictly for informational purposes. The material may include information, products, or services by third parties. As such, the Author and Publisher do not assume responsibility or liability for any third-party material or opinions. The publisher is not responsible for websites (or their content) that are not owned by the publisher. Readers are advised to do their own due diligence when it comes to making decisions.

DEDICATION

To those who have a story in their heart and need to share it.
And for those who allow me to share mine.

PREFACE

aves of heat drifted up from the desert floor, blurring the men working below. Heat so overwhelming, even the smallest breeze seemed mocking.

They moved slowly about their work, hauling rock and wooden support beams across the open area to the mine. Sweat poured off their bodies, and they moved as if in a hypnotic trance. No relief was awaiting them at the end of the day. The heat suffocated them in the darkness of the night as well.

Bodecia stood at the door of her tent, watching the workers pushing themselves to their tasks. She fanned herself with her straw hat, but it did little to bring any relief from the heat. Her body was wet with perspiration, just as those of the men below. In fact, she had just returned to her tent for relief from the blazing sun after working with the men to clear the opening of the mine.

How did a lady of the House of Lord Gwilim come to this?

Of course, she knew. Her heartbeat quickened as she thought of him. Balak!

Leaving this cursed land and her revenge on Balak kept her mind focused on this dreadful task. It drove her to near oblivion, thinking of the hate she felt for the man and the sweet promise of release from Exiled.

A scream brought her attention back to the men below. One of the workers had strayed beyond the safety of the work area and was being attacked by the hungry insects living in the scalding sand.

He was covered with them, biting and pulling chunks of flesh away from his body. He tried in vain to brush them away, but they had found their prey and were fast taking him to his knees.

He would be dead soon, with nothing left but a bony skeleton.

She sighed heavily. One less man to do this task. It could take weeks to get a replacement, and she had little time to waste. It was her only regret for the passing of a life.

Gold was the important thing. It was everything. She knew the true value of what she had and was sure to use it to her advantage. Nothing would stop her.

She sent shipments to both Gwilim and Andro. Both needed the gold for the same reason. Escape! It mattered little to her which one would make the golden tunnel through the Barrier, but she knew one of them would.

As she sat on top of the smoldering hill above the gold mine, she smiled to herself. The heat meant nothing, the death meant nothing, her suffering meant nothing. It was all about to end.

Now, all she needed to do was decide which of these men would better afford her freedom.

Chapter One

Before Blue left camp, she dressed as a man, a wool rag tied around her head to cover her new golden hair. Two men traveling would be less suspect than an old man and a young girl.

She caught up with Jep in a few hours. He sat on the side of the trail, watching as she approached, as if he had been expecting her to disobey Jack's orders all along.

He shook his head and smiled knowingly, "Well, you are a stubborn one, I will give you that! I cannot imagine disobedience being part of your education and programming."

"Doctor Salto said I must decide what was important to humans and what was not. I decided this was most important indeed."

"Just the same, she will have both our goats when we get back. You always stay close to me and listen and do everything I say."

Blue smiled as she followed the old wizard, remembering Doctor Salto standing on the ridge watching as she made her way to follow Jep.

Jep talked most of the night explaining what to expect when they reached the village. He had played the minstrel in many villages, so he knew what to look for when it came to acquiring information. He also knew how drunken soldiers acted around a young woman and gave the proper warnings on how to protect herself.

"We'll say you are my daughter, and we are looking to work for a few days until we can move on," explained Jep as he moved carefully along the slick trail. "Hopefully, those drunks will think twice before making any advances toward you."

"Your daughter," Blue grinned, "I suppose someone will believe that." She pulled and tugged at the scratchy wool rag covering her head.

Jep grinned as he looked at the pretty woman. "I suppose an ugly, old man like myself could be lucky enough to have a lovely daughter. Why, I knew a woman once so homely she made the flowers in a field dry up when she looked at them. Yet she bore three of the most beautiful girls I have ever seen. Men begged for their hands in marriage."

"How can that be? Are the children not brought from the parents?" asked Blue.

Jep smiled, "You would think so, but sometimes the Creator holds back his best surprises and showers them where least expected."

Blue gazed at the stars above, "What must it be like to be born to parents?" she whispered in wonder under her breath.

Jep walked on, pretending he did not hear and wishing his heart did not feel the pang of sadness for the creature.

They traveled throughout the night, only stopping once for Jep to take a breather. Animals had worn down the path they were traveling, so it made it much easier to travel, but they also worried the tracts could also be raiders moving up the mountainside toward their friends.

They reached the village by dawn and hid in the tree line to see what was happening inside. When Jep finally decided it was safe, they made their way through the back gate.

Jep told Blue the first order of business was to see she had proper clothes to wear. They scouted the little shops along the backside of the village and stopped into the first dress shop he could find.

The shopkeeper was a kind, chubby little woman who seemed overjoyed to have a man and his daughter visit her shop. She quickly found Blue a woolen, brown skirt and began to measure her for the hemming.

"It will not take but a minute, love," she said to Blue. "By the way, my name is Mrs. Lyn."

"We do appreciate your kindness, dear lady," smiled Jep. "My daughter was given the trousers by a kind man on the road. Her clothes were torn to pieces after she fell during the ice storm."

"Oh, you poor dear. I hope you were not hurt too badly," she said sympathetically. She looked curiously at the small, shiny silver triangles on the side of Blues face. "Of course, you will need a proper bonnet as well."

"Have you lived here long," asked Jep, hoping to draw her attention away from inspecting Blue.

"Oh, I have lived here all my life. Why, my parents owned this shop before me."

Jep decided Mrs. Lyn could prove to be a useful source of information. "We noticed a lot of soldiers in the village. Is that normal?"

"Bah, they show up from time to time. Animals! They make a terrible mess and cause all types of problems, but they bring money into the village, so some say it is worth the bother."

"Do they stay very long," he asked.

"Not usually. They have been here longer than usual, perhaps because of that terrible ice storm," she said, looking out of her small window. "If the truth be known, you would be better off moving on as soon as you can. We have been troubled more than usual by these men this trip." She lowered her voice to a whisper as if someone might be listening, "They can be very ruthless, especially for a lovely girl such as your daughter. Most of us make sure our doors are bolted, and we are safe in our homes before dark. This time, they brought some kind of beasts with them. Never did that before. We are more than a little worried, but what can we do? There are too many of them and too few of us."

Jep walked to the window while she continued to make the hem for Blue's skirt. She chatted away, hardly noticing Blue did little more than respond with a yes or no.

Jep watched the soldiers as they walked toward the main gate. He could just see through the gate at the army camp beyond. He wanted to get a closer look but decided he and Blue should try to find a good, busy tavern to start their search for Owyn. That is where Owyn would have started his investigation.

Within a few minutes, the skirt was hemmed.

Mrs. Lyn provided not only a sturdy wool cap, but also a good cotton under-cap that tied beneath the chin. "A good lady needs her head covered," cooed Mrs. Lyn, "to avoid catching her death of cold, and no need to be fancy about it. Not with this lot around."

As they made their way toward the center of the town, Blue pulled and tugged at her bonnet one minute and the skirt the next. "These clothes are too binding," she complained. "And they scratch the skin."

"We all have to make sacrifices," smiled Jep, pulling his colorful rag coat out of his travel pack, pushing his arms through the sleeves. "We will at least 'look' the part," and did a quick little dance in the middle of the street.

He stared at Blue for a moment, then reached down and grabbed a handful of dirt. He began to smear the mud on Blue's face to make her appear a little less attractive.

"I don't suppose you could alter your looks a bit." He asked as he turned his head, looking at Blue. "Shabby teeth, or something of the sort to make you. . . . less attractive.

Blue listened attentively, a look of concern on her face. "Do I offend you, Jep. It was my intent to be of help to you."

Jep smiled and answered, "It is alright, my dear one, you are more help than I could have imagined."

They visited several taverns around the village, asking for work. A few places needed a waitress, but no minstrel, and some needed a minstrel but no waitress. Blue tried to talk Jep into splitting up, but Jep declared Jetta would have his head if they did, so they kept trying.

Finally, they found a tavern quite a bit larger than others they had tried. The owner of the Crusty Hound was a dirty, sweaty man who was more than glad to hire them both. He said he had a spare room in the cellar they could share for sleeping.

He immediately put Blue to work, cleaning mugs and wiping down dirty tables. Jep, although an entertainer, was not spared other work and was told to douse the floor with soapy water and set up tables and chairs. It was a much-needed job since the place reeked of old alcohol and sweaty bodies. They worked most of the afternoon before the soldiers began to pour into the tavern.

Within a few hours, soldiers packed the tavern. Blue ran mugs of ale to every corner of the room. Jep was told to lend a hand until it was time for him to perform, so he strapped on an apron and pushed his way through the crowd, his hands full of mugs.

When they had a minute to spare, Jep pulled Blue aside, "Blue, listen for talk of a stranger coming through here a few days ago. Knowing Owyn, he made himself a bit obvious, so someone is bound to remember him. Just keep your ears open."

Blue thought it was a curious thing to say since she did not realize her ears were closed, and she briskly rubbed her ears.

They worked non-stop for most of the night. Jep performed his best songs and told his most adventurous tales. He even collected a few coins for his work. Each time he tried to sit and rest, the old tavern keeper would slap his head and scream for him to get to work.

Blue was behind the bar, filling mugs with warm ale, thinking about what they were going to do about Owyn. They would never find him if they had to stay here all night to serve this foul-smelling ale to these drunken soldiers.

Blue missed Owyn and his funny, crooked smiles. She remembered the time Owyn had given him the first ale he ever had and how silly it had made him feel. She remembered how hard Owyn laughed when he sang the Fox and the Rabbit. Smiling to herself, she began to sing it again softly to herself.

"Hey, wha's that ya singin', lass?" slurred a toothless old drunk.

Blue looked up and give him a quick smile, "A song I used to sing with my friends a long time ago."

"I heard that song before." He said, scratching his dirty head. "Yeah, it was that funny little guy a while back. Remember him, Jaspas?"

"Ho, yeah, I kind of liked the little bugger. What wus his name, Stell?"

"Aw, I don' member. But I member Commander Voxx takin' him outta here by his coat tails."

Both men shuddered and gave a frightened shake of their heads. "Poor fella," one of them muttered.

Blue furiously tried to get Jep's attention across the barroom. He finally noticed and hurriedly made his way through the crowded room.

"They just said they saw a young man here several nights ago who was dragged out of here by a Commander Voxx," Blue hurriedly explained in a whisper, just as she spotted the tavern owner headed her way.

"See what else you can find out," she called over her shoulder as she grabbed both fists full of mugs of ale and began making her way across the room.

Jep turned to look around the bar trying to decide which men she was talking about. The bar was full of men. Which ones was she referring to?

He looked toward her helplessly, shrugging his shoulders. Blue saw his confusion at not knowing which men to seek out, so she pointed to her teeth, hoping he would understand.

From behind him, Jep heard, "Oden, no, it was Own, wadn't that right, Jaspas?"

"Owyn, his name was Owyn; funny lad," he said leaning forward on the bar, shaking his head.

Jep scooted closer to the two men. "Yeah, I saw the same guy that night. He was a funny one. What did that fellow, Voxx, want with him anyway?"

"Shhhh..." Stell warned, "that not jus any fellow. Thas Commander Voxx. He's the Commander of our troops. Gwilim's main man."

Jep's heart shuddered to be so close to people who served Gwilim. These drunken men looked like any other drunken soldiers, more or less. Some were human enough, while others bore resemblance to beings he did not recognize. He had to remind himself they were all ruthless butchers.

"What do you think he wanted with that young fella anyway?" he asked.

"What do you want at know for?" growled Jaspas as he drooled ale down the front of his shirt.

"What else do we have to talk about?" smiled Jep in his friendliest smile.

Both men began to laugh loudly and slapped Jep on the back. "Thas the truth!" they laughed as sloshing their drinks on the bar and the floor.

"So," Jep continued, "what do you think happened to the poor fella, that Owyn?"

"Took him to the holding building, I suspect. Where they take people for *questioning*," offered Stell. He swayed heavily, and Jep worried if he were to get any more information from these two, he had better work fast before they both passed out.

"Poor guy," Jep said, hoping his sympathetic nature would keep them talking.

Blue returned, listening to the conversation. She quickly filled fresh mugs for the two, "I didn't think there was a building so large in the village," she innocently smiled and gave them a flirtatious stare. The two drunks grinned foolishly back at the pretty maid.

"Voxx uses the old supply building in the rear of the village square. Keeps it guarded all the time. Won't even let most of us near. He is a mean one, that one. Kill you for a thought," said Jaspas smiling shyly at Blue.

Blue and Jep shot a look at one another. That was it! They both nodded and began to move away from the two drunks. "Hey, where ya's going? Are we done talking?" yelled Stell as they moved away.

"We must complete our work," Jep yelled, pulling Blue through the crowd toward the rear exit and into the ally. With a slam of the big door, they left the noise of the bar behind.

"We need to get going now before anyone starts looking for us, too," warned Jep. If they found out who Owyn was, they may also be suspicious of us.

Blue nodded just as the fat tavern owner came bursting through the back door, yelling, "What do you two think you are doing? Get yourselves back inside and get to work! I'm not paying you to come out here and...."

"We do not have time for this," growled Jep, lifting his hand and placing it on the man's head. Immediately, the man's eyes glazed over, and his mouth sagged open.

"You do not need us. You have all the help you need inside. You will go back inside and busy yourself and leave us alone," suggested Jep, weaving a memory spell.

The fat tavern owner blinked his eyes, then slowly turned and walked back into the crowded tavern.

Blue looked at Jep and smiled, "That was very enjoyable. Why can not you use that skill more often?"

"Any use of my power almost depletes me for a while. Hopefully I have retained a bit for rescuing Owyn."

They began to work their way toward the back of the village where the supply building was located. Soldiers were everywhere, drinking and gambling in the streets. They called and whistled at Blue as they hurried along their way.

From the tavern behind them, a voice began shouting.

"There, there they go," yelled a voice coming from the Crusty Hound. They turned to see Jaspas pointing toward them, and several soldiers began running in their direction.

"This way," yelled Jep darting down a nearby ally. They cut between houses and doubled back toward the back of the village toward the supply building. They crossed streets and changed directions, trying to lose the raiders. As they tried to catch their breath in a doorway, they spotted a group of soldiers making their way directly toward them.

Jep spotted an old barn nearby and pulled Blue inside. He pushed her behind him into a dark corner. He peered outside to see the soldiers searching nearby buildings around them.

"Keep against the wall and cover yourself with straw until they pass," he whispered. He turned to Blue and froze, his eyes opening wide.

"Jep, what is it?" cried Blue, ducking to avoid whatever caused him to alarm.

"Your hair," he stammered, "it's glowing."

"What?"

"Glowing! Like a light; a <u>bright</u> light. Blue, they will see your hair from across the street!"

Blue grabbed her head, and found her cap was missing, "But it is golden, like the woman at the tavern in Serenity."

"I would think not exactly like hers. Quick, find something to cover your head!" He peeked outside and saw the soldiers quickly approaching their hiding place.

They grabbed everything they could find to try to cover Blue's glowing head, with no avail. Outside, he heard the voices of the soldiers closing in. Finally, Jep spotted an old oil cloth used to cover supplies in rainy weather. He tossed it over Blue's head and, pushed her into a heap against the side of a wagon, and pushed himself against the barn wall, throwing handfuls of straw over himself just as the soldiers began to enter the dark barn. He wished again his magic were stronger so he could weave a spell to protect them, but the spell he had used on the tavern owner had weakened his power.

He thought there were three of them and held his breath as they moved farther inside the barn. They took a quick look around, then hurried out of the barn and moved on to the next building.

Jep sat up, brushed the straw away from his clothes, then crawled to the wagon. He pulled away the oilcloth from Blue's head and helped her stand. "We are going to have to split up. I will make a distraction, and you make your way to the supply building. I'll keep them busy as long as I can. You will find Owyn. If you can, free him. Otherwise, wait for me at the supply barn and I will hurry there to help you.

Jep knew Blue had a good head when it came to directions and was more than capable of manhandling a few soldiers. She was incredibly strong and fast. She was the right person to go after Owyn.

Jep looked out of the barn door and saw the soldiers making their way down another street. "Go," he said, "and find something to cover your head!" Jep rushed from the barn and headed toward an alley across the square.

Blue looked around until she found some old rags and bundled and twisted them around her head, hiding her glowing locks.

She took the closest street leading to the back of the village. Several times, she hid in doorways and alleys to avoid soldiers. She was not sure if they were looking for her and Jep, but she did not have time to worry about them.

Finally, she spotted the large supply building. Several wagons were lined up along one side, some still filled with goods waiting to be unloaded. Four soldiers stood talking in the opening at the front of the big building.

She crouched down in a nearby doorway, thinking of ways to get past them, when suddenly, a large explosion a few streets away rocked the buildings, knocking mortar and roof tiles onto the streets below.

Blue smiled as she recognized Jep's handiwork and watched as the soldiers rushed to investigate.

She quickly crossed the receiving area in front of the building and hid next to the supply wagons parked along one side of the building. She felt well protected by the shadows and wagons. Slowly, she made her way along the side of the building, looking for a place where she could see inside. Finally, she found a place where some boards were broken and pulled apart, allowing her to get a fair view of the area inside.

Several men inside paced back and forth, barking at one another as if they were arguing.

"Well, what was it?" a loud voice snarled as the four soldiers guarding the building returned.

"Some idiots set fire to a keg of brandy blew up a whole wagon," one reported. "Don't think any of our guys were hurt."

"Go, go on then, and do your jobs. I have my own work to do," he yelled at the men, and they scurried back to their posts.

The large man in the center of the room wore the uniform of a commander. Unlike some of the soldiers on the street, he wore a battle uniform. He was a huge man beyond any Blue had seen before. His muscular body looked as solid as a rock, and from what she could see and hear, all the men with him feared him and scuffled nervously when he approached.

Commander Voxx struck the side of his leg with a thick leather strap which had small metal disks dangling from it. He paced silently back and forth near the opening where Blue lay watching.

"Wake him! I cannot wait here all day!" he shouted.

One of the men picked up a bucket and tossed the water at a nearby chair.

Voxx moved away from the opening, allowing Blue a better look into the barn.

At first, she did not recognize him. At first, she did not recognize it was a man at all. But finally, as he lifted his head toward Voxx, she saw the crooked smile that was Owyn's.

She felt her heart stop as she stared at the battered man sitting in the center of the room. His face was bloody and bruised. His eyes were almost completely swollen and closed, and the front of his shirt was blood-soaked.

"Good morning' Commander. Have a good night's sleep?" greeted Owyn.

Voxx lifted the heavy leather strap and struck Owyn directly across his swollen face.

Owyn yelled out in pain, then turned back to Voxx and smiled, "<u>Not</u> a good night's sleep then?"

Voxx stared at Owyn with such hate that Blue was sure he was about to strike Owyn again. "You seem to think you are quite a jester, but I assure you, I have no sense of humor. I will be here all day, again, if I need to be in order to get the information I want."

Owyn hung his head, and Blue could see he had very little strength left in him. She knew if he had been beaten and starved for the past days, his life was slowly ebbing away.

Her mind was in a whirl, trying to calculate the possibilities of what could be done to rescue him. There were four guards at the front of the building and four men standing around Owyn. She knew she could manage at least three of the men, but Voxx looked as if he were a very formidable opponent.

She began desperately looking around the inside of the building to see if there was another entrance. She spotted a loft which ran above one side and over the front of the building. On the loft, she saw a pulley with a rope attached to a large frame, probably used to lift heavy loads from the wagons brought in for unloading.

She watched as Voxx continued to scream questions at Owyn, "I ask you again, little man, where in the Valley of Shadows are you planning to meet with Doctor Westin? You can spare yourself anymore pain if you will just answer me."

Again, Owyn looked up and gave the man his crooked smile and shook his head.

Voxx struck out with his leather strap, this time hitting Owyn square in the chest. The breath was knocked from him, and he threw his head back, gasping for air. The shirt he was wearing was torn away, and Blue could see huge black and blue marks covering his chest and stomach.

She had to help Owyn!

She worked her way around the back of the building, looking for another opening, but found nothing that would give her access inside. The other outside wall was well lit by torches and afforded her no safe way to find an entrance.

Each time she heard the leather strap strike she became increasingly desperate, and she realized her face was wet with tears. "Owyn!" her heart screamed. "Hold on, I am coming!"

She worked her way back to the side of the building where she was hidden by the wagons. As she backed away a little, looking up, she could see an opening at the top where the loft was located. Blue thought it was used as a ventilation door to keep the supplies from getting too hot.

A long rope was strung between the warehouse and a small house next door. Most likely, it was used to hang the family's wet laundry. The wagons sitting below just might give her a little footing, if she could use the rope to climb into the opening above.

She crept behind the last wagon and made her way to the little house next door. When she reached the back of the house, she gave the door a hard shove. It broke from its' lock with a snap and opened.

Working her way through the house, she tried to recall exactly where the rope would be located. She rushed through the main room of the house and saw a woman and her two children crouched in the corner. The mother had her arms around her children and cried out in fear as Blue entered the room.

"Do not worry," Blue whispered, trying to console the woman, "I will not hurt you. Please be very quiet. I need to go into the building next door. Please do not make a sound."

The woman slowly nodded her head looking at Blue, "Are you going to try to help the poor man they have over there?"

Blue nodded. "He is my friend. I must try to save him before they kill him. Will you help me?"

The woman looked at her children and then at Blue. She stood and hurried her children to a bed nearby and told them to keep quiet. She turned to Blue, "What do you want me to do?"

Blue explained she wanted to get to the loft next door and needed the use of her clothesline to climb up. "The woman nodded then offered, "I will cut the rope from my window and let it drop to the ground. I am sorry I do not have weapons for you, but please help that poor man. We have heard his screams for many days. They have no right to harm anyone like that."

Blue placed her hand on the woman's shoulder and gave it a friendly squeeze. "The Creator will bless you for your help."

The woman smiled and said, "Just as long as he removes these animals from Harmony, it will be blessing enough." She rushed up the stairs then turned once again, "Please destroy the rope when you are finished so they will not be able to find out how you entered."

Blue nodded and quickly headed out of the back of the house, relieved to find someone to help her.

She stopped below the window and caught the rope before it struck a wagon and drew the attention of the guards. The woman looked out to make sure Blue had the rope, then gave her a small wave and closed the window shutters.

Blue took a quick look around the front wagon to make sure the guards were occupied, and when she was satisfied they would not be a threat, quickly grabbed the rope and took up the slack. She climbed onto the wagon just beneath the window. She was only a few feet beneath it but too far to reach the opening. She placed her feet on the side of the barn, testing her weight against the rope. She hung there for a minute, then began walking herself up the side of the wall, pulling her weight, hand over hand. Slowly, so not to make any noise, she finally made it to the opening and stepped into the loft. She quickly untied the rope from the top of the window, as she had promised the woman, and coiled the rope around her arm, looking across the ally. The woman was standing at the window, peeking through the shutter. She smiled and gave Blue a wave.

Blue looked around the loft and saw it was stacked with barrels, bales of hay, and all sorts of bolts of cloth and other supplies. She stepped carefully onto the flooring to make sure she did not make any noticeable noise but decided it best to crawl on her belly to be sure.

She made her way to the front of the loft, where she could get a view of the scene below. She saw the men lined up around Owyn, with Voxx pacing back and forth. Owyn's head was leaning on his chest, and Blue worried he was unconscious again. The men were arguing with Voxx, and several times he charged at them, as if he intended to harm them also.

"If you kill him before we find out Westin's location in the Valley of Shadows, then we'll never find him!" one of the men argued. "That place is a maze."

"He is right, Commander, he has had all he can take. Let him get some of his strength back, then you can begin his questioning again. You have been at questioning him for days," added another.

Voxx grit his teeth, glaring at the men around him. "I have been doing this since before you were sucklings. I think I know how to question a prisoner without your advice! If you do not have the stomach for it, leave!"

The men shook their heads, and one of them began again, "You know we are not bothered by blood; we have been a part of much worse than this. But, if you kill this man, you also kill our chances of locating Westin. I, for one, do not want to face Gwilim with that news!"

Voxx grabbed the man by his throat and growled, "Are you threatening me, Chambers?"

The man glared back into Voxx' face and hissed, "Balak is the one who threatens you, Voxx, not me. He is the one trying to take your place at Gwilim's table. We will not have you endanger our lives because of your blood thirst!"

Voxx pushed the man to the ground, glaring wildly over him. He walked over to Owyn who still sat with his head leaning against his chest. He reached down and grabbed something from Owyn's neck and gave it a quick snap. He held up the gold-capped bear tooth Owyn wore for good luck. "This will make a good souvenir for a friend of mine; in payment for services well done!"

Voxx turned to the men and barked, "Very well, we will give him a few hours to rest. But know I will get the information I want from him!" He closed his fists around the bear tooth and stormed out of the building.

Blue heard the men talking among themselves below her. By their voices, she could tell they hated Voxx and worried for their own lives. They did not care what happened to Owyn afterwards, but they had to keep him alive until he gave Voxx the information. One of the men walked back over to Owyn and poured more water over his head. "You're a tough little bugger, I'll give ya' that," he said.

Owyn shook his head slowly and looked up at the man. "Is it bath time again?"

The man stared at Owyn and sighed, "You are a likable sort, but you know he is going to kill you, do you not?"

Owyn looked at the man and nodded.

One of the other men walked forward, "If you tell him what he wants to know, we will make sure it is quick. You have our word as soldiers. You have fought a hard fight, we respect that in a man. But now it is time to be done with it and face your Maker."

Owyn looked at the floor as he asked, "Why do you do these things? You men do not seem like animals, yet you allow him to treat you as such. Why?"

Chambers looked at Owyn, then at the other two men before answering, "We are soldiers, and we do as we are ordered. No better and no worse than any other."

"Owyn pulled his head up and looked at the man, "I know this man, Balak, you spoke of. He was from my land. He is a traitor and a butcher, and he has ordered you to be butchers as well. He is destroying his own people and his own land. Do you think he has any loyalty to you? He will deal with you in the same way. Is he worth your allegiance?"

Chambers stood looking at Owyn for several minutes, then answered, "You think we have a choice. We do not. Gwilim holds our very souls in his hands. He holds the souls of all his men."

Owyn frowned as he tried to understand, "How can he hold your souls? A man's soul is his own."

One of the other men stepped beside Chambers, "We do not have to tell this man anything. Why bother anyway, he will be dead by tomorrow eve."

Chambers turned to look at the man and answered, "Because I need to say it. Out loud. I need to remember why, or else we are no different than Voxx." He looked back at Owyn. "Gwilim holds the souls of our families. Not just their lives but also their souls. He knows a man will fight harder for his family than for his own life, so he holds them hostage against us. That is why we blindly obey his and Balak's every command. Not to obey means eternal death to our loved ones."

Blue sat in the shadows of the loft, listening. Her mind began to think back to her questions to Dr. Salto about good and evil. She had a hard time understanding why some things were considered evil at one time and not evil at another, such as their killing of Gwilim's men over their killing of the Homelanders. Blue knew Gwilim was evil, and if Balak was at his side, then he was evil too. Looking at the treatment of Owyn, she knew Voxx was also evil, but she felt a sorrow for the men standing around Owyn. In a way, they were prisoners as well.

Owyn shared her thoughts as he looked into the eyes of the men and said, "Then you need to get rid of Gwilim."

None of the men answered but slowly turned and walked out of the building.

Owyn watched them go and sat painfully, trying to catch his breath.

When she was sure the men were gone, Blue stood slowly from her hiding place so Owyn could see her.

He stared up at the young woman in the loft in shock. He then whispered, "Girl, what are you doing here? If they find you, you are as good as dead. Go while you can."

Blue slowly turned her head, hoping his eyesight had not been damaged. When the light from the torches flashed on the shiny silver triangles on the side of her head, she heard Owyn gasp.

"Blue? Is that you?"

"Shhhhh...," Blue hissed. "Jep is out there somewhere. We have come to get you out of here."

Owyn grinned and shook his head. "No, it is too late for me. They have torn me up pretty bad. You and Jep need to get back to the others and warn them. They know we are here, looking for Westin."

Blue hurried to the pulley at the top of the loft and lowered herself to the floor. She was greatly relieved to find the caretaker of the building had kept it greased so it did not make a noise. When her feet touched the floor, she ran and hid behind a stack of barrels."

"We are not leaving without you, Owyn!" she hissed.

"Hey, you make a pretty good-looking girl," flirted Owen as he gasped for gulps of air.

Blue had forgotten Owyn had not seen her as a woman. She smiled back at her friend. "It is just temporary," she said.

"There is another thing," he added, "I heard Voxx tell his men the Veil has fallen. He said they would not have to worry about being left in the Homeland to die anymore. They could stay there forever."

Blue felt panic building inside her as she listened. The Veil down! The Homeland was now open to raids at any time. She knew Stevien must be warned as soon as possible.

Blue stuck her head from around the barrels to see if any of the men were within sight. When she felt it was safe, she began working her way to Owyn. There were stacks of barrels near him, hiding her until she was right next to him.

"Blue," Owyn begged weakly, "Please, you must get out of here. Go, find Jep, and get back to Jack. He needs to know what is going on. Somehow, they know our every move, always have."

Blue reached out from behind Owyn and began to untie his hands. The ropes were bloody from his struggling, and she had a tough time loosening them. At last, his hands were free, and she crept around to try to untie his feet. She looked toward the open front of the building to make sure no one was coming. When she was satisfied it was safe, she untied the ropes.

Owyn was so weak he could not lift himself from the chair. Blue put all her weight under his arms and pulled him to his feet. "We must move now, Owyn. Can you help at all?" she asked.

"Well, now," Voxx' voice roared. "It seems a lovely lady has joined our little party."

Blue looked up to see Voxx and his men standing in the doorway.

Chapter Two

"Quoto just rode in; that makes all our scouts returned. We should gather everyone and decide what to do now," reported Soulo.

"Right, let the men know we will meet right after we eat in my tent," answered Jack, looking down at the valley below.

Soulo agreed to let everyone know about the meeting. He watched Jack with a look of concern. He knew the loss of three of his friends weighed heavy on him. He noticed the wild man, Luka, sitting nearby and shot him his usual look of disgust, then walked back to his men.

Luka made a sucking sound as he cleaned dinner from his teeth, "I do not believe the man likes me," he observed.

"He has nothing against you personally, he is a military man. Your way of life seems frivolous to him compared to the hard, defined life of a soldier," explained Jack.

"Well, if he thinks my life is easy, I would like to have him travel with me for a while. At least *his* food is cooked before he eats it."

Jetta turned her head in distaste at the thought.

"Sorry, ma'am," he offered. "I sometimes forget my manners. My wives do not give it a second thought."

After the men were fed, Jack and Zi walked to their tent to meet with Soulo's scouts. The men were eager to hear the report and were curious as to their next move. Jack knew they were all worried over the delay of Owyn's return.

They filed into the tent, sitting on the ground or leaning against boxes or barrels of supplies. The scouts looked weary and ready for a full night's sleep.

"Glad to have everyone back," said Jack. "Quoto, you gave us a bit of a scare, coming in so late. Did you see any signs of Owyn on your way back?

Quoto looked around the tent and shook his head, "No, have not seen him since he left here a week ago. The trails are getting treacherous, he may have been forced to take a different route back."

Jack nodded thoughtfully. "We have been holding off meeting up with Doctor Westin to see what the raiders were going to do. We hoped they had lost the scent of their group and be forced to search for him the hard way. We would then have the advantage over them. But first, we needed to make sure we were not being watched or followed. The last thing we want to do is to lead them to Westin. That is why we have asked you to check the areas ahead and around us. We need to make sure we are not being observed.

"We must reach Westin and his group as soon as possible. The weather has been a big factor in slowing us down, but we will have to push as quickly as we can to reach him before that army does."

Soulo took up the discussion, "We will need to keep up the scouting assignments to make sure no one follows our tracks. You men have done a great job so far, and I have no doubt you will continue to provide your best. I will be making new scouting assignments before morning."

"When will we be leaving to meet up with Westin?" asked Quoto.

"We want to give Owyn a little more time to catch up with us. Hopefully, we will be able to leave tomorrow," answered Jack.

"But, if time is important, we need to go ahead and start making our way," said Quoto. "The trails are getting worse, so the sooner we move, the better off we will be."

He walked to the map table and pointed at a location on the map, "It will take us a good three days of hard travel to reach the Valley of Shadows, so Owyn will have plenty of time to catch up, and we can take advantage of the weather while we can."

Jack suddenly stiffened and looked at Quoto. He stared without moving for what seemed like minutes. The group became deathly quiet, alarmed by Jack's sudden silence.

Concerned, Zi walked over to Jack and placed his hand on his shoulder, "Jack, are you alright?"

Jack looked up, and Zi's heart pounded heavily at the look on Jack's face. He had never seen that look before, and a fearful dread fell over him.

"Yes, ... I...," he stammered for words, rubbing his hands over his face, "I am just a little tired. Could... we meet again a little later?"

Soulo looked worriedly at Jack, then quickly dismissed his men, shooing them out of tent.

"Is he alright?" asked Quoto, standing at the tent's opening.

"Yeah, I think he is just worried about Owyn," answered Luka.

Zi and Soulo watched Jack with concern as Jack stared into the distance.

"Jack," worried Zi, "what is it?"

Jack continued to remain silent, and the men moved closer. Zi reached out and took him by the arm. "Jack, what is wrong?"

Jack turned to look at the three, "I think Owyn is dead."

The men's eyes shot wide as they stared at Jack in disbelief.

Zi was the first to respond. "What do you mean? Jack, the boy is just late returning. There is no need to jump to that kind of thinking!"

Jack shook his head as tears began to stream down his face. "And I think Quoto killed him."

Soulo stared in shock. "Jack, this makes no sense. Why would Quoto kill Owyn, they were friends."

Jack shook his head as he focused again on his friends. "Then why is he wearing Owyn's good luck pendant?" he reached inside his shirt and pulled out his gold-capped bear tooth, which matched Owyn's.

"What? Maybe Owyn gave it to him as a gesture of friendship," Soulo argued, trying to put together the possibilities.

Zi stumbled forward and grasped the edge of the table next to Jack. "No, Jack's right. Owyn would never part with that tooth. It was his greatest treasure," the big man's voice trembled with rage and grief.

Soulo rubbed his hand across his head as he paced the floor. "But you cannot make those charges against a man without facts. He could have found it. You cannot be sure Owyn did not give it to him."

"Oh yes, I can," Jack said as he gripped his pendant, "Owyn was wearing his when I saw him off six days ago; we always gave it a tug for good luck. Quoto did not leave for scouting duty until the next afternoon. You just heard him say he had not seen Owyn. He lied."

Everyone stood quietly as they tried to put the pieces together in their minds. Jack knew Owyn would never be parted from his charm without a fight. And he must have lost the battle if Quoto was wearing it.

Jack walked across the tent and dropped into one of the chairs. He bent forward and held his head in his hands.

"We cannot condemn Quoto as a murderer just because he has Owyn's bear tooth. It does not prove he hurt Owyn," Soulo tried to reason.

"Maybe, but there is more proof. I think Owyn sent a message to us through Quoto, a way to trap Gwilim's army."

Soulo shook his head, trying to understand what was happening. "I do not understand Jack. What are you talking about? What message?"

"Quoto suggested we begin traveling for the Valley of Shadows as soon as possible to meet Westin," said Jack.

"Yes, so what?" asked Zi.

"We are not meeting Westin there. But Quoto did not know that. In fact, he never knew _any_ of the places we considered meeting Westin. But it _is_ the first place I ever suggested. Westin suggested we should meet at a different location."

"Maybe Owyn mentioned it to him at some time," added Soulo.

"No, Owyn hated the idea of meeting at the Valley of Shadows. He is terrified of caves. He told me the only way he would ever go into the Valley of Shadows was to set an ambush for the raiders. I think as his final act, he directed them there so we can use it to our advantage."

Soulo and Zi looked at one another in alarm. Was it possible?

"Jack, maybe Quoto just guessed we were heading to the Valley of Shadows. It is the most obvious landmark. It does not mean he harmed Owyn." argued

Soulo. "Besides, why would they even bother with us now if they thought they knew where to find Westin? Wouldn't they just go there themselves?"

Jack stared at the ground, still thinking of his friend Owyn. He slowly shook his head and answered, "It was the reason we changed the location. Westin's man said the Valley is filled with hundreds of twists and turns. It would be next to impossible to find their exact location. No, they would need us to lead them to the exact location."

Soulo closed his eyes and shook his head, "We need to get to the bottom of this. Let me call Quoto in to find out what is going on!"

"NO!" shouted Jack, jumping from his chair and grabbing Soulo by the arm.

"Owyn has given us the advantage, one which has probably cost him his life. I plan to use it."

He walked back to the table and rolled out the old maps. The others came and stood beside him. Jack looked into the faces of the men around him. He saw mixed feelings of grief, anger, and betrayal on their faces. His own hate and anger would have to wait for its revenge. Owyn was trying to help them, and Jack was not about to let him down.

"This is what we are going to do," and Jack began to lay out the plan Owyn had given them.

CHAPTER THREE

The work on the mine was moving along as scheduled and Bodecia hoped soon she could allow herself a few days away. More than anything she wanted to treat herself to a few relaxing days to be treated as a true lady. She was, after all, a lady of great standing in Gwilim's palace, or at least was in the past. And, she had given up as much as those sweaty men hammering and hauling rock.

This land had proved to be more treacherous than she had believed.

The nights and the days held their own particular dangers. During the day, they were surprised by huge insects, as large as a man's hand, which were almost invisible in the white sand. They lay flat under a thin layer of sand until they felt the vibration of footsteps nearby; then, they would spring up on their long, spidery legs and make a dash for the person. At times, there would only be a couple nesting nearby, but most often, they traveled in large groups. If a man were not careful, he would find himself covered with the white creatures, stinging and pulling away lumps of flesh. They lost four men before they understood what they were. They fed heartily on the half-dead who roamed nearby, leaving bony skeletons behind, eventually falling in heaps on the desert floor, finally at peace. But the warm flesh of the living was especially appetizing to them.

Bodecia made sure her tent was reinforced to keep the little demons away. She never walked anywhere without a long, hollow wooden rod designed to send strong vibrations through the earth, making the insects scatter in the other direction.

She had men place the wooden rods around the perimeter of the camp, with stones dangling from ropes. The constant hot wind, which blew here, caused the stones to strike against the rods, sending out vibrations. But she wanted to be doubly sure they didn't get a chance at her, so her rod was a constant companion.

The night brought its own special nightmares.

The mines were a dumping spot for the people and creatures Gwilim had used for his horrid feeding. Bodecia was surprised at first that Gwilim should show mercy to anyone, but of course, this was not mercy. This was damnation. They were the walking dead.

They came mostly during the night. They cried out to the men in their hollow voices, moaning and crying for forgiveness as if Gwilim could hear and help them.

Their wasted bodies could barely hold them up as they came every night. Their skin was dried and gray as if it had been draped over withered bones. Their white, shriveled heads gleamed in the moonlight as they shuffled their way toward the mining camp. Glowing, milky eyes looked out of black eye sockets, begging for release, begging for death.

Gwilim used them for his own nourishment. He drained them of their youth and lives so he might regain his own, then sent them here, like rubbish needing to be disposed. He would not release them, even in death.

Bodecia hated the night most of all. The groans and crying filled the night. She set up barricades to keep the ghouls away, but it did not stop the noise they made. She ordered the men to kill a group one night, but they only stop long enough to feast on the dead then began again. There were so many of them that it was impossible to kill them all.

At least the re-routing of the water had been a success. Eos had been good at his word about the water filling the gulch. It had filled quickly, and the men were able to work harder after they had a chance to cool off in the water. It was also a great help to wash the ore as it was brought out of the mine.

Bodecia was pleased with the work she had accomplished so far. As soon as the men broke through into the main chamber, Eos said they could move into the mine shaft and get away from this heat, the spiders, and the ghouls. He told her the temperature inside the mine was even cool enough for a shawl. She found it hard to believe it after sweating for months.

In Gwilim's palace, there was always a chill. She supposed it was the way Gwilim wanted it. She could not imagine how the temperature could bother a man who had very little blood coursing through his veins.

She recently received a message from Andro. He would be at his palace in Bandelon, a large city near the mine where they were working. He arranged for her to stay in his palace while she was visiting, and it sounded like a holiday to her. She had never had to endure such a primitive lifestyle as she had endured since arriving at the ore mine. She was a lady, after all, and accustomed to being treated as such.

Eos gave a quick bow as he entered her tent. The formality had existed between them in the beginning had turned into a tolerated sense of duty. She realized, of course, without his heavy hand over the men, she would have been killed and the mine deserted months ago. Eos was a hard man and took no disobedience from the workers. She supposed if the men had detected any sign of weakness,

Eos would be as good as dead. She respected his ability to exact so much fear in so many.

Eos held out a huge rock in his hands and let it drop heavily on her worktable.

Bodecia caught her breath as the gold streaks glistened in the sun falling over its' surface. The sheer beauty of gold always captivated her.

She picked up the rock and held it in her hand. "Is this it?" she asked as she turned the rock over in her hand.

Eos nodded his head and smiled. "It is the real thing, all right. We found it lying in one of the passageways leading down into the mine. It must have fallen off one on the flats being hauled to the surface. But it means there is more. I told you this old mine was full of it. There is no way it could have been completely mined out."

"How soon before we can begin our own digging?"

"We should reach the main chamber in a day or two.

We lived and worked there the last time I worked this old hole. I ordered double duty in the washing of the rocks being brought out. We have found some decent size nuggets already, but nothing as large as this."

Bodecia smiled as she held the heavy rock. According to the plan she had laid out for Balak, she was a good two weeks ahead of schedule. Two weeks would give her the time she needed to get the gold moved to another location.

She felt a plan begin to form in her mind as she turned the glittering rock over in her hands. She would take this opportunity to escape. She had to! She would not stay behind the Barrier forever!

She felt a chill rising up her back as she thought about the ghouls which came each night to the wall they had built around the camp. That would not be her fate.

"Two days, and then we can all move down into the underground chamber. Good. I will be gone for the next couple of days on a trip to Bandelon to meet with some of Balak's people," she lied. When I return, I will look forward to moving into our new camp, away from this heat!

"Eos, make sure all precautions are made to keep the men from stealing any of the gold they find. They're a slimy bunch who may try to hide a few nuggets for their own gain."

Eos shook his head and answered, "I will do that, of course, but there is really no need. Gold will do these poor beggars no good. They would rather have a loaf of bread. Anyone caught with gold besides 'Gwilim's chosen' are given a fate worse than death. These men want none of that."

"All the same, make the proper arrangements," she ordered, never taking her eyes off the glittering rock.

Eos nodded his head. "I will keep the men working while you are gone. If we break into the main chamber, I'll have this camp broken down and moved inside."

"Good, but keep the barrier up. I do not want those ghouls following us into the mines and trapping us there. Now, would you pick a couple of men to accompany me to Bandelon. I will be leaving before midday. Make sure they bathe and put on their trooper's clothing. I do not want to look like beggars when we arrive."

Eos said he would take care of everything and left her standing with the rock still in her hands. She debated on whether to send the rock to Balak to show him she was making progress but decided to send him a few nuggets instead. She did not want him to get the idea they were as far along in the excavation as they actually were.

She placed the rock on the edge of her desk and continued to pack for her trip to Bandelon. She held out several beautiful, brocaded silk dresses, trying to decide which to carry. They looked hot and heavy to her, so she decided to only take two and packed several of the cooler and lighter-day dresses. She did not care what she looked like for Andro, but a Lady was always expected to look like royalty. She looked down at her hands and was appalled at the dirt and grime accumulated on her nails. She most definitely would have to do something about that. Of course, gloves would cover it for a while.

She walked over to look in the mirror at her dressing table. She rubbed her fingers over her face. Gloves would cover her hands, but nothing would cover the sun-browned skin on her face and body. Even when she covered herself or stayed in her tent most of the time, she still found her skin browned.

She grimaced as she looked at her face. A noblewoman never had sun-browned skin. Their skin was pale and flawless, like a statue. Only people of low standing had the skin of a lizard.

Her fingers moved to the corners of her eyes as she noticed the small creases there. This land was slowly baking her alive. "No matter," she said aloud, "it will be a small price to pay to be gone from this land and returned to the land where I will be treated as a queen again."

She looked away from her mirror and finished packing.

By mid-day, four troopers waited at the bottom of the hill for Bodecia. She was surprised to feel her heart jump inside her to be traveling to Bandelon. It was a town she had held disdain for in the past. Now, she could hardly wait to be there.

A soldier loaded her trunks on the coach, which she insisted they take, and she climbed inside, fanning herself against the heat. She wore one of the pretty day dresses, which would be cooler, but she was afraid it would be wet with perspiration before they reached Bandelon.

She gave Eos one last wave as the coach took off with a lurch, sending her flying to the floor. She quickly climbed back onto the seat and looked to see if

Eos and any of his men had noticed. They were back at work, so she straightened herself and sat back as the coach rocked its way down the bumpy road.

Bandelon was a large town and served as a center of commerce in this region. From her coach window, she saw at least three palaces. It was not as desolate here as it was in the mine region. There were trees and, flowers and crops growing around the outside walls of the town. A large river ran right beside the town, providing it with water for drinking as well as irrigation for their crops. She marveled at the landscape, recalling the barren land where she was now living.

They passed over a wooden bridge and crossed into the city. Bodecia sat as regal as a noblewoman, but inside, her heart jumped with the excitement of a child. A bath, a proper bath; having her hair done; she checked off the list of indulgences she intended. She could scarcely remember a time when she had not been a pampered woman. Even when she was growing up, her magic abilities had afforded her many luxuries. That seemed like a hundred years ago. A few months at the mine could erase a lifetime of splendor.

The coach rumbled down the streets, causing people to move to the side of the road to let them pass. She spotted dress shops, leather goods, silk shops, and cobblers. She so wanted to stop and buy her some of the beautiful things she saw in the little shops, but they would do her little good at the mines. She decided the best purchase would be a good pair of boots to protect her feet from the rocks which cluttered the camp.

When the coach finally came to a stop, Bodecia found herself in front of one of the palaces she had seen coming into Bandelon. The coachman opened the coach door and helped her down.

Immediately, Andro made his way down the stairs toward her. "My dear!" he exclaimed," you have made it at last."

He lifted her gloved hand to his lips and kissed it. "I have arranged the best quarters in the palace for you. Your maids are waiting for your orders. I have also arranged a wonderful dinner for tonight." Andro smiled as he helped her up the steps.

"You are very kind," she offered in her haughtiest voice. It would not do to let this toad of a man know how desperate she really was for this fine treatment.

"Not at all. Now, would you rather rest up from your trip before our meeting, or would like to meet now?"

"Later, Andro. I would like to clean this travel dust off first," she answered. She could see he noticed the tanned skin and deep wrinkles burned into her face.

"Of course. I will see you are shown to your rooms right away," he said, and he barked an order for one of the servants to lead the way.

"I will see you at dinner tonight, my dear. Enjoy your rest," he waved as she followed the squire down the walkway to her rooms.

She walked through the palace halls and began to feel her regal self again. The palace was not nearly as grand as Gwilim's, but it was nicely appointed, with rich tapestries decorating the walls and shiny buffed marble floors. Statues were stationed along the walkway giving it an outdoor courtyard feeling. The halls were bustling with servants from all sorts of civilizations. Bodecia recognized some as the stocky dwarf people from the far northern regions, and others were the fragile nymphs from the woodlands. Gwilim found them amusing to have around his palace as well.

When they reached her rooms, two maids assigned to her stood waiting. The first order was for a cool bath with rose oil. She could hardly wait to lower herself in the fragrant water.

Her quarters were as large as the ones she had at the Dark Palace. She had been assigned two rooms, and both were tastefully decorated with gilded furniture and deep, rich colors. Thick rugs covered the floors, and she was tempted to take off her shoes and rub her feet across them. A long mirror hung at the end of the room, and she gasped aloud when she caught sight of her full reflection. She could see in full what months in the sun, wind, and sand had done to her.

One of the maids unpacked her things while the other tended to her bath. She stood impatiently waiting for the ornate brass tub to be filled with water. When it was filled, she lowered herself into the cool, sweet water and dismissed the maid. She fully intended to soak until her skin was totally softened.

She was curious about the news from the Dark Palace and knew Andro would have all the gossip. He may be a disgusting little man, but if he had the informants he claimed, he would know what Balak was up to.

Bodecia slipped beneath the cool waters, letting her hair submerge with her. She knew sand was plastered to each strand. You just could not get away from the sand. She called for one of the maids to come in and wash her hair for her. She intended to use up every luxury this palace had to offer.

The rest of the afternoon, Bodecia allowed herself to be pampered like a queen. She had oils and lotions rubbed into her face and body, her nails painted, and her hair styled into the customary Bandelon style. She found it a bit quaint, with small braids wrapped behind her head, falling down her cascade of auburn hair. She thought she looked like a small child.

When she went to her closets, she found Andro had provided several dresses for her. She was quite surprised to find the old ogre had fairly good taste when it came to women's clothes. To do away with the little girl image she believed her hair gave her, she chose the most provocative dress in the closet. It was a rich dark blue silk, with a full flowing skirt. The bodice was embroidered with shiny silver flowers and scrolls. The cut of the bodice was extremely low, much more than she usually wore, but she wanted to feel beautiful again after spending so many months in that dusty, dirty pit.

She sighed as she looked into the mirror. Her skin was still darker than usual, but with the help of face paints, she thought she looked quite lovely, even if it was wasted on Andro.

A young man came to escort her to the dining hall. He bowed in respect but never gave her appearance a second glance. She was a bit irritated when he did not give her an approving look.

Andro stood as she entered the dining room, "Ah, Bodecia!" he wooed, "Your beauty makes this room shine."

She found her cheeks growing warm from the compliment and scolded herself. "He is an ugly little man. He would think any woman beautiful if she could stand sitting with him for more than a minute!" she reminded herself.

She took her seat in the large, overstuffed chair at the elaborately set table. The wine goblets were of the finest silver, and the dinnerware looked as fine as any at the Dark Palace. Andro had freshly cut flowers all around the room, filling the area with their fragrant scent. Bodecia began to feel that wonderful feeling of being special again.

A servant brought wine and began to fill their glasses. Both she and Andro waited until all the servants had left the room before they began talking. She realized he knew just how easily Balak could plant his own 'spiders.'

Andro finally walked to Bodecia and set his wine glass on the table. He put his finger to his lips and walked to the doorway. He looked down the corridor in either direction, then returned to the table, facing the door so he would be able to see anyone coming.

"Did you find your rooms to be satisfactory?" he smiled.

Bodecia hated the fake formalities she had to endure for the sake of society, but boring chitchat was always proper before diving into the main conversation. "They are very nice, Andro, thank you," she offered.

"I hope you do not mind my providing you with a few dresses. I see you wore one of my favorites, and may I say it looks lovely on you. I own many shops which design clothing for the lords and ladies of this land, so I tried to pick a few I thought would be becoming to you," he smiled genuinely.

She found herself surprised he knew about beautiful things, but she had to admit the dresses he had chosen were some of the finest she had ever seen. She looked at him in wonder. He was most definitely one of the most common-looking men she knew, but perhaps there was more to him than meets the eye. He had already proved to be surprising with his network of spies against Balak.

"What do you hear from the Dark Palace and Balak?" she questioned.

Andro looked at her solidly for a moment, then began, "Gwilim has taken on a new life. He must have drained the life source from dozens of innocents to revive his youth. He has shown himself in public many times in the past few weeks. He is eager to be moving forward with this thing. Balak is always at his side, acting the pet dog he is."

Bodecia was concerned Gwilim was making public appearances again. It usually meant he was ready to take some sort of action. Balak must have given him the impression the time for the opening in the Barrier would be soon. She felt her heart race at the thought of her own escape plan coming together.

"What is the purpose of these appearances?" she asked.

"He is organizing his troops for invasion and has sped up the production of the demok. Hundreds of people were killed for nothing more than trying to move their families out of harm's way. He takes delight in reminding the people he is their master and has no mercy for anyone who is not willing to die for him," Andro grit his teeth as he stared at the table. "During the time he kept to himself, the people became content with their lives and forgot what a harsh, demanding master he can be. They remember now. He is withhelding food from them to force their devotion to his cause. When he feels they are more penitent, he claims he will open the food sources again. Meanwhile, the weak and sick are dying by the hundreds while he again raids the villages of their young men to train for the army's invasion of the Homeland."

Bodecia made a mental note to step up work at the mines as soon as she returned. It sounded to her as if Gwilim had his own timetable for the opening of the wall and may not be as easily fooled as she had hoped.

"What of your spies? Have they any news of Westin?" she eagerly asked.

Andro quickly changed the subject, talking instead of Bandelon and the sights to be seen there, as several servants began to bring platter upon platter of food. They placed the platters of roasted pig, potatoes, and other delicious foods around the table. Bodecia had forgotten how famished she was and licked her lips hungrily.

Andro smiled, "I thought a grand celebration was in order. You have made great sacrifices for the cause. You should receive a little reward in advance. I hope you do not mind if we dine alone tonight. I thought it would be better to have our discussion alone instead of with my noisy family."

She looked up at him and wondered if she had made a mistake about the man. It had been a long time since she had met anyone who had a spark of kindness in them. She had always been suspicious of any kindness toward her in the Exiled. It was, after all, a place where evil had been resident for hundreds of years.

When the servants left, they each filled their plates before Andro continued.

"My spiders tell me Balak's army has an approximate location of where Westin is located. It is in an area where there are many canyons and caves, so unless they know exactly where he is, they may have a hard time finding him."

"How will we get to him first if they do not even know where he is?" she asked, as she threw proper etiquette away as she used her fingers to fill her mouth with the tasty pork.

"Let me worry about that. I understand there is another group of people trying to rescue Westin also."

"Who are they, and why do they want Westin?"

"They are from Homeland, I believe, from the Palace of Ages. I am sure they want Westin so they can seal the Barrier once and for all. If they have their way, we may find ourselves sealed here forever as well."

Bodecia did not like the sound of that. Her work at the mine would soon be completed, and she certainly did not want to return to the Dark Palace to spend the rest of her life at Balak's whim.

"How are things at the mine proceeding?" asked Andro.

"I am ahead of schedule. I told Balak it will be another month before we have the gold ready, but I believe we will have our precious gold any day. Hopefully, we will have Westin by then. After we make it through the Barrier, I want to make sure he seals this place up tight forever. I want Gwilim and Balak to feed off each other!"

Andro stared at Bodecia for a moment and then responded, "Not a bad notion. I told my family to prepare to move quickly. Is there anyone you would like for us to bring here to join you?"

"No, not anymore. Balak took the life of my only friend. However, I want to see I am compensated for my work. I intend to live the rest of my life as a queen, so see to it I get my reward. If we take half of Gwilim's fortune, what do we care if he is enraged? We will be safely beyond his reach after we escape and seal the Barrier for good."

Andro stopped eating and looked solemnly at her, "Bodecia, our plan is not to seal the Barrier but to destroy it. We must free the people in Exiled from Gwilim's control. I thought you understood that. Too long have the innocent been suffering under his reign. Many of the people here were sent for good cause, but the children of those people should not have to suffer for the sins of their fathers. They should know what it is like to be free. For so long, innocent people have been condemned to live here for crimes they had no part of. It is an unfair exile for them. Gwilim, Balak, and their evil followers must be destroyed, and there are many here who will happily help in that fight. You and I must also stand in this fight together."

Andro looked in Bodecia's eyes, searching for an understanding in their cause. Of course, she had misunderstood. She had believed Andro and his followers were working for escape for themselves and their families. It never occurred to her he wanted to destroy the entire Barrier.

She smiled her sweetest smile, "Of course, it would be wonderful to free the people of Exiled, but Andro, there are *things* here that should not be set free. Gwilim has created creatures which are not human and would cause chaos in a civilized world. How can we destroy them all? Don't you think it would be better to take only the ones who deserve to be free?"

"And who, my dear, will make the decision of who is to go free and who is condemned to stay?"

She looked at him and sighed. "Some sacrifices are always necessary, Andro. And there are always an acceptable number of casualties. If we free the monsters of this land on the rest of the world, they will find a way to send us all back and seal us up here forever."

Andro smiled and sat back in his chair. "Do you remember when we first began our talks with the Homeland? We had selected a group of councilmen who, at the time, were working on a solution for the people here to be able to return to their homelands. We were working with Westin and Balak. That council still exists. Even though Gwilim was able to sway Balak into becoming his second in command, the people on the council have never given up their dreams of release from this place."

"So, the council still exists?"

"It does. And though the talks with Homeland ended when Balak joined with Gwilim, Westin never stopped working with us. He communicated with us from his prison at the Dark Palace, encouraging us to stand and fight for our freedom. He told us the people of the Homeland would send their armies to help destroy Gwilim's creatures and followers."

Bodecia did not know if she believed it was possible or not. There were many types of beings in this land, not all human, and it was hard to know which were trustworthy and which were not. It sounded too good to be true to her. She thought Andro and his people were being very naïve if they believed the leaders in the Homeland would ever allow them to return there.

"We still need Westin, no matter what," she told him. "He has the means to engage the Barrier's magic. If you believe evil can be separated from the good in this land, then I will leave that little chore for you. I have enough worries at the ore mine. But hear me now, Andro," she hissed, "I will leave this land, with or without you. You have about three weeks before Gwilim and Balak come for their gold to open the Barrier on their own. So, whatever you are planning, you had better get on with it."

"Remember," she offered. "Gwilim feeds on power and magic. That Barrier was created from some of the most powerful magic ever used. If he has a chance to feed on the power from the Barrier, then the entire world will be doomed. He will be unstoppable."

Andro looked alarmed at the thought of Gwilim gaining even more power than he already possessed. "Then he must be stopped *before* the Barrier comes down."

She nodded as she stuck a succulent roasted potato in her mouth. She watched him as he appeared to be making decisions within his own mind. Of course, she had reservations of taking the Barrier down. She could not believe he and his followers would be able to defeat Balak and Gwilim. It seemed she had her own decisions to make.

"Has Balak made any new attempts at opening the Barrier?" she asked through her mouthful of potato.

"If he has, we have not seen any evidence. I think his last attempt shook him. He not only lost a troop of raiders, but it was obvious the magic of the Barrier sensed his attempts and re-wrote the magic in the wall. Westin has the only true knowledge to control the Barrier's magic.

"Gwilim is a most impatient master, so I am sure Balak has his hands full, keeping him convinced he is still capable of making it happen."

Bodecia hoped Gwilim *had* shown his wrath to Balak. She would have to return to the Dark Palace to face Gwilim again, but with the promise of gold, she was sure she would stand as one of his favored again. Of course, she fully intended to kill Balak before she made her escape. It would be a sweet gift she would give herself as a reward for a job well done.

They finished their meal and made plans for their imminent escape to freedom. Bodecia decided Andro had more uses than she first anticipated. It looked as if they had a profitable partnership after all.

Chapter Four

Blue stood in the middle of the old warehouse holding Owyn as Voxx and his men entered the building.

Owyn raised his head and groaned at the sight of the men. He turned to look at Blue and was surprised to see the look on her face. It was not one of fear but of amusement; like a cat watching a mouse approach.

She gently lowered Owyn to the chair and stood waiting for the men to approach.

"Owyn, you did not tell me you had a lady friend looking for you. I am sure we will find some use for her among our raiders," he sneered.

Owyn tried to stand, but Blue put her hand on his shoulder and pushed him back down. There was no strength in him to fight right now.

"I was hoping I would get the opportunity to meet you," Blue began. "I wanted the chance to tell you how I feel about your treatment of my friend, Owyn."

Voxx looked at the pretty girl in astonishment for a moment, then tossed back his head and released a peal of laughter. The men behind him stood watching Blue with interest. They did not share his mirth. Their hands were already holding their swords.

"I am going to take Owyn with me now. You are to stand aside and let us pass," Blue stated in a voice as calm and controlled as if she were asking someone to pass the bread at dinner.

Voxx stared in shock, then again began to laugh as he turned to his men, "The lady wants us to let them pass. Perhaps she would like for us to saddle a horse for them to ride also!"

Blue looked between the men and answered, "That will not be necessary. We will walk."

The entire situation was wearing on Voxx as his eyes narrowed. "You will not be leaving this building; you or your friend, Owyn."

Owyn raised his hand to Blue and said in a weak voice, "Blue, go, there are too many of them."

"He is right, woman! How do you expect to stop us? You are in the same trouble as your friend."

"Not really," replied Blue as she took a step toward the men. When she was within arm's length, Voxx reached out and grabbed her arm. His eyes shot wide open as a sizzling sound filled the air. His mouth opened to scream, and his body began to shake furiously.

From outside the building, a powerful wind poured through the open door. Chambers and the others were blown against the walls of the building, falling unconscious to the floor.

Jep ran into the warehouse and looked at each man to make sure they were no longer a threat. Voxx had fallen on his back like a mighty turtle upended. His clothes smoked on his body.

Blue reached down, put her arms under Owyn, and lifted him to his feet. He looked at her in surprise, "Wha' the heck? Did you do all that?" he asked.

"No, she did not boy. Let's give credit where credit is due!" Jep came running to Owyn's other side.

"Hurry, Blue, before more soldiers come to see what the ruckus was about!" They pulled and carried Owyn through the barn doors and into the streets.

Inside, the men were crawling in the dirt; all their senses disoriented. Because of the intense blast of Jep's power, they could not see, hear, or speak. In fact, they were so disoriented they did not even seem to know where they were.

Jep looked back in the building and then at Blue, "You never said you had magic."

"That was not magic, Jep, that was science."

Jep gave a low, respectful whistle as they helped Owyn along the dark streets toward the back gate.

Owyn was barely able to move his feet, and it was becoming more difficult to pull him along.

Jep hoped he would be able to heal Owyn a bit if he had time to stop, but the streets were full of soldiers, and it was only a matter of time before the men in the building got their senses back and sent out an alert.

"What are we going to do, Jep?" worried Blue. "We must get Owyn somewhere safe!"

Jep was about to answer when Owyn finally collapsed in the street. He and Blue tried in vain to help him up. He had lost a lot of blood and was too weak to go any farther.

A nearby door opened, and a woman's voice whispered, "Here, old man. Bring him in here."

Mrs. Lyn, the seamstress who had made Blue's skirt just that morning, held open the door to her shop and waved them in.

When they were safely inside, Mrs. Lyn grabbed a bucket of water and rushed to the street to wash away the blood left by Owyn.

She hurried back inside and quickly closed and bolted her door. "Well, I thought there was more to you two than meets the eye," she declared with her hands on her hips.

She walked over and looked down on the unconscious Owyn. "Bring the boy back here," she instructed.

Jep and Blue again picked Owyn up and pulled him to the back of the shop. Mrs. Lyn had a pot of water on a nearby stove heated and brought warm, soapy water to clean the blood away from Owyn's face. It revealed deep cuts and bruises.

"Poor dear," she said in sympathy. "Those men are nothing more than animals. They have brought nothing but chaos and destruction to our village. We are afraid to leave our homes at night, or day for that matter."

Jep kneeled beside Owyn and looked at his face. He moved his hands over Owyn's chest and stomach. "He has a lot of damage inside. I think he is bleeding internally. I must act fast, or we are going to lose him."

The woman looked at Jep curiously, "So, you are a wizard, are you? I thought so. I have a gift of foretelling, and I have been expecting someone like you." She looked at Blue and smiled, "But I never could have predicted you, my dear."

Jep took her hands and asked, "Will we be safe here for a while? Even after I heal him, it will take a while for him to get enough strength back to allow us to leave."

"Take all the time you need. I have rooms in my basement where I store fabrics, there is plenty of room for the three of you."

Jep nodded and looked back at Owyn. He put his hands on his chest and began to move them. When he found a spot which concerned him, he stopped. A warm golden glow began to radiate from his hands, penetrating Owyn's body. Owyn stiffened as the flow of healing magic entered him. After a few minutes, Jep moved his hands to other places and began again.

"There are so many," he sighed, frowning, "I am surprised he had not already died. If only I had better healing magic. I am afraid I am not talented enough to help him." Jep cried out in frustration.

Blue held her breath as she realized how close Owyn was to death.

"Can you save him, Jep?" she asked worriedly.

"I will do my best, Blue. Now, please sit quietly while I look for all the injuries. If I miss even one, it may cost Owyn his life."

The healing was tedious work, taking hours. Jep sat next to Owyn, slowly moving his hands, stopping every inch or so, allowing the golden glow of healing to enter. Several times, he returned to an area to re-heal the broken places inside. "He is so fragile. The wounds keep opening again."

Mrs. Lyn quietly made herself busy, making hot cups of caff and tea for them, always returning and sitting with Blue, holding her hands. Occasionally, she would put her arms around Blue and give her a pat.

Blue was afraid to breathe. She watched helplessly as her good friend Owyn lay close to death.

His breathing was so shallow it was hard to see his chest rise and fall. His color was dull and pale; as blue as she had once been.

Finally, Jep stood, swaying from the use of so much magic. "I have done as much as I can. Some of the wounds were made days ago, so I tried as best as I could to heal them. He must rest for a while, and we shall see."

Mrs. Lyn took Jep to the table and sat him down. "Now, wizard, you need to care for yourself, or you will be in as bad a shape as the boy. I am going to bring you some stew, and I expect you to eat all of it, the girl, too. If you are going to care for him, you both will need all your strength."

She brought two large bowls to the table, along with a loaf of bread. She stood waiting with her hands on her hips until Blue finally left Owyn's side and went to the table to eat. Ms. Lyn did not look to be the kind of lady who would take 'no' for an answer.

"Now, while you're eating, I want you to tell me what brought you here," she demanded as she sat at one of the chairs at the little table.

Jep nodded, then began telling the story of their quest.

***

"Whew," she said, shaking her gray head. "To think all this is happening around us, and we were not aware. In years past we lived a peaceful existence here in Harmony. We raised our own food and had peaceful relations with nearby villages. But then 'they' came. We believed they were from another kingdom somewhere in the Grand. It never occurred to us that they were an invading army since they never harmed us or our land. But, of course, now I see the invasion is meant for your land; we seem to have <u>given</u> our land away.

"They have always passed through our village. They cause the same problems as any army would, I suppose, fighting, drinking, and such. But, the last few times, they have brought those 'things' with them; those animals. That is when we began to believe they brought evil. Some of our men mingled in the army camp to see those creatures up close. They came back with horrible stories. We were genuinely concerned they could turn them loose on our village. We are a peaceful people, and there was no reason to fear for ourselves. Most areas of the Grand are that way. We would be helpless against them."

Jep closed his eyes at the thought of the demok ravaging the peaceful village. He had seen it before in his own land and knew the horror that could be visited upon them here.

"I am convinced it is the reason Gwilim chose the Grand as his next kingdom. No one in this land would know how to fight him. What have your people decided to do?" he asked.

"We built the wall which surrounds us," she pointed out. "We don't believe for a minute it would be able to keep them away, but perhaps it would give us time to arm ourselves in case of attack."

Blue and Jep looked at one another, knowing the wall was of no use at all against Gwilim's men. The light cannon they carried could wipe them away like a mist on the moor.

Jep looked at the old woman, "Let your people know they need to set traps for this army. You know your land better than they, and you can begin to cut down their numbers before they even reach your walls. They are battle soldiers, and in an all-out fight, your village would not have a chance. Your defense needs to be long-range. Begin your defense as far away from your village if you can. Also, begin to look for places where you can hide your old and young, far away from the battle."

She sighed a long sigh. "It may be hopeless. As I said, we are a peaceful village and never had the need to defend ourselves."

Jep gave her hand a squeeze, "Well, if we are successful, the invasion will be over. But we still have this army to contend with. They are a vicious group on their own, even without Gwilim, and those demok must be destroyed."

They took turns sitting with Owyn while the others slept. Mrs. Lyn took the first turn, saying she had to clean the kitchen anyway. Blue insisted she only required a small amount of sleep, but Mrs. Lyn pushed her to a mattress and covered her. "Sleep while you can, child," she insisted. "I do not require much sleep either. When you are as old as I am, it is a good idea to keep your eyes open as long as possible! Otherwise, some kindhearted person will be shoveling dirt on you."

Jep found he was totally exhausted. The use of his magic had weakened him greatly. He worried the soldiers would try to search the shops and homes, but Mrs. Lyn said that she would warn them if she heard anything.

Blue also found she was tired. She supposed the use of her power surge had worn her down a bit. She decided to close her eyes and allow her body time to recharge. She placed herself in a state of 'ready' in case she needed to react quickly.

Jep woke several hours later to find Mrs. Lyn sitting quietly beside Owyn. She worked on a piece of needlework and occasionally reached over to wipe the sweat from Owyn's face.

He sat up from his bed and stretched his arms. "How long have I been asleep?" he asked.

"Just a few hours," she responded. "Owyn has not stirred since you lay down.

Jep stood and walked over to Owyn, putting his hands on his chest again. "His heart seems stronger, and his color is better. Hopefully, he will wake soon. We really need to get back to our group as soon as possible."

"Will he be able to travel?" she asked surprised.

"Hopefully, if I have been able to heal all his serious injuries. He will not look too good for a while, but he should be able to travel."

Blue sat up from her mattress, listening to Jep and Mrs. Lyn.

"Where there any sign of the soldiers," she asked.

"Oh, I heard them in the streets off and on. It began to snow quite hard for awhile, so I expect they will think your tracks have been covered. Hopefully, they will give up their search."

"I hope you are right. Now, dear lady, it is your turn to get a little sleep. It will not do to have your shop closed down on account of us," he declared.

She smiled as she stood, "Tomorrow is our worship day. My shop is always closed then, but I think I will get a little rest now. Make yourselves at home. There is food and bread if you are hungry." She then folded her needlework and made her way to her bedroom.

Jep and Blue discussed ways to get out of the village and meet Jack and the group. Jep was not at all sure Owyn would be as strong as he had claimed he would be. He had some serious injuries and was weak from loss of blood.

"What will we do if Owyn can't travel for a while?" worried Blue.

Jep scratched his head and yawned, "I was thinking one of us would have to stay here while the other went back to camp. Jack needs to know what happened here. He is also expecting us back tonight. I do not want him sending anyone else here."

"You should be the one to go back, Jep," said Blue. "I will stay here and care for Owyn."

"Nonsense, I should be the one to stay, after all, I am the healer. He may need me again; besides, Jetta would have my head if I left you here," argued Jep. "And Jack may need your help to get to Westin. Owyn and I can catch up with you."

"Will you two please quit yammering," came a familiar voice.

Both Jep and Blue jumped from the table and ran to his bedside. "Well, it's about time," joked Jep. "We didn't send you here for a rest, boy!"

Owyn smiled at the two. "Blue, whatever possessed you to become a woman?" he asked.

"I thought no one would notice me," she grinned.

"I told her she would stand out in any crowd, but with me acting the protective father, she didn't do half bad."

Owyn tried to sit up and held his head in pain. "I had a pretty rough time of it. Thanks, you two, for coming for me. You saved my life."

"Of course, we would come," said Jep, inspecting the purple bruises on Owyn's face. "We just need to stay out of sight until they think we are gone. Then we can make our way back to camp."

Blue looked at Jep for a minute, "We need to do more than that. They were willing to kill Owyn to get the information they wanted. I do not believe they will stop looking for us now. And do not forget, if they want to track us, they can use the demok to locate us."

Jep looked up in alarm. "I had forgotten they could use the demok for tracking. I am sure they have Owyn's scent. There was plenty of blood left in that warehouse. What do you have in mind."

Chapter Five

Jack and Soulo waited inside the tent as the troopers began to pour in. The scouts sat near, waiting for their instructions.

"We will be moving out this morning to meet Dr. Westin," Jack began. "I have received word from him, and we agreed on a place for us to meet.

The men stood quietly, but Jack could sense they were eager to finally complete their mission.

"We will leave this morning and travel to a place known as the Valley of Shadows. It is an area filled with long, deep canyons and caves. Westin will be waiting for us in a place known as Silver Cave. It is a day's travel to the area. I will take a few men with me so we can get in quickly, get Westin and his group, and be off again. The rest of you will be waiting outside in Blight Canyon. We will meet back up with you there and then make our way to the Barrier by way of the Northern Portal.

Soulo continued, "It will take us two days to get to Blight Canyon, and Jack and his group should be able to make it to Silver Cave and back in a day in a half.

We will camp outside the area and wait for them there. Half a morning's travel should be enough to get Westin back with us."

Jack took the lead again, "Once we have Westin, our journey is almost done. When we get him to the Barrier, we will once again seal the wall for the last time."

They waited for a minute, then Soulo asked, "Any questions?"

The men sat quietly, then Quoto spoke, "What about the scouts? Will we still need to go on our scouting details?"

Soulo nodded, "More than ever. You men who returned last night will be relieved, and we will let the backups make the runs to Blight Canyon and the Valley of Shadows. You deserve your rest now. We will need you again later."

The scouts nodded, all except Quoto. "If it is all right with you, I would rather be on scouting duty. I'm not the least bit tired."

"Quoto, you were the last one to return last night," said Soulo, "you must be exhausted. Why not let one of the other scouts take your place?"

"I feel better out there scouting than I do sitting here, Commander. If it is all the same to you, I would like to go back out."

Soulo looked at Quoto, then nodded, "If that is what you want."

They rolled out the maps and began marking the locations where the main group of soldiers would wait for Jack and pointed out the location where Jack and his group would camp with Westin before heading back to meet them.

As the men began to leave the tent, Quoto approached Jack and Soulo. "Where is Jep and Blue? I have not seen them since I rode in last night."

"Luka took them with him to scout out the far eastern side of the mountain. He promised them good hunting, too," lied Jack, gripping his sword tightly. Jack felt anger and hate filling him as he answered Quoto, and it took everything he had to keep from ripping the throat from the man standing in front of him. Instead, he reached out his hand and placed it on Quoto's shoulder.

"We appreciate your going back out so soon. You know how important this is."

Quoto clapped Jack on the back, "Sure, no problem. I am at home on the back of my horse now. I was never very good at sitting around waiting for something to happen."

"You had better get yourself ready then," said Soulo. Jack detected a tremor of anger in his voice as he turned his back and began rolling the maps up.

Quoto walked away to prepare to leave.

"He should be gone in an hour or so," said Soulo, watching Quoto walk toward the trooper's camp.

Jack stared at the man, his body shaking, "That was the hardest thing I have ever done. I wanted to kill the man more than anything in the world. You realize he most likely killed Bragos, too. He must have been an obstacle for Quoto when he needed to communicate with the raiders."

"I agree, and Bragos was his friend. But we can use him. It gives *us* the advantage this time," said Soulo. He placed his hand on Jack's shoulder and gave it a gentle squeeze.

Quoto was quickly on his way, as Jack and Soulo had expected. They anticipated he would want to get back to Gwilim's men as soon as possible with the news they had the exact location where Westin could be located.

When he was out of sight, they again called all the troopers together.

"We have a change in plans," Soulo announced, and he began to give them their new instructions.

They were packing up their camp to leave when Zi spotted Jep coming down the mountainside. "Jack," he pointed, "It's Jep."

Jack looked to see Jep making his way up the steep trail. He was wearing his old travel cloak and held it tight against him as the wind began to pick up. Walking behind him, Blue gave an exuberant wave to the group.

Jack was relieved to see them back. He had worried they had also run into the same problem as Owyn. Jack's heart sank, remembering the loss of Owyn. He and Owyn were like brothers.

Zi felt the same, of course, and had kept to himself after learning of Owyn's death; even avoiding Jack.

As Jep and Blue turned the corner and continued up the hill, Jack noticed a black and blue face following them. His eyes could hardly believe what he was seeing as Owyn lifted his hand to wave to him. Jack blinked his eyes and looked a second time but only saw the snow-laden bushes around the path with Jep and Blue. Was he seeing things? Finally, he spotted Owen, slowly making his way around the clump of bushes.

He heard Zi yelp with joy as he bound down the hill, throwing up great clumps of snow with his big feet. Jack stood frozen, staring at the battered face as it came ever closer. He realized his eyes were filled with tears as he watched Zi reach Owyn. Zi grabbed Owyn and spun him round and round, laughing and crying at the same time.

"Careful, you big oaf, you'll open up all his wounds." Fussed Jep.

Owyn looked at Zi, then at Jack, touched by his homecoming reception. "So . . , you missed me then?" he asked.

Jack walked over to Owyn and put his hand on his neck. "We thought you were dead," he said in a broken voice, blinking the salty tears from his eyes. "You look like you may have been close."

"I guess I was," offered Owyn as he gave Jack and Zi one of his crooked smiles.

Jack put his arms around Owyn's shoulders and gave him a tight squeeze. "Do not ever do that again," he said, clearing his throat, then turned and walked back to his tent.

Jetta and Soulo also ran to greet the three. Jetta tenderly reached up and touched Owyn's face as he described how Blue had rushed in to save his life. Jetta smiled lovingly at Blue.

The entire company of troopers ran to welcome Owyn. It was a grand homecoming, and Owyn was more than touched by the men's attention.

Finally, Jack, Zi, Soulo, and Jetta pulled the three aside and listened to their story.

"I got your message about the Valley of Shadows," said Jack.

"Oh, I hoped you would. I heard them talking when they thought I was unconscious and found they have a spy in our camp. They kept asking for Westin's location, so I figured if I gave them only half the information they needed, they would send their spy back for the other half. It was the only way I had to get a message to you. I guess I figured right."

Jack told Owyn about Quoto. Owyn was shocked to find out one of the men he had called a friend had betrayed him. "Why would he do it? What would he have to gain?"

Jack shook his head. "I can not imagine anything so important to allow a friend to be tortured to death. We believe Bragos did not die at the hands of the raiders but that Quoto killed him so he could meet with the raiders. I believe Bragos suspected what he was doing."

Soulo slapped his hand against the side of his leg. His anger had been under control as long as it could be. "I will have his head. Bragos was a fine soldier!"

Everyone nodded. It was a personal betrayal to each of them.

Jack put his hand on Owyn's shoulder, "Thanks to you, we will be ready for them."

Chapter Six

Balak looked down into the demok courtyard as they feasted on their meals. Lately, there had been plenty of opportunities for them to feed. There had been much talk among the people of rebellion since Gwilim placed them on food rations. Nothing makes people more discontent than a hungry belly.

Balak did not believe in it himself. He had always found the promise of wealth and prosperity to work better than punishment. Besides, hunger kills, and they had better use of these people than to be food for the demok.

He turned away from the feeding below and walked toward the front of the palace. He hated these creatures. They were Gwilim's creation, not his. They reminded him of the horror he had allowed to visit upon the Homeland. These creatures were once human beings. Now, after Gwilim had breathed his evil magic into them, they were mindless animals. Of course, they had their uses. They had always worked very well in the raids on the Homeland. They terrorized villages while the soldiers used the light cannon to collect all the rich bounty the land had to offer. Everyone benefited from that collaboration.

He knew he had sold his very soul to Gwilim. The price was high, but the rewards would be worth it. He would have his own kingdom and would rule it forever. He would be far away from Gwilim and his evil empire. Of course, there was the promise from Gwilim that he would live forever. The price was more than acceptable to him.

He reached his quarters and tossed his cape across a nearby chair. A young servant boy was awaiting his return. He held a letter and a shiny, black box. Balak snatched them from his hands and quickly dismissed him. The young man bowed and eagerly left the room.

He could tell by the wax seal the letter was from Bodecia. "Ah, news from the mines," he stated sarcastically.

He read:

Lord Balak,

We have tasted success at last. After much toil, we began to make our way into the mine. It was an exceedingly difficult task, considering the ceiling of the mine had collapsed and kept us from entering more than a few feet into the mine's opening. We have, however, removed most of the larger rocks from the opening and are now preparing to build the new walls and ceiling to make the mine secure enough for us to work. I estimate another three to four weeks before you have the gold that you require.

I am sending a few nuggets found when we cleared the opening. I wanted to assure you of our imminent success.

I will soon require several wagons for transport of the ore back to you. I assume you will want the gold sent to the Palace. Please advise.

-Bodecia

Balak tossed the letter on the table and opened the lid to the box. His eyes twinkled as he stared at the nuggets. It was filled, and they gleamed brightly in the light of his room. He took a few out and held them in his hand, admiring their bright beauty. He placed one between his teeth and bit down. Completely pure! With this precious ore, he would have the ability to open the Barrier once and for all.

"Very beautiful," came a voice from behind him. He turned his head to find Gwilim and two of his slither-men confidants standing in his room. He was always unnerved when Gwilim seemed to suddenly appear, never giving warning of his approach. Balak bowed deeply, turning to face Gwilim. He found it difficult to lower himself to bow to anyone, but to disrespect this man could mean death. Or in his case, worse, since Gwilim could not afford to kill him.

"A gift from our Lady Bodecia?" Gwilim asked, tilting his head to one side. He snapped his fingers, and one of his servants quickly ran to fetch him a chair.

"Yes, she reports they have finally been able to clear the opening of the mine. She sent a sample of things to come," confirmed Balak.

"Well, it seems she knows what she is doing after all." Gwilim smiled as he looked at Balak. His teeth had been freshly filed and looked as sharp as knives. Balak had always hated the look, but after seeing him feed, he knew it was a proper look for him.

"I still say we should keep an eye on her. She has a treacherous heart," said Balak.

"Who is to say I am not doing just that," smiled Gwilim. "Bodecia is not as clever as she thinks. She will do an outstanding job of bringing us the gold. When it is time, I will deal with any treachery she may harbor or richly reward any loyalty. It is my call to make."

"Of course, Master. Bodecia may indeed prove to be a faithful servant. That is my hope also," he lied.

Gwilim stared long at Balak before answering. "I am sure it is. I think it may be worthwhile to pay her a visit in the next few weeks. Let us give her a chance to get the mine in full production. We would not want her to think we have forgotten her." He stood, walked to the table, and lifted one of the gold nuggets from the box. "Lovely," he purred. "Tell me again how this will work."

Balak sat at the table with Gwilim and began, "When the Barrier was created hundreds of years ago by the great wizard Elidor, the magic guarding the wall was set in constant motion, ever moving, yet solid. Because of the constant changing of the surface, any attempts to solve its' mysteries and find a way to destroy the wall was impossible; But, Westin discovered, through ancient texts, an opening could be made using the combination of gold and magic. The purity of the gold infused with runes of magic inscribed upon it will allow the flow of the Barrier's magic to pass over it."

"At least it *was* the plan until Westin escaped," hissed Gwilim. "His departure put a stop to everything! You failed to mention that detail. He holds the inscriptions, which must be etched in the gold to keep the opening safe. Without them, we may end up like your last attempt to open the wall.

"I hope your sources are correct when they claim they know where he is located. We need him back here to complete his work." Gwilim's eyes narrowed threateningly.

Balak winced at the reminder of his past failures, making an opening in the wall. He hated failure and hated being reminded of it even more.

"It is only a matter of time until he is ours again. Do not discount my abilities, I will one day have the same knowledge Westin now holds," assured Balak. He wanted to make sure Gwilim still regarded him as a necessary ally. "Once he is returned and Bodecia has supplied us with our gold, we will be ready to move forward with our plans."

Gwilim seemed lost in his own world for a moment, and Balak was cautious not to disturb his thoughts. Finally, Gwilim looked back at Balak. "That is my hope. I suppose I can wait a few weeks since I have already waited many lifetimes."

He placed the nugget back in the little black box. "Make sure all arrangements are ready so when we have the gold and Westin, we can move immediately."

Again, Balak bowed in submission to Gwilim.

"And the raids on the Homeland, how do they fair?" inquired Gwilim.

Balak smiled as he reported, "The Veil has fallen, so our men can make their attacks anytime without any ill effect on their health. We have drained the rich resources from many areas and safely deposited them in the Grand. You will have your new kingdom soon."

"Good," smiled Gwilim, "we still have much to do to prepare for our occupation of the Grand and the Homeland. Production of the demok must be hastened. They will become the Honor Guard of the New Land."

Balak gave a silent shudder as he considered Gwilim's words. A world where demok were the peacekeepers sounded like a nightmare world to him, but what did he care as long as he had his kingdom and an eternity to rule it. He would set the laws in his own land. Gwilim would stay in his part of the new world, and he would stay in his.

He heard new cries coming from the back courtyard of the palace. It was something he had never been able to get used to. People knew their fate with the demok and screamed in terror, awaiting their doom. He wished the keepers would just take their lives before they entered the arena to avoid having to listen to their cries, but he realized it was that very thing which excited Gwilim.

CHAPTER SEVEN

"**O**wyn's rescue was quite a feat, but how were you able to escape the soldiers and demok in Harmony?" asked Zi after hearing the details of Owyn's rescue.

Jep and Blue smiled as if each were bursting to tell the story. Owyn had been scurried aside by Jetta, who was applying herbal ointments to his battered face.

"We realized we would not be able to hide from the raiders for long. Since they thought they had the location of Westin and his group, they feared if we reached you, we would give away their plans. They could not allow that to happen.

"We had to convince them we were no longer a threat. It was important they proceed with their plans. Owyn suffered greatly to make sure they would do so. Near dawn, when Owyn was stronger, we left Mrs. Lyn and made our way toward the back gate. She brewed a strong potion, made with the last of her spices, pepper, and such, and we used it to cover our scent from the demok after we threw them off our tracks.

"Blue and I were able to overcome three guards patrolling the outside wall. We dressed them in our clothes, which gave them our scents, loaded their bodies on horses, and left a trail up the side of the mountain. We discovered an area on the trail which had recently been avalanched by the heavy snow. We threw the bodies over the side into a deep chasm and released the horses. We covered our trail and our bodies with peppers and spices to make sure our own scents would end at the spot where the bodies were left. I added to the deception by using a bit of magic to dump several feet of snow from the cliffs above over our footprints and closing the path we took."

Blue nodded, then added, "We waited on the other side of the trail, covered in pepper potion and snow, to make sure it would work. The bodies of the three below were only barely visible and too far down for them to identify. The demok, who had been given Owyn's scent, howled and clawed, trying to make it down the mountainside after the bodies.

"We dressed one of the men in Owyn's bloody clothes, so his scent was very strong." Blue smiled as she looked at Jep, "And I think when they saw Jep's colorful rag cloak, they were convinced it must be us.

Jep looked at Jack, shrugged his shoulders, and continued. "Once we were sure they were gone, we hurried to meet you. We prayed you were able to get the clues Owyn sent you."

Zi shook his woolly head. "We have quite a surprise for them waiting for them. It is time they found out the people of the Homeland are not going to take their barbaric actions lightly. We are also a fierce people."

Jetta and Owyn returned to the group. Owyn's face was covered with salves. Jetta assured him it would take away the bruising. He had deep cuts on his face, which would leave scars, but he seemed to have much of his strength back. "I am ready to move whenever you are," he announced, a grim determination replacing his boyish demeanor.

Soulo gave the first group of men their orders, and they moved out hours before the others.

After Quoto left, they called the men together again and gave their new change of orders. Jack was worried over their reaction to the news of Quoto's betrayal. They were overcome with anger when they heard Quoto was a spy for Gwilim, and when told he was responsible for the death of Bragos, they could hardly be contained.

Soulo reminded them that anger was an army's best motivation. The enemy had a face now, and it would work to their benefit. They would need it in the days to come.

Jack's group was finally on their way again. He forced Owyn to ride a horse, and reluctantly, he had given in. "Just for a few hours," Owyn argued, but he knew Owyn had not fully regained his strength. Jep quietly cautioned everyone Owyn was still in an extremely fragile condition.

Jetta and Blue chatted and laughed along the trail, looking like two average village women. Blue told her stories about waiting tables at the tavern and the silly old tavern owner. She described in detail everything she had done during her stay at Harmony. Jetta smiled and tried to explain a few details, which confused Blue. She was turning out to be a very curious "human" after all.

"I am so proud of you, Blue," she said." You have become very independent. You had to make your own choices and decisions, and you did quite well. I suppose you do not need me anymore!" Jetta looked out of the corner of her eye at Blue's reaction.

"Oh, Doctor Salto, I will always need your instructions! Making my own decisions was challenging, but I am not altogether sure _why_ I made some of them. Sometimes, it seemed unreasonable for me to do some things, yet I found myself doing them anyway. Is that a normal human trait?"

"Oh yes," Jetta laughed, "it may be one of our most endearing traits. And, you will find it will get you into all sorts of situations."

Jack and Zi smiled at one another as they listened to the two talking. It was good to get back to a normal kind of life. Even though Blue was nowhere near normal, she was becoming a welcome addition to their trip, and it was nice for Jetta to have another female to spend time with.

"All the same," reminded Jetta, "it might be better to tone down that hair! Perhaps a nice brown color will attract less attention!" They both laughed at Blue's silly, bright hair.

Owyn seemed to wear down quite quickly and Jep stopped several times to make sure he was healing properly. "The magic can only hold for so long. Then the body must do the rest," he said. "I have never been strong in the magic of healing. It really is not my strong talent."

The weather was warming as they began to work their way farther west. The snow had thinned and left deep muddy trails.

"Looks as if we may be finally leaving the snow for a while," Jack called to the troops, hoping the change of weather would lighten their spirits. Their faces seemed dour remembering the recent betrayal of their comrade.

That evening, after Soulo divided the troops, he and his men moved on ahead, leaving the others to complete their part of the plan.

Jack and his group, along with the rest of the troopers, moved along the ridge of the Valley of Shadows.

He surveyed the landscape and noticed the earth looked as if it had been carved and gorged out by a great sculptor, using cutting tools to make the twisting, turning canyon along the valley floor. For miles, tendrils of offshoots coursed their way through the land as if they were a writhing body of snakes wrapping around on themselves. Hundreds of caves dotted the tall, ragged walls of canyon walls.

Jack understood why the local villagers believed this place to be haunted. The wind whistled eerily through the canyon and up the white, rocky hillside, promising foreboding danger.

They traveled on through most of the night. It was treacherous work, but Jack knew they must reach their destination before dawn. The entire plan depended on keeping a precise schedule.

Several times, they were forced to stop and look again at the old maps to make sure they were heading in the correct direction. Once, they were forced to backtrack and take a different route to descend to the canyon floor. The canyon proved to be a confusing tangle, just as they were told it would be.

Luckily, there was a bright moon to light the night, so at least they were able to see where they were going, but the canyon remained deadly quiet, except for the wailing wind, which always blew.

Troopers looked around nervously as they rode along the bottom of the canyon, staring at the looming rock walls around them. The rock seemed to close above them, leaving them with no view of the sky at all. It felt as if they were being swallowed by the rock itself.

Zi was the only one who seemed at home among the rocky landscape. He took his rough hands and gently slid them over the walls smoothed by the wind and water. He felt the canyon was a holy place.

"I tell you, this place is as sacred a place as ever I have seen," he muttered in a tone of quiet awe.

"Yeah, it may be a place of wonder, but give me an open area so I may catch my breath," whispered Owyn so his voice would not echo through the canyon.

"No fires tonight, no tents either," Jack ordered. He posted guards on the high cliffs above them and cautioned everyone to stay together for the rest of the night.

He walked the cliffs all night, checking with the night guards, unable to sleep himself. He searched the horizon, looking for any sign the enemy may be close. It was difficult to see anything moving among the twists and turns in the canyons, and Jack could see why Westin's man had discouraged a meeting here.

Tomorrow would be a time of death for many. He knew some of the dead would be his own men, and he dreaded the responsibility of pushing them into battle. Soulo was sure both their groups were ready, but the raiders numbered more than ten times their number.

Jack found a quiet spot looking along a particularly deep and twisty part of the canyon and looked out over the landscape. He closed his eyes and began to pray to the Creator to care for the souls of his men who would be offered to paradise tomorrow. He prayed for the wives and children who would never see their husbands or fathers again for the parents waiting for the return of their sons.

A great weight of sadness fell on his heart as he thought of every man who traveled with them and mourned for them. How did their world get so out of control? Men never seemed satisfied with what they had. They seemed willing to take the lives of peaceful innocents in the hope of what? Superiority? Prestige? What could make any man or wizard believe he had the right to cause such devastation to others for his own cause?

Jack shook his head. He knew his men would give anything if they could to go home and live in peace with their families. But there were always people like Gwilim who planned to destroy everything wonderful and good about their land and their lives.

Of course it is why they were here. Gwilim and Balak must never be allowed to destroy the land again. If it was not possible to seal the Barrier, then he would enter the Portal into Exiled and kill them both, himself. He would never be able to return home, sealed behind the Barrier, but at least his life would have been sacrificed for something of great importance. "It beats dying of old age," he whispered aloud.

Dawn was only a few hours away when he finally made his way to his bedroll. He looked at his friends Owyn and Zi, snoring loudly, and felt a pang of despair over almost losing Owyn.

Blue sat, as usual, next to Jetta, watching Jack. She lifted her hand in a wave but remained quiet. Jack was glad. More often than not, Blue wanted to sit and talk for hours about everything, from the dirt on the ground to the stars in the sky. Jack was in no mood.

Chapter Eight

Commander Voxx and his men crept slowly and quietly toward the camp which lay ahead. The wind was their friend today, blowing in their faces covering any noise they made.

He motioned to the men behind him as they moved in closer. They saw the campfires still burning in the grayness of dawn. He smiled to himself as he looked on. "These fools are so clueless they didn't even post a guard," he whispered to Quoto, squatting next to him.

Quoto nodded, "As I said, they do not believe we are anywhere nearby. Why should they bother? All the scouts are out looking at the trail ahead. I told you this would be easy, just like robbing a blind man. Jack's men will be no problem at all under a surprise attack. And, now that they have recovered Westin, the hard work is done for us."

Several mounds of sleeping men were spotted around the campfire. Voxx estimated sixty or seventy men. There were two tents set up, so he supposed one would be the tent for the woman and one for Westin. A cold smile crossed his face as he thought of the reward he would receive when he delivered Westin to Gwilim.

The demok in the far back of the group began to growl, and Voxx turned quickly to their keepers. He gave them a fierce sign, using his thumb, making a cutting motion across his throat. Immediately, they hushed the creatures. They were much too close to success to have them ruin it now!

Voxx checked to be sure his men were ready for attack. They were closely confined by the canyon walls, but he knew it also meant Jack and his group also had nowhere to run. He stood tall and gave a loud battle cry, commanding the raiders and demok to rush into the sleeping camp.

The canyon shook with their screams and heavy boot steps. Swords and spikes slashed and cut at the sleeping bodies, ripping and tearing. Demok howled with hunger and rage as they were freed to rampage the camp.

Voxx viciously slashed into one of the sleeping bodies when suddenly, his confused mind began to warn him. Something was not right. There were no screams of pain, no smell of hot blood or body parts thrown through the air.

Just as he began to understand, he heard a loud rumble from above. He looked up in the dim light of dawn and saw a wave of boulders and rock sweeping down toward them. He did not have time to shout a warning to his men as he covered his own head and ran for cover in a nearby rock crevice.

It sounded as if the earth were being ripped apart, as rocks rolled over and mercilessly crushed the demok and men on the canyon floor. Man and animal screamed in pain and terror as the huge boulders raced down the hillside, crushing them beneath their weight. In the misty gray light of morning, it was impossible to see them coming until they crashed into them.

The survivors had just begun to gather themselves when a second volley of rock came raining down on them, knocking some on their knees and pinning others against the sides of the canyon walls. Men raced to exit the canyon but found it blocked by huge rocks.

Voxx peered out from his hiding place and saw his men trying to gather themselves. Men and demok lay crushed on the hard rock floor, clouds of dust rising around them. Most could not be identified as man or animal anymore. Their ambush on Westin had turned into their own graveyard.

"Here! To Me!" he shouted, trying to get his men's attention. A few of the men looked his way and slowly began to stumble toward him. He could not tell exactly how many men he had left, but the ground was littered with raider bodies. He felt sharp pain as he tried to stand and found he had received a deep gash in the top of his leg. "Hurry, men! To Me," he shouted.

He heard another battle cry and at first thought it was from his own men, but then he saw, through the clouds of dust, men running toward them with their swords raised. A hail of arrows began pelting them, and more of his men fell.

"We are under attack," he yelled, lifting his own sword. "To arms!!"

Quoto, who had also found cover within the rocks, ran to try to escape the hail of arrows. Voxx grabbed him as he tried to run past. "You will stand with us or die by my hand," he growled.

"If they see me, they will know!" he begged, tugging his coat to free himself from Voxx' grip. "Let me go!"

Voxx looked out to see his men engaging the Homelanders. Demok were savagely grabbing men and tearing their bodies into pieces. No-one had a defense against them. His men heaved their heavy broadswords against the troopers, and the sheer weight of the weapons felled them like saplings.

There was still a chance they could win this. The Homelanders had been outnumbered in the beginning; they still had more fighting men than they could overcome. Voxx felt his hopes begin to rise.

He released Quoto and shoved him into the protective crevice. "Stay there. They should not be able to spot you. It may be necessary to use your services again!"

Voxx quickly left to join the battle.

Soulo knew these men were no match for the demok. His men were a hardened army, but an arrow could still bring them down. But these creatures were more than mere man. He watched as two troopers battled with one of the creatures, hacking at it with their swords. A man would have been dead after the first two hits, but this creature kept fighting as if it did not know it was supposed to die.

When, at last, they took it to the ground and finally cut its throat, both men fell over the body in exhaustion. The battle raged around them, but the enemy thought they were as dead as the demok.

Soulo called for another volley of arrows, this time carrying vials of oils set ablaze. The arrows streaked through the air like shooting stars, then a sickening thud followed as they found their mark in the bodies of men and animals. Screams filled the air as the burning oil covered the men. Flaming bodies ran in all directions as they frantically tried in vain to put out the flames.

Men on both sides tumbled and crawled over boulders and rocks, which the soldiers had been collected days before and stored on the cliffs above the mock campsite.

The rocky floor of the canyon was now slippery with the blood of the dead and wounded.

Soulo scoured the area, searching for Quoto. He wanted to kill him himself. Quoto had been one of his finest scouts, and he had trusted him. Now, he wanted nothing more than to take his life.

A sharp command for the enemy to fall back sounded, and the raiders began their retreat toward the back of the canyon opening. He had expected more raiders and demok from the accounts Jep had given him, so he thought they may have left much of their troop in Harmony. But, nevertheless, the larger part of the army was here; at least what was left of them.

Soulo had been a soldier all his life and could easily estimate the number of men in a troop. As he looked out at the departing enemy, he decided they had about two hundred left to them. Not a bad day's battle; especially when they were battling man and beast.

The demok screamed in rage as their keepers called them into retreat. They had the taste of blood now and fought their own masters to continue in the kill. These mindless creatures knew nothing else, he supposed. He would have to think of another battle plan if he were to meet them in battle again. They did not die like ordinary men. He was overcome with their bulk and brutality.

He called to his men, and they slowly lowered their weapons and watched the enemy make their way out of the canyon.

For a moment, all was quiet, then a loud cheer rose within the troop. It began to swell until the walls of the canyon echoed their victory cry. Soulo hoped the raiders could hear the sound of their defeat.

As the last of the enemy climbed through the fallen rocks blocking the canyon opening, Soulo recognized the form of Quoto, running to catch up with the men. He fought back the urge to catch him but knew Quoto was too far away, and he would be giving himself into the hands of the enemy. "It would almost be worth dying for to get the traitor!" he roared as Quoto disappeared through the rocks.

Soulo walked among the dead and injured. Captain Valco commanded his men to check every raider. The only mercy given to the enemy was a quick death. He lost almost twenty men, and at least another twenty had been injured in some way or another. Many would not make it through the night, but each man he stopped to check on grinned and shook his hand. "We did it, Commander! Did you see them run!"

He had never been as proud of a group of men as he was of these men. He swore to them that every man's family would know of their brave actions on this day.

When he and Jack devised this plan, Soulo made sure he and his men set up the ambush just as Owyn had planned it. Owyn's quick thinking had given the enemy the false information that Westin would be waiting here. He marveled at how well Jack knew Owyn's mind and how sure Owyn was Jack would make the connection.

Time had been on their side, allowing Soulo and his men two days to set up the elaborate ambush. They moved heavy rocks and set up a catch lever to release the rocks to the enemy below. It had been hard work, but the men were filled with excitement to at last be fighting again.

The false camp had been tricky. It had been Valco's strategy to set up the site so the enemy would see a sleeping camp and would be prepared for them at just the right time. Jack made sure Quoto overheard where they would be meeting Westin the night before and would make camp there until the next morning. That left very few hours for the enemy to make their attack. If they attacked too soon, Westin might not be with them. If they attacked too late, they might miss them altogether. He also thought early light would be the probable time for the enemy's attack, and he had been correct.

Soulo set up a line of guards at the far end of the canyon and began to work on the wounded. The bodies of the enemy were dumped into the woods on the far side of the canyon. His own men were buried in one of the small caves in the mountain side. They piled rocks at the opening to keep wild animals from disturbing their comrades. It was a trick they had learned from their friend

Towak of the Rogel tribe. Soulo took one of the Homeland flags, attached it to a large tree limb, and placed the limb in the center of the mound of rocks.

He and his men went back to work caring for the injured. Now, it was Jack's turn to complete his part of the plan. Soulo wished him well.

***

"Where are we going now?" yelled Quoto as he rode his horse up to Voxx."

"Back to Harmony. We'll pick up the rest of our troops and then catch their trail. We do not have enough men to overtake them now, but when we do catch them, there will not be one left alive! He looked at Quoto, "Except for Westin, of course. But only because he still has a duty to perform for Lord Gwilim."

Quoto did not like the look in Voxx's eyes.

Quoto thought of the Homeland soldiers who had just died at the Hall of Shadows and realized he was mourning their deaths. He had been friends with those men for many years, and their loss was as keen as if he had been fighting alongside them. His heart sank at his betrayal to them.

He supposed it had to be this way. The agreement had been made without his input, and he knew if it was possible to save any land in the Homeland, he wanted it to be his land.

When Governor York had approached him with the plan before he left Baka Ton, he was at first apprehensive. But as the Governor explained the treaty he made with Gwilim to spare their land and its' people, Quoto knew he had to do as York asked. Of course, no one would be able to defeat Gwilim, especially now that Balak had joined him and would open the Barrier to allow their escape. It was foolish to think otherwise. The protective Veil had already fallen! No, it was wise to make peace with Gwilim before the invasion on the Homeland.

He was not a traitor! He would be a hero to his people! When all the other regions of the Homeland were conquered by Gwilim and Balak, his people would live in peace, all because of his sacrifice.

He rode on, feeling a lot better about himself, almost able to forget the faces of his dead Homeland comrades.

Chapter Nine

Everyone stared in awe at the strange orange and pink spires jutting up from the earth. The group was completely surrounded by them. There were thousands of them in every direction, like great towers of a mighty kingdom, reaching up into the sky. They made the travelers seem more like ants than human beings.

Zi groaned as they passed through the shifting sand beneath one of the mighty spires. "We should not be here. This is a cursed place. Can not you feel it?" he almost tumbled from his saddle as bits of rock rolled down a nearby hillside. "I have no desire to carry a curse for the rest of my life," he grumbled.

"It would be a waste to put a curse on something as ugly as you," said Owyn as he peered up from the wagon he was riding.

Jack was glad to hear Owyn back to his old self. For the past few days, since his return from Harmony, he had been withdrawn and quiet. He ate only after Jetta fussed over him and practically pushed it down his throat.

Jack knew he hadn't been sleeping very well either. He heard him crying out in his sleep many times. He wanted to talk to Owyn about what had happened to him in Harmony, but Owyn seemed to always shy away from him when he tried, so he finally decided to wait until he was ready.

Blue walked close to the wagon, always keeping an eye on Jetta as well as Owyn. She sensed Owyn was not back to normal yet and was very protective of him. Jetta tried to distract her and coax her away from Owyn, but he seemed comforted by Blue's presence, so, after a while, Jetta did not bother.

Jep seemed more worried than anyone for Owyn. The old wizard was afraid he might re-open some of the wounds he had received in Harmony. He was forced to use his magic several times on Owyn when the movement of the wagon had become intolerable.

"That boy should be dead, by all accounts," he worried. "I suppose if he were not so hard-headed, he would be. I suppose it is a good thing to be stubborn after all."

Jack worried about Owyn, too, but was more encouraged this afternoon. He had more energy than before, and his teasing with Zi was the proof everyone needed to relax a little.

"All I am saying is, we should meet up with Westin and leave as quickly as possible. There is no need to borrow trouble when you have it chasing you!" Zi continued.

"We'll leave Needle Rock as soon as possible," Jack replied. "I have a creepy feeling about this place too."

Jep looked thoughtfully around the arches and spires. He stopped several times and stood perfectly still, as if testing the air, then hurried to catch up with the group.

"What is it, Jepthya?" asked Jetta, frowning. "You act as if we are being watched or something. Are we in any danger?"

"I am not sure," he said uncertainly. "But I do not think we are alone."

Jack stopped and looked at Jep. "What do you mean? Have you seen something?"

"No, not that....." Jep's voice trailed off as he looked around him again. "It is more like.... I can _feel_ something is wrong."

"A wizard can't be wrong!" huffed Zi. "What did I just say about this place being cursed!"

Jep walked slowly through the spires, stopping and listening. "You may not be far wrong, my friend."

Zi's mouth sagged open as he looked at Jep. "This is one time I would not mind you lying to me, old man."

"We cannot be too far away from Westin's camp. They must know we are near. Once we have him, we will be gone from this place," Jack declared as he, too began to feel increasingly uncomfortable.

Although it was only mid-morning, the sky began to darken. Gray clouds moved slowly over their heads, and the wind began to whip the sand, stinging their faces.

Blue suddenly stopped in her tracks and shouted, "Jack, what are those?"

Jack strained his eyes to see where she was pointing and, through the haze of swirling sand, saw the ground rising before them. A loud, shrill whine sounded, and the earth was thrown into the air, revealing a group of giant, eight-legged insects. Their eyes glowed red as hungry mandibles snapped menacingly at the new intruders. They held gossamer wings tight against their bodies and began a deadly swaying, back and forth, always eyeing their prey.

Jack gaped as he looked up into the fierce, cold eyes. The creatures were taller than five men standing on one another's shoulders. They resembled huge locusts, and locusts were always hungry. He had seen entire fields leveled in just a few hours in the Homeland by their much smaller cousins.

The shrill noise got increasingly louder, bouncing off the walls of the tall spire, causing them to cover their ears in pain. Men were trying to push themselves into the crevices of the spire walls to get away from the creatures and the noise. The locusts dug at the ground with their spiked legs, stirring up even more sand, trying to get to their prey. Their wide abdomens heaved in and out as their piercing song continued.

"What should we do, Jack?" screamed Jep through the ever-mounting noise.

Before he could answer, one of the creatures sprang into the air and pounced on a helpless trooper. The locusts held the trooper against the ground with its wings as its giant mandibles ripped the man's head from his body. A long tube-like extension shot from its mouth, jamming into the man's chest as the thing sucked the blood from his body.

The group scattered, looking for any kind of protection within the spires.

Another scream from the horses told them more of the locusts were also feeding.

Blue grabbed Jetta and Jep, pulling them between two of the orange spires, while Zi pulled Owyn under the wagon. Jack and several troopers found shelter between the spires as the locusts rammed the towers, clawing at them.

"Jep!" yelled Jack, "This may be one of those times you may want to use you magic!"

Jep stuck his head around and took a look at the chaos. The men scurried for shelter, but the horses were left in the open. They screamed and bucked as the locusts attacked, some breaking away and running for their lives. Another horse was taken down as Jep warily stepped from behind his shelter.

One of the locusts spotted him and made a leap. Jep threw up his hands and sent a wave of light toward the creature, causing it to explode into slimy pieces. Nearby locusts scurried to the remains of their fallen comrade and began to feast.

"Jack," yelled Jep, "I cannot fight them all, there are too many. Get your men out and fire a volley at them."

Jack shouted for the bowmen to ready their bows, and soon, a hail of arrows was flying toward the creatures. Loud clinking noises sounded as the arrows bounced off the hard bodies of the locusts Not one arrow had made its mark.

Jep looked out helplessly as more locusts began to spring from the desert floor. The noise from the creatures was beginning to shake the spires around them, threatening to topple their only refuge.

Jep sent more waves of light, destroying many more and temporarily distracting a few of the others, closing in on them.

Jetta screamed in terror as one of the creatures tore at the coat she was wearing. Its mandibles snapped menacingly, trying to reach her. She pulled at her coat and clawed at the sandy wall of the spire, trying to get away from the hungry maw.

Blue was at her side in an instant, slashing at the creature's face with her sword. Jack did not even know Blue had a weapon and was surprised to see Blue was quite talented in her use of it.

She stabbed at the red eyes of the creature as it leaned in to make a grab for Jetta. Her sword pierced the unprotected eye, slashing it open. Bright liquid shot from the eye, and the creature twisted and turned away in pain, its tiny front legs wiping at its eye while the huge body twisted and slammed against the giant spire protecting the three.

A deafening cracking sound filled the area as the towering spire snapped and tumbled down, covering Jetta, Blue, and Jep.

"NO!" screamed Jack as he tried to work his way to the three trapped under the rubble. His path was blocked by several of the hungry creatures, who leaped toward him, causing him to go back into his hiding place.

A trooper shouted to the others, "Try for their eyes!"

Another volley of arrows filled the air, and several arrows found their mark in the eyes of the creatures. They shrieked in pain and twisted and rolled in the sand. The other locusts? began to attack their own fallen immediately, jamming their tube-like extensions in the bodies and feeding.

Jack looked helplessly at the spot where his three friends were trapped. He realized there was no way he would be able to cross the area and get to them without becoming a victim himself.

"Jack!" he heard Zi shout. "We could use some help!"

Straddling the wagon, a locust had its legs strapped around the wagon bed. It pushed and rocked the wagon, trying to lift it off his friends hiding beneath it.

"A volley to the wagon!" he yelled, just as the men released a stream of arrows on their own.

The locust lifted its body upright just as the arrows were released, spreading its wings to take flight. The wagon began to lift, exposing the men beneath it. Two arrows slammed into each of the creature's eyes, causing it to release the wagon crashing it to the ground. Zi flinched as the wagon rested only inches from his face.

Suddenly, the locust was forced to the ground as a giant wolf tore at its legs. The wolf pulled and gnawed until the leg snapped from the body, and it lay twitching in the sand. The wolf clamped onto another limb.

Soon, the area was filled with wolves, snarling and biting at the giant insects. The legs, while arrow-proof, were not sturdy enough to withstand the bite of a ferocious wolf. The insects began to topple, and the wolves then tore at their wings and necks.

Locusts began to take flight into the sky, preparing for a fresh attack, when suddenly, one of the creatures was snatched from its flight by a pair of strong talons.

Jack looked into the sky to see Luka sitting on the back of a fearsome dragon, waving his arms and yelling like a madman.

Dragons were coming from all directions, swooping and grabbing locusts, one in each claw. They bent their long, slender necks and snapped at their bodies, easily ripping them in half, feasting on the vile insects.

Jack could hardly believe what was happening. He yelled for his men to pull their swords and join the fight.

The sound of the crunching of insects was sickening, and the smell was worse, but they kept slashing at the creatures until, at last, it was quiet. At least Jack thought it was quiet. His ears were still ringing from the song of the locusts.

Luka landed his dragon nearby and jumped down, giving his wolves a call. The animals began to pull away from their kill and trotted over to the big man, who rubbed each one's head in affection.

Jack quickly rushed to where Jetta and the others were trapped and began digging. The spires were petrified sand and very heavy, even though most of the rocks were no bigger than his hand. Troopers joined him as they frantically dug with their bare hands to reach their friends.

Jep was found first, coughing and gagging from the sand which covered him. Jack pulled him free, and the troopers hurriedly carried him to the wagon. Blue pushed away the rock and sand covering her, as soon as she heard Jep's cough, and soon she too was pulled free. She fought madly to free herself from the troopers when they tried to carry her to the wagon. "I must help free Doctor Salto," she screamed as she pushed them away and joined in the digging.

"She was next to me when the tower fell," Blue yelled as she dug harder.

Jetta's hand began to move under the thick layer of sand, and Blue cried out, "She is here! We found her!"

They dug the rocks away and soon uncovered Jetta's still form.

Jack quickly turned her over and wiped away dirt and sand that covered her face. Her eyelids began to flutter. "Shhhh...." he said. "We're getting you out of here."

He gently lifted her small body from the rubble and hurried toward the wagon. "Jep! We need some help!" he called.

Jep, already tending the wounded in the wagon bed, looked up, his face revealing alarm, as he saw Jack holding Jetta's limp body.

"Put her here," he said as he cleared away a place in the wagon for her.

Jep wiped her face clean with water and saw blood trickling from the side of her mouth. He pressed against her ribs, and she cried out in pain.

Blue squirmed in sympathy as she hovered next to the wagon, peering over the side at Jetta.

"Jetta," Jep said softly, "Can you hear me girl?"

Jetta's eyes slowly opened, and she looked up at Jep. She opened her mouth to answer him and was racked with a spasm of coughing. Droplets of blood splattered against the side of the wagon.

Jep laid his hands on her body and began moving them slowly, letting his magic reveal the damage done to her. Everyone stood close, waiting.

Battle-hardened troopers wrung their hands as they nervously waited for news of Jetta.

Jep looked up, "I need more time with her. She is badly hurt. Is it safe to stay here for a couple of hours while I try to tend her? Will those evil creatures return?"

Luka looked over Jep's shoulder, his forehead wrinkled in concern for Jetta. "Not as long as my friends stand guard. Take the time you need, wizard."

They erected a tent right over the wagon so they would not have to move her again. The wind still blew hard, and they wanted her protected from the stinging sand.

The troopers pulled the carcass of the dead locusts away from the area and quickly set up make-shift defenses from the wind. Afterward, they sat quietly, waiting and tending to their own wounded.

"You were a beautiful sight on that dragon, if I say so myself," said Zi as he greeted Luka. "You never said you had a way with them too!"

Luka smiled at Zi's fuzzy, sand-covered face. "You know I did. Remember when I told you I flew over the Barrier with the aid of a friend? Meet my friend, Scala."

Zi looked warily at the huge, scaled creature as it turned its giant head, eyeing him.

"Pleasure," he offered timidly, giving a quick nod toward the dragon.

"How did you find us?" asked Jack, giving Luka's hand a hearty shake.

"You people leave tracks a blind man could follow. Scala and her fellows let me know you were coming here. It has been some time since these demon locusts have been here, and it was your misfortune to pick the wrong time to visit. Scala knew they were about the area, so she warned me."

Owyn walked over to Zi and Scala. "Well, make sure you thank her for us," he said.

"Tell her yourself," Luka chimed, "she can understand every word you say."

Owyn's eyes widened as he glanced over at Zi. Zi returned the look with a smile.

"And a lovely lady she is!" he commented.

"We circled over a fierce battle a day or so away," he said, "thought I recognized that sour faced man you call Soulo. We made a stop to check on them."

"How are they?" Jack asked anxiously as he tried to slow his heartbeat.

"They lost a lot of men, most of them, but he said to let you know they did the job proper," Luka replied. "I only wish me and my group had been around then. There is nothing more I would like than to get my hands on a few demok."

"Most of their men!" Jack looked at the ground in stunned silence. He did not know what he had expected; they were being sent against ten times their number, but still, he felt the loss keenly.

Luka sensed Jack's distress and continued, "He said he would meet you as planned. They were aiding the men who could be mended. I took several back to my compound to stay until they were healed. I can tell you they do not take well to riding on the back of a dragon."

Luka looked around at the troopers left. "Your numbers are dwindling. How many men do you have left?"

Jack did not know, and right now, he could not bring himself to think about it. Gwilim's men were still out there somewhere, albeit many hundreds less, thanks to Soulo and his men. The thought of another battle was more than he could handle at the moment.

Owyn stumbled over to Jack, "We should set up camp here for the night if you think it is safe enough. This fight has taken its toll on everyone, and Jep could use the time to help Jetta."

Jack agreed and asked the men to look for firewood and set up tents to shelter them from the sandstorm.

Jep pushed back the opening of the tent and looked over the group, looking for Jack. When he spotted him, he motioned for them to come to the tent.

Jack and the others approached a solemn Jep as he let the flap of the tent close behind him.

"I cannot save her," he said in disbelief, shaking his head as if he could not believe it himself.

The group stood in shocked silence as the words slowly sank in. Jack felt his heart catch in his chest when he saw Jep's grieving face.

"Is there nothing you can do?" he asked. "Your magic.... Can your magic do something? You were able to heal my arm with it."

"And me...." added Owyn, concern written on his face, "I was near death too, and you were able to save me."

It was the first time Jack realized how badly hurt Owyn had been. He had avoided talking about it, and Jep and Blue had respected his wishes and kept quiet about his ordeal in Harmony.

His head was whirling with the amount of death that had befallen them, and now Jetta!

"Her body is too injured for me to be able to hold her together for long. My magic uses the forces of nature. I was only barely able to help you, Owyn. If you had been injured any more than you were, I would have been helpless to help you, too. Jetta is bleeding inside and in many places. I cannot stop them all. She is dying."

The words stung like a knife, and everyone gasped back their grief. Little Jetta, who had become the mother of everyone, was being taken from them.

Owyn stepped forward and took Jep's arm, "Where's Blue? Does she know?"

Jep nodded. "She understands Jetta is hurt badly. She has some medical understanding, but I do not think she is accepting the inevitable. I tried to explain it to her. She refuses to leave Jetta's side."

Troopers sat heavily on the sand, and Jack saw more than a few tears on the faces of the battle-hardened men.

Zi and Owyn both turned their backs to avoid having anyone see their faces.

Zi had taken a kind hand with Jetta and cared for her whenever Blue was not around. He watched her steps on the trail and helped her along the way when she tired. He had shown a soft and caring side seldom seen by most.

"Jack, she wants to see the three of you. You had better hurry. I do not think she has much time left."

Jack stood numbly for a second, then hurried into the tent, with Owyn and Zi following closely behind him.

She laid limply in the bed of the wagon, with faithful Blue holding her hand, a troubled look on her face. The shiny triangles on the side of her head seemed dull to Jack, and he began to worry for Blue as well.

He stepped closer and sat on the open tailgate to be closer to Jetta. Jep had entered the tent with them and stood on the other side of Blue, his hand on her shoulder.

"Jack, it seems I have made a terrible mess of our mission," she whispered. "There is so much left to do, and it seems I have run out of time." She sadly shook her head, and a tear trickled down her cheek.

"I know you will succeed. You are good and dedicated men, and you know the consequences of failure. You will find Westin and his group. Please understand the real reason for this quest. There is so much more you need to understand, but I will have to leave that to Dr. Westin."

A fit of coughing took her for several minutes, and blood once again splattered on her chest.

When she was able to continue, she looked at Blue. "I have given my friend, Blue, all the knowledge I had to aid Westin at the Barrier. She knows what I know now, so protect her with all your strength. Once you reach Westin, he will need her. She is the best chance we all have." She smiled at Blue and stroked her face.

"One thing more," she stopped and looked at Jack and the others, "you have been my dear friends, and I love you all. I had such a wonderful time with you. May the Creator protect you all." She smiled a weak smile.

It took Jack a minute to realize she was gone. Her sweet smile was still on her lips.

Blue finally broke the silence, "No! This is unacceptable," she stated. "This is unacceptable."

"Blue, she is gone. There is nothing more we can do," comforted Jep.

"This is unacceptable," Blue repeated over and over as if it were the only words she knew.

Everyone stared at Blue in alarm as if they expected her to explode. Over and over, she kept repeating the phrase as if she were trying to convince death to change its mind.

Owyn walked over and stood next to Blue. "She does not hurt anymore Blue. She is safe now. No more heat or cold, no sickness, no demok, or locusts. She is safe and happy in the arms of the Creator."

Blue looked at Owyn, her face wet with tears. "She was _my_ creator, Owyn..... my mother."

Owyn put his arm around Blue, and to the surprise of everyone, Blue cried in grief. It was an odd sight, seeing something that was once not human act in such a human way, but Jack knew Blue had a good teacher in learning how to be human.

Jep walked over to Jetta and closed her eyes. "She asked that we burn her body so the animals and locusts would not feed on her."

Jack nodded slowly as he looked at her sweet face one last time.

Chapter Ten

The group moved about their duties in a daze as they prepared to continue toward their meeting with Westin. Everyone seemed confused and unsure as if they had never packed for travel. They stumbled around silently, picking up their scattered supplies and then just standing, looking at them as if they had never seen them before. They were lost.

Jetta had added more to the group than anyone imagined. She was not just a brilliant doctor and Blue's teacher but was mother to them all. Her presence made this foreign land less hostile. Her gentle spirit made even the hardest part of the journey tolerable.

Now, as the funeral pyre died away, they knew they would have to finish the long trip without her. The thought left everyone confused and frightened, especially Blue.

Owyn spent the remainder of the day comforting Blue, who could not accept the reality of being without her Jetta. She seemed alarmed at leaving Jetta's ashes to fly away into the desert, so Jep collected them and placed them into one of Jetta's fine metal tins she had brought along to carry her precious herbs. Together, they buried her ashes near a great arch, which seemed a majestic place to leave dear Jetta. Blue made a marker with her name on it, followed by the simple word "Mother."

Afterwards, Blue left the group to be alone, to grieve for a final time. Owyn wanted to go with her, but Blue asked to walk the spires alone and gather herself before the journey. The troopers were a bit alarmed for Blue to wander off alone, but Jack assured them Blue would be back soon, and they would be on their way. They had come to think of Blue as the little brother/sister they had left behind in the Homeland and knew how lost she would be without Jetta. He marveled at how they all had changed since they left Baka Ton.

Their numbers had dwindled drastically since then. They had lost a quarter of their men and horses. He recalled how he feared losing men when they were crossing the Wilds. It had been a hard trek, but, looking back, it had not been as treacherous as the rest of the journey had proved to be.

Owyn and Zi loaded their things into their travel packs, then began packing Blue's. They stopped several times when they went going through Jetta's things, and finally only packed the herbs and spices she had brought. Jep looked through the supplies she brought with her from the Palace of Ages and kept a few things he thought were important to give to Westin.

Zi sat heavily as he lifted the pair of small boots from the pack Jetta had counted as a prize possession when they had stopped in Serenity. She had braved the snowy mountains in her old boots and was thrilled to acquire the new pair.

He folded them fondly and placed them aside.

No one seemed surprised when Blue walked back to the campsite as a man. He shed the feminine appearance for one of an old man. His hair was no longer golden blonde but gray. His face was lined with wrinkles, the eyes were older, sadder. He walked with a slight stoop, much like Jep. He walked to his pack, picked it up without a word, and stood waiting for Jack to give the word to move out.

Owyn stared at Blue sadly, then shook his head. He walked over and gave his shoulder a small squeeze, as the group began making their way out of the spired canyon.

Jack knew the big question on everyone's mind was whether they would be able to continue without Jetta. She had been Blue's instructor and, with Westin's help, were the only people who could train Blue to put a stop to Gwilim and Balak's plans.

Jetta told them she had transferred the information needed to Blue, and Jack supposed they would have to believe it was enough. Jetta would not put them in danger without doing her best to provide the assistance they needed.

Luka walked next to Jack, discussing the area they were to find Westin. Once they passed through this canyon, they would find the long narrow valley called Needle Pass. Soulo and his men were to meet them close to the mouth of the valley, and Jack would be glad to have all his men together again.

The rain had not yet begun to fall, but it appeared it wouldn't be long. The sky seemed ever threatening, with dark clouds moving swiftly overhead. The wind was becoming stronger with each mile, sending the sand slashing at their faces.

Blue walked beside Jep most of the day. Jep talked quietly with Blue, who only seemed to respond with nods of his head. Jack did not know what Jep was saying, but it did not seem to upset Blue too much, and he hoped Jep would know what to do to help Blue with his grief.

"It was the entertainer at the Crusty Hound. That's where Blue got the idea for his new body. There was an old fella who told stories, like Jep. He worked at the tavern where I met those troopers," said Owyn. He nodded his head with approval over his apt memory. "I could not quite put my finger on it, but that's who it is. A funny fella, as I recall."

Zi looked back at Blue and Jep, "But why pick an old man? Why not a young one, like before?"

Owyn shrugged his shoulders as he adjusted the pack on his back. "Guess he feels old right now. Losing someone you love takes the life out of you."

They all could appreciate that. Each of them knew the empty, hollow feeling when you lose someone you love. Changing into a person who reflected a sad person was a natural choice for Blue.

When the rain drops began to finally fall, it slapped at their faces like a whip. Between the blowing sand and rain, they were forced to cover their faces to protect their eyes.

Luka sent his wolves ahead while the dragons were sent to scout for Westin. The rain and wind never bothered the animals. They kept their steady pace, occasionally reporting back to Luka.

The spires were thinning out, and soon they left the sandy canyon and emerged into an area gratefully spotted with sage brush and scrub trees. It was always good to see something green growing again.

The ground soaked up the rain as fast as it could fall, but Jack knew soon even the sandy ground would not hold the water back. He recognized high water marks where flooding had once occurred. Twigs and leaves were caught in the lower branches of the scrub trees, indicating water had risen to that level. He asked Luka to keep a close eye for any indication of quick rising water. Luka was vastly experienced and knew what clues to look for to predict any change.

Jack found himself, more than once, turning to check on Jetta and was abruptly reminded she was gone from them. He met Blue's eyes, who understood what Jack was doing. They would smile sadly at one another and force their way on through the storm.

Near late afternoon, a huge dragon swept down from the sky and landed across their path. Jack was momentarily shaken and going for his sword before he recalled they were friends of Luka.

Luka approached the huge dragon as it tucked its huge, leathery wings against its body. Its snake-like head moved from side to side as Luka approached. "Scala," he purred, rubbing his big hands along her scaly neck. For several minutes, Luka caressed the animal's head as it leaned into him. They whined and moaned to one another until, finally, the creature let out a mighty bellow and heaved a column of fire into the sky.

Jack and the others jumped in fright, Owyn falling to the ground. They still worried about the creatures, though Luka seemed quite comfortable with them.

"Hard to think of these creatures as being tame." Owyn declared.

"I would never call them tame, frog." Offered Zi. "Let us say they tolerate us."

The troopers crowded close to the tree line in case a hasty retreat from the dragon was needed, but Luka gave it a pat it on its long neck, then turned and walked back to them.

"There's trouble, I fear," he shouted over the wind. "Scala says they spotted Soulo and his men up ahead. They have already made it to the mouth of Needle Valley. Unfortunately, there is a squad of soldiers nearby. Voxx's men, I suppose. They have demok with them."

"How soon before they reach Soulo?" Jack asked.

"They are not heading for Soulo but toward a smaller group nearby. Westin and his people, I expect."

Jack thought for a minute, "We must get to our men. At least if we get Soulo we will have a fighting chance of protecting Westin when we get there."

Jep stood to the side, listening, "How many men do you think?"

Luka raised his eyebrow, "My dragons only think in terms of meals, not numbers. They say there are many days food following Soulo."

"Considering how much a dragon eats, it must be quite a few," Jep offered. "What about the wolves? Will they be able to give us a better head count?"

"Ay, they should. I expect them anytime."

"One more thing, Scala says they are bringing a large wagon with them. She says it is holding a large arrow."

Jack and Jep looked at one another in realization. "The light cannon!" whispered Jack.

Luka looked between them for a minute, then asked, "Is it the weapon you were telling me about? The one that destroyed the Tourashon village?"

"I am afraid so," said Jack. "We need to make some plans if that is the case. They will not need to get close to destroy Soulo's area."

"No, that is not quite true. They need to get an exact location to achieve a proper aim. We will just have to hope they cannot spot Soulo and his men before we reach them," reminded Jep.

"Regardless, we need to move at double speed to reach Soulo _and_ get to Westin."

"How much time do we have before the raiders reach Westin?" he asked Luka.

"Scala says maybe half a day."

"And how long till we can reach Soulo?"

"About an hour or so."

Jack made some quick calculations in his head, then turned to his group. "Have the men mount their horses, double up if they have to," Jack ordered, he moved to Owyn and Zi to let them know what he was planning.

They rode as fast as the rough terrain would allow them. The wind was not merciful and blew strongly in their faces. The rain, at least, was not pouring but falling in a slow drizzle. Another heavy fog began to lift from the ground, covering the hooves of the horses as they made their way toward Needle Pass and Soulo.

Scala led the way above, drawing them closer. Many times, she was lost in the gray, fluffy clouds as she lifted and fell with the wind.

At last, they spotted a scout from Soulo's camp waving in the distance. His wide smile was evident even before they reached him.

"You guys are a sight, let me tell you!" he yelled over the storm. "Soulo has worn a path around the camp pacing. Maybe he can relax now that you are finally here."

"No quite!" Jack answered. "Lead us to him as quickly as possible!"

The scout's smile faded as he saw the serious expressions on Jack and the other's faces. He turned his horse and quickly led them back to his camp.

Soulo jumped straight into the air as he spotted them. Jack sensed the soldier was accurate in describing Soulo as anxious.

He ran to greet Jack and his group as they dismounted their horses. "Am I ever glad to see you guys," he said as he took Jack's hand and shook it heartily.

Jack looked around at the men with Soulo. So few had survived the attack on Voxx's men at the Valley of Shadows. He knew there would be losses, but there could not be more than thirty or forty men here!

"How many?" he said as he looked around.

Soulo looked at Jack and answered, "Twenty dead, and seven sent to Luka's. We took a hard hit, but they took a harder one. For every man we lost, they lost ten. We cut the number of demok they had with them too. They learned a hard lesson of respect for the Homeland, I tell you."

"We had a few casualties ourselves. We lost three of our troopers," Jack hoped he was delivering the news in a proper way, "and Jetta."

The breath left Soulo with such force it was as if someone hit him in the chest. His eyes widened in disbelief as he stared at Jack. His eyes searched across the group until they found the old man that was Blue.

"How did it happen?" he said softly.

Jack explained the attack of the giant locusts and the tragic death of Jetta. He found himself surprised to see water fill the eyes of the scarred and weathered face. It was like seeing a flower blooming in a rock. Something you never expected to see.

At last, he nodded his head. "She was a fine woman, a fine lady."

"Soulo, Luka's dragons reported a large group of raiders nearby. They are no more than a few hours back and heading straight toward Westin. They have the light cannon with them."

Soulo looked at Jack, trying to comprehend everything thrown at him in the last few minutes. At last, he shook his head and pulled his thoughts together. "Can we get to Westin first?"

Jack shook his head, "They are a few hours closer than we are, but I may have a plan."

Jack motioned for Luka to join him, Soulo, Jep, Owyn and Zi. He began to hurriedly pour out his plan.

"Luka, how many men do you think your dragons can carry?"

Luka's eyes narrowed as he looked questioningly at Jack. "I would say six easily, maybe eight. What are you thinking, Jack, boy?"

Jack smiled as Zi began rubbing his hands together excitedly. "Now we can show them which end of a bear to kiss!" he growled.

Chapter Eleven

The earth was a blur below them as Jack and his men clutched the thick scales of the dragons. They whisked through the thick gray clouds, which quickly soaked their clothes. Soon, they found themselves flying high above the gray fluffy mass. The sky up here was brighter, and the clouds were not as thick. Jack pulled one of the dragon's scales in front of him to shield himself from the rushing wind. He found it sucked the very breath from him whenever he tried to sit up and look around.

He looked to the right of him and saw Zi and Owyn on their dragon. Zi tucked his head and as much of his bulky body as he could hide beneath the tough scales. Owyn, however, was having the time of his life. His body lay low along the back of the dragon, and his arms stretched out to either side as if he were flying like a bird. Occasionally, he yelled out a whoop, causing poor Zi to cower in terror under his scale.

Jep, Luka, and Soulo were each on dragons on either side of Jack's and Owyn's. Jep looked quite at home, but Soulo was not fairing much better than

Zi. The rest of the men cowering behind them were almost invisible beneath the dragons' protective scales.

There were six dragons in all which Luka had convinced to carry them. It had been quite a discussion since the dragons did not seem to like the men anymore than the men liked them. But finally, Luka's persuasive manner won them over.

Only forty men were able to make the trip, and Jack hoped it would be enough. He had to arrive at Westin's camp before the raiders, and this was the only way to do it.

The huge creatures swayed and swooped, gliding on the currents of the winds. Jack tried to spot mountains and other landmarks to show him where they were, but the clouds would only allow fleeting glimpses of the ground below.

"I can't tell how high up we are, but we must be far above the mountains!" yelled Jep.

"Probably for the best," he yelled back over the wind. "If we saw how high we were, we would probably all die of fright before we had the chance to face the enemy!"

At last, the dragons tilted their leathery wings and dipped back down into the gray mass of clouds. Again moisture covered them as they broke through the clouds to the earth below.

Jack spotted a small group of people camped against a jagged alcove of rock which seemed to stretch to the sky, Needle Rock.

When the group spotted the dragons, they scattered like frightened mice into small openings and outcrops as the six giant dragons landed softly on the ground. Jack did not blame them a bit. It must have been a frightening sight to see sweeping down from the sky.

The dragons lay flat against the earth to allow their riders closer access to the ground, but it still proved to be quite jump. Men dismounted immediately, but none as fast as Zi, whose feet hit the ground as soon as the dragon's.

Owyn grinned at Jack as he dismounted, sticking his thumbs in his waistband, "Well now, that was as about as much fun as I have.......". He was hastily shoved aside as Zi rushed to a nearby clump of bushes and lost his stomach.

Jack looked toward the frightened people and waved his hands. "It is alright!" He shouted. "I am Jackson Creed, here to see Dr. Westin. I am here to help."

Before he could finish, a little white-haired man stepped out and approached Jack. "The Creator be praised; you have finally reached us." A broad smile spread across his face as he reached out and took Jack by the hand. "We were so worried. We were afraid something had happened when you did not arrive yesterday. I have tried to reach you several times but with no success."

"We ran into trouble, and I am afraid more trouble is heading this way. The raiders will be here in just a few hours," Jack explained to the old doctor.

Jep walked over to the old man, and Westin let out a whoop. "Jepthya! How good it is to see your face!" The two men gave each other a hardy embrace as the rest of Jack's men joined them.

"And where is Jetta? Don't tell me you got the poor girl on one of those things!"

Jep took Dr. Westin by the elbow and led him away from the others to break the sad news. Jack saw Westin shake his head sadly upon hearing the news of the death of his friend.

After a few minutes, they re-joined the group. "And what about Blue," he asked, "which one of these men is our Blue?"

Owyn stepped forward, "Blue is waiting back at the camp for you and your group to join him. I think he will be awful relieved to see you."

Westin looked around the group, then cocked his head to the side and looked at Jep. "What do you mean 'he is waiting' for me to join him?"

Jack put his hand on the old doctor's shoulder and began, "Doctor Westin, have you ever wondered what it would be like to fly?"

Chapter Twelve

Commander Voxx and his group prodded their horses through the tall, sharp blades of exotic grass which covered the ground. The blades cut and ripped at the legs of the animals, so they had to be forced to move forward every few minutes. He gazed back over his shoulder at the men following him. Some were not so lucky as to have saved their horses in the battle with the Homelanders, and they also suffered the sting from the grass as they pushed their way through.

The demok seemed to notice little discomfort, he noticed. They swayed their big bodies back and forth as their handlers herded them on. They lifted their snouts high in the air from time to time and growled, letting their trainers know they were still on the right track.

They lost several demok in the last battle. Voxx was not particularly fond of the beasts and would much rather lose them than soldiers, but they did have their uses. They never tired, for one thing. Even when the men had to stop for rest, the empty eyes of the demok always seemed to stare out into the unknown countryside, hungry to move on. Voxx could not imagine what their life was like, but it mattered little to him as long as they remained his weapons. But still... he glanced again at the closest animal near him.

The creature, as if sensing his curiosity, looked back at Voxx. Its' cold black eyes stared defiantly at him for a minute, then its' mighty body shivered into a whimper, and it bowed its' head to avoid any further eye contact.

Quoto, riding beside Voxx, watched the encounter with the creature. "Where do these things come from?" he asked in disgust. "I've run into creatures similar who raided our villages for years, but I have never seen any such as these."

Voxx turned back in his saddle and prodded his horse along the grassy trail. "Unless you come from the other side of the Barrier, you would not. They are Gwilim's doing."

Quoto spared a look at a group of demok huffing beside his horse. "He made these things?" he asked. "Why make such monsters? How could he even bring such things to life?"

"He made them for exactly what you see; mindless killers who live only for his purpose. *How* he made them is his own concern."

Quoto curled his upper lip as the scent from the group reached his nose. "He can still control them even when they are on this side of the Barrier, and he is on the other?"

"We had better hope so!" grunted Voxx. "We would be as good a meal as any to these creatures. As long as Gwilim is alive, there will be demok. They are his most ruthless soldiers."

Quoto looked back at the wagon being pulled behind them carrying the long cannon. There were ten demok pulling the heavy load, grunting and pulling, the muscles in their arms and legs looking as if they would explode.

"And that thing? Is that one of Gwilim's creations also?"

"Actually, the cannon was a 'gift' to Gwilim from your good Doctor Balak. It was a way of endearing himself to Gwilim." Voxx's voice took on a tone of hardness.

"Balak created the light cannon?"

"He and Westin. When he left the Homeland to join us, he brought the plans with him, as well as Dr. Westin. It seems Balak still needed the old man to complete the cannon. It works quite well, I am pleased to say. We have several here in the Grand and the Homeland."

Quoto rode quietly beside Voxx, remembering the destruction of the Tourashon village. The little village was utterly destroyed. He remembered the horror he felt at such power. He thought again his governor must believe it important for his region's safety, to make a secret agreement with Balak. Cannons, such as these, had destroyed thousands of acres in every region of the Homeland, drying up rivers and lakes and sucking the precious nutrients from the earth. Nothing grew where the cannons had taken their deadly aim. Followed by the raids of the demok, life was very quickly snuffed out in the hands of the raider army.

He wished he could somehow contact the governor of his region. He did not like Voxx or his men and knew they hated him. It made this an unhealthy duty. He could not be sure Gwilim was not even now giving orders to attack the Northland Region. Nor was he sure his land would remain safe after the opening of the Barrier. Quoto was a scout, and a good one, and he knew very well how to read signs, and what he read of this group made a deathly dread spread over his soul.

Voxx gave a satisfied grunt as they reached the end of the long grasses and prodded his horse to a mound of rock close by. Quoto was relieved to be rid of the sharp blades, too. The legs of his tough, animal hide pants were shredded, and his legs had several cuts.

Voxx heard a whistling sound, and from over the hill, another group of men came bounding down the hillside toward them. Quoto was surprised to see the group approach. He did not know Voxx had more men meeting up with them.

"Commander, the group is camped no more than a few hours ahead," reported one of the men. They show no signs of leaving anytime soon."

"Good! We found them then!" said Voxx as he rubbed his hands together, his eyes wide with anticipation. "Any signs of the others?"

One of the other men from the group stepped forward, "They were spotted more than half a day away. We will have Westin and be long gone by the time they arrive."

"I do not want any more surprises like the last time. Westin and his group are no match for us. I do not care what you do the others, but Westin is to be taken alive. Is that clear?"

The men around Voxx all nodded. Balak had given the order, and no one wanted to incur his wrath. In the brief time he had been in Exiled, his orders were as Gwilim's.

Voxx walked over to the demok handlers and to the other officers. He often left Quoto out of the conversations, but this time, Quoto was determined to know what Voxx planned. The last battle had almost cost him his life.

Voxx laid out the attack plan as Quoto nudged his way in with the others. Voxx glanced at him for a moment and then proceeded. "These creatures must not harm Westin in any way. They have his scent. Remind them of the penalty they will receive if they harm him. As for the others, let them have their fill. We have no time for prisoners. Gwilim is most anxious for our return with the doctor."

The handlers herded the demok in a circle and repeated the same orders Voxx had given them. The creatures seemed to understand spoken commands even though they were mostly animal. Clothing that had belonged to Westin and still held his scent was passed among the creatures.

Each of the demok handlers wore a heavy leather belt around their waists, with a metal disk at the center. The men touched the disks, and the demok shrieked in pain. The creatures curled up on themselves and rolled on the ground, gasping for air. The scent of the animals was gagging, as the pain caused them to release urine and feces while they screeched and howled in the dirt.

Quoto ran from the horrid spectacle. Never had he seen such torture. The creatures clawed at the ground and each other to find release. As their howling filled the air, the birds in the surrounding trees flew away in a panic.

Finally, it ended. The creatures lay panting and whimpering in the dirt as the handlers screamed at them. "Remember the scent! No harm comes to the man with this scent!"

Quoto mounted his horse but knew his face must show the fear and loathing for the torture he had just witnessed. He hated the demok, but nothing should suffer such pain.

Voxx looked at Quoto as he also mounted his horse. "From time to time, it is necessary to remind them who has the power here." He looked ahead as he motioned his men forward. "It is a good lesson for 'everyone' to remember."

Quoto got the message.

Chapter Thirteen

Andro paced nervously, back in forth across the short hallway in front of his rooms. He knew he looked like a man who had not slept for days, and he supposed it was better than he actually felt.

He spent the past month meeting in small homes, behind storefronts, and out-of-the-way taverns to keep his people informed. He knew each meeting could bring him closer to being discovered by Gwilim's spies, but there was no other recourse.

Bodecia had been good on her word of keeping him posted on the progress at the mines. She was a very capable woman, he decided. Of course, he still worried whether he could trust her, but he really had no choice, her part in this plan was of the greatest importance.

Andro's wife sat watching as he muttered to himself. She had spent many years as his wife in Exiled, and she would follow him anywhere he went. Even to death, she supposed. She sat quietly, not wanting to disturb him. She could tell his mind was working on a plan of some sort. He confided everything to her. Sometimes, she wished he would hold back on some details, but she knew the passion he felt for his people, and a man without a confidant would soon explode with no release. She worked hard along his side to make sure his plans would come to fruition.

As if sensing her thoughts, Andro stopped his pacing and looked at his wife. "They should have been here hours ago," he said in frustration. "I think you should go, my dear, you and the girls. Go to the safe place I set up for you until it is time."

Helen smiled and shook her head, "Now, what good would that do? If they know about us, they will track us down anyway. Besides, what kind of life would we have without you?"

His eyes filled with tears as he looked at the dear woman. She was as motherly a woman as he had ever known, but he had always found her the most sensual creature in the world. She was confident and supportive of him, always offering him good counsel. Of course, he knew at one time she had been condemned as a witch for telling fortunes. She had given some particularly bad warnings to a nobleman, which he failed to heed, and he claimed she had cursed him. Thus, she had been sent to Exiled.

He walked over and placed his hand on her cheek, "And what would my life have been without you?" he wondered aloud.

A sharp knock at the door made them both jump. Andro looked at her, then rushed to open the door.

Zackos and Keyok pushed their way past him and shoved the door closed behind them. Both men looked frightened but relieved to see Andro.

"We were beside ourselves with fright!" Andro said, placing a comforting hand on the men's shoulders. "Is everything going as planned?"

Zackos, the older of two, nodded, "Everything is fine, it just took us longer than we thought to get away. Balak seems to be in a mood lately. He watches us as if he knows what we are planning. Even Gwilim makes his way around the castle more often than ever before. Every man, woman, and child cowers at the sight of him."

Young Keyok stood nodding at Zackos and wringing his hat in his big hands. "But he does not seem to suspect anything as far as we can tell. He just keeps bringing more and more demok for us to train."

Andro looked at the floor and shook his head. "We must move quickly. Underestimating Gwilim is a terrible mistake."

Another knock at the door made everyone jump. Andro's wife stood and walked to the door, opening it only slightly.

A man dressed in a messenger's clothes nodded and held out a letter. Helen thanked the man and took the letter from him.

"It is from Bodecia!" she whispered.

Andro quickly took the letter from his wife and broke the wax seal. For several minutes he read the letter before he finally looked up.

"It is time," he simply stated, looking at the others.

***

Bodecia watched the messenger ride away with her message to Andro. Finally, this could be over. She was sick to death of this mine and the dust and dirt and the infernal heat. She had worked these men almost to death. Even after they entered the mines and took up residence there, it afforded few luxuries. The ghouls did not enter the mine area, but every night, their wailing echoed off the walls of the cave.

The welcome cool she had anticipated was not there. In fact, the mine seemed humid and hot, like the steam baths she had once enjoyed back at the Dark Palace. Only here you could not rise and have cool water poured over your body to relieve the heat. Here, you wore the heat like a heavy, wet cloak, suffocating your every breath.

She cut most of her long hair, hoping to make herself cooler. She knew she appeared more like a man than a woman now. Her short hair crowned a body once soft and delicate. It was now muscle-hard. Her arms rippled as she helped dig and pull the precious gold from the mountain. Her once long, slender legs now pulsed hard as she pulled a pallet to the separating area. Her hands, once dainty and pampered, were covered with tough calluses.

The men no longer even looked at her as a woman. She was just one of them now. She was their Captain; she ordered, they obeyed. No questions. At first, she was a little confused by their sense of loyalty to her. She was even more surprised to find she had developed a bond to them, too.

Sweat trickled down her dirty face, and she wiped the dirt from her eyes. She looked at the gold lying in the finishing room. There was no denying the beauty of it. It glistened and sparkled like the morning sun. "No," she thought, "there has never been a sunrise this beautiful."

Balak made a surprise visit several weeks back to check on the progress of the mine. While he assumed it was a surprise visit, she had ample warning of his arrival and made the proper adjustments to the mines. Andro had been good at his word about having his little spiders in the Dark Palace. Even before Balak left the palace, she was preparing for his arrival.

He was shown the mining area, collection, and separating areas, and, of course, to the finishing area. At least to one of them. Bodecia in no way wanted Balak to see the full scale of their work. He had been pleased enough to see the work progressing as well as expected and quickly gathered the finished loads of gold and had them sent to the foundry at the Palace.

He seemed more than a little amused to see Bodecia dressed as one of the toughened miners. She could see in his eyes he held no thoughts of carnal pleasure for her now. In fact, she looked as if she could easily beat him to death with little or no effort.

He brought with him new tools and additional recruits in hope of speeding up production of the gold. He was in a hurry to complete his plans it seemed.

He was not the only one.

Eos lumbered slowly toward her, bearing a huge smile across his face. "Not a bad day, lady," he purred. "We passed our quota yesterday. We are digging up the profit now."

"We still need to get this shipment to Bandelon as soon as possible. Andro will have his men waiting to receive and process it," she ordered as she made her way to her tent.

"Will you be traveling with the shipment this time, Lady?" Eos called out as she continued her way.

"Oh yes," she answered with a smile, "I will be going this time."

Chapter Fourteen

Stevien hurried toward the meeting chamber with several of his most trusted guards close behind. The winds outside rushed through the long windows, lifting the ornate rugs from the floors.

A dusty, yellow sky threatened to bring even more destruction on Baka Ton. For days now, severe storms had battered the city until the people, fearing it to be cursed, fled to the surrounding hillsides.

Stevien called for an emergency meeting of the Region Council, hoping for a bit of good news from their territories and, even more important, help to fight back the treacherous Governor York.

By the time he reached the Chamber the councilmen had settled themselves in alongside their governors. York's councilmen stood uncomfortably waiting for Stevien. He shot them a heated look then told the group to be seated.

"It seems our enemy lives within us, as well as beyond," he began. He sat silently for a moment, eyes closed, trying to gain composure. He dared not speak about the hate and anger he felt right now. It was a fragile time for everyone.

"I once asked for your help in fighting this war with Gwilim. We stood as brothers, fighting the same evil, determined not one of our lands should fall. I trusted the oath given by each of you. I could not allow myself to believe one of you would betray us all."

The group nervously waited for Stevien to continue. York's absence was obvious, and each region seemed to pull away from the others as if fearing they might be a traitor as well.

"The Northern Region has decided to pull away from the safety of the Homeland and make its' own alliance with Gwilim. They feel it is safer to make a pact with evil than to fight with the just. They will of course, be lost."

The group muttered between themselves as their rumors were confirmed.

Stevien continued: We cannot count on the help from the Northern Region. We can only protect our borders to the West and South. Since the fall of the Veil between us and The Grand, our borders are left wide open. We must set up heavy patrol lines to cover as much of the territory as possible."

Governor Rufus called out, "Stevien, the Southern Region still stands with the Homeland! We will send our troops to cover as much of the southern border as possible.

The others all stood and re-confirmed their oaths to the Homeland, promising to stand against Gwilim's raiders wherever they tried to cross.

Stevien sat heavily in his chair and smiled at his countrymen. He had not slept in almost three days and knew these men and women hadn't slept in quite a while either. The passion on their faces was undeniable. In the past years of wealth and plenty, they had forgotten the passion of battle. That passion had been awakened, along with the anger of being betrayed by one of their own.

Generals from each region were assigned to meet with Stevien's honor guard to set up the perimeter outposts. He was relieved he would not have to worry about those assignments.

"A soldier in a battle fever is a holy sight," he thought to himself. "It is like a call from the Creator."

The group had mostly disbanded to meet with their own men when Governor Atlan approached Stevien. She placed a gentle hand on his shoulder. "Stevien, is there any word from our border rangers?"

He shook his head, "We have not spoken in weeks. We feared Gwilim could locate them through our communications and agreed not to contact one another until they had Westin. My guess is they do not have him yet." He smiled weakly as he looked up at her.

"Yet!" she assured with a smile. "They will find him. I am sure of it."

She gave him a pat and returned to her group. Stevien was, in truth, worried sick over the fate of Jack and his group. He had tried several times to reach them but without any luck. Could they all be dead? Did they know of the treason of the Northern Region? Were the troopers from the Northern Region spies sent to kill off Jack and his group? He wished a hundred times he could have given them more warning, but he did all he could and hoped they were on their guard.

He stood from his chair and swayed for a moment, weariness overcoming him. He knew he desperately needed sleep, but with imminent invasion, his mind would not allow that precious escape. His people were out there somewhere, cowering in terror, waiting for the enemy to overtake them. These hellish storms were only the first round to weaken them. Next would be the death. Next would be the end.

Stevien steadied himself until he felt his appearance gave the impression of a confident leader. He stared defiantly out the window at the gathering storm as if he could frighten it away with his will.

Fear is a terrible thing to see on a leader's face. It makes the mightiest of soldiers fall to their knees, willing to give up. He wasn't about to give up to Balak and Gwilim without a fearsome battle. If he must die, he would be ferocious about it.

Chapter Fifteen

The scream from Gwilim made the skin on Balak's skin prickle. He had never seen Gwilim so driven. In the past weeks, he had been working non-stop, building his army of demok to prepare for the invasion of the Homeland, and the anticipation was driving him mad.

Balak was no fool. He knew his relationship with Gwilim was strained. His knowledge had been of vital importance at one time, but once the invasion was under way, his usefulness would end, and Gwilim had little use for people who had nothing to offer.

Gwilim promised to reward him with a kingdom of his own, anyone he preferred. But, of course, even that would be in jeopardy if he could not find a way to endear himself to this monster.

Balak watched Gwilim walk among the hundreds of demok in the courtyard below. He touched and caressed them as if they were his children. In many ways, they were.

He was always repulsed when Gwilim created his demok. He had seen it repeatedly, yet still, his mind rejected the manner of their existence.

Gwilim required Balak to watch. He enjoyed the sense of terror and awe his transformations brought, and he looked up now to see it again on Balak's face.

He fed earlier that morning; ten this time, ten people who had displeased him in some way or another, or maybe another ten innocents this time. It really did not matter to Gwilim. He needed his demok, and the sacrifice of a few lowly lives was of no consequence to him.

Balak knew the truth of it. The people were becoming more enraged as Gwilim took their family and friends for his hideous army. Their ancestors had been sent here for unspeakable crimes, but these people no longer felt they were deserving of the punishments dealt to them. They had families now and wanted nothing more than to live and raise them in peace in Exiled.

Gwilim was more than happy to remind them they were his for the taking, and they held no other purpose in life but to serve his cruel whims.

Gwilim walked to the center of the courtyard, where a wild boar was chained. The animal lunged toward him, trying to rip him to pieces with his sharp tusks.

Gwilim smiled at the animal as it squealed in frustration at the long chain which held it. He reached his hand out to the animal, touching it, and it became still as death. He slowly circled the animal, now quiet and still, and laid his hands on the tough, hairy hide.

"A good one, don't you think Balak?" he called out.

"Yes, quite a large specimen," returned Balak, wishing the ordeal was over. He had much to do to get this invasion moving, and watching Gwilim work his magic was wearing on his nerves.

Gwilim nodded his head, his eyes wide in anticipation. He knelt before the ugly creature and held its' snout close to his face. He opened his mouth wide and a swirling, bright mist of green poured from him and entered the body of the boar. A long wail accompanied the mist as the life source of the person Gwilim fed on earlier realized their fate. The mist continued to fill the beast until it expanded and grew larger, changing shape. The legs became long and muscular, as well as the arms. The back straightened and grew until the creature was able to stand on two legs as a man. The face, always distorted, retained the long tusks, as well as the thick snout. But the eyes revealed the terror behind the creature. It was no longer human, no longer animal.

At last, the whimpering ended, and Gwilim stood before the 'thing' he had created. He preferred the boars for his hideous transformations, though Balak had witnessed bears, mountain lions, wolves, and other unfortunate animals. But the boar always brought him a particular kind of pride.

He stroked the creature and soothed it as if it were a new pup. Soon, the creature calmed and whimpered, comforted by its' master's touch. It belonged to Gwilim now.

Gwilim finally turned and climbed the stairway out of the courtyard to make his way to Balak. Immediately, the animals began to cry and weep for him, making the unsettling noise of a creature, not animal or human.

The handlers herded the creatures into a holding area to begin their blood thirsty training.

Gwilim took Balak by the arm, and they began to walk the long corridor back toward his dwelling.

"How long before the work on the opening is completed?" he asked impatiently. "My army is ready, and I find I grow ever tired of the wait."

Balak knew Gwilim had been planning this invasion for hundreds of years. He and Westin had been the last piece of the puzzle to accomplish his plans.

"The last shipment of gold is on its way. I should say by the end of this week, perhaps before. I have instructed the foundry to work without pause so everything is ready for the last piece to be laid."

"Good," purred Gwilim, "I shall have my armies moved to the Northern Portal and wait for our arrival. When the opening is made, there will be nothing to hold back the army of the Exiled. We will be free at last to claim what is owed us!"

"How many men are waiting our arrival in the Grand," asked Gwilim.

"There are at least five thousand men and demok there now," answered Balak, feeling the weight of the destruction of the Homeland bearing down on him. Some of the troops are in the Homeland to secure the land after the light cannons destroy their villages; Baka Ton is under attack as we speak. Others search for Westin, and still others are making their way to the portal to await our arrival."

"At last, I will conquer that cursed wall!" spat Gwilim.

Gwilim understood the powers of the Barrier. He tried for hundreds of years to find a way to escape, always without success. In fact, his attempts helped to strengthen the wall, sealing Exiled completely because of his inept attempts. Contact between him and his army left in Homeland had only been possible through messaging birds for over a hundred years. That was until Balak and Westin were able to break through from their side. To Gwilim's surprise, the first pinhole in the Barrier had finally been made, by his enemies.

He smiled to himself at his great fortune of finding men who wanted to work out a treaty with him and the people of Exiled. Gwilim played the part of a concerned leader for many years, feigning interest in making an allegiance with the Homeland, who hoped to send trading caravans back and forth through the Barrier. He knew if Balak and Westin knew of a way to make an opening through the Barrier for trading purposes, then he would be able to use it for escape.

Unfortunately, Westin had perceived his intentions and began to pull back from their negotiations. Balak had not been so easily put off and continued secretly working with Gwilim while Westin took on other projects at the Palace of Ages.

As usual, Gwilim was able to see an opportunity with Balak. His greed, his hunger for power, mixed with his gift of magic and science made him easy to entice. Soon, plans were set in motion for his defection to Exiled.

Balak was overconfident from the beginning he could bring down the Barrier alone. It was by Gwilim's uncompromising insistence that Balak had been forced to take Westin when he left. If not for Gwilim's foresight, they would be stuck behind the wall forever.

Gwilim found his long, sharp nails squeezing into Balak's arm as they continued walking to his rooms. "Fool of man," he thought. "And still, we wait for the real master mind! Without Westin, we sit, like children, waiting." While Balak conceived the technology of penetrating the wall, Westin had been able to withhold the most valuable information. The precious inscription to re-route the magic which protected the wall. Without it, they faced certain failure again. He needed more than the few minutes Balak had previously provided to keep the wall open to move his mighty armies into the Grand.

"So, once the gold is molded and Doctor Westin is delivered back to us through the Portal, how much longer should we have to wait?"

Balak gritted his teeth and took a deep breath. He knew Gwilim relished reminding him he was useless without Westin. He had worked hard to negotiate a place of honor and respect in Gwilim's house and to be revered as his second in command. It was a position he had insisted on even before he left the Homeland, but still Gwilim enjoyed making him humble.

"Once the old man is returned to us, we should be able to proceed within a week!" he responded. "It should not be too hard to convince him to complete his final part now that he understands escape is impossible for him. How soon do you expect your men can deliver him?" Balak smiled as he cunningly placed the shoe on the other foot.

Gwilim, realizing Balak was also pointing an accusing finger, raised an eyebrow, "I should say in the next day or two, at the latest."

"Have the light cannons in the Grand been set against the Homeland," asked Balak.

"Ah, yes, even as we walk these halls, the people of the Homeland are tormented by the fury of the cannons. We have taken the very air they breathe and turned it into a mighty, destructive storm, destroying their villages. The attacks will continue until we make our victorious entrance. They shall see storms such as they have never known. Their every nightmare is soon to be realized. They will be so thankful for the reprieve when we arrive that they will welcome us with open arms."

Balak felt his heart skip a quick beat of regret when he thought of his own village being destroyed.

"Then I should say, yes, you should most definitely move your men to the Northern Portal," he offered.

Chapter Sixteen

With only a few hours to work, Jack and his men moved as quickly as they could. They did not bother to camouflage their tracks since Westin and his group had been there for a while, a few more footprints should not matter.

Before they flew away on the winged serpents, Jack asked Westin and his group to leave their old clothes at the campsite. He wanted to make sure the scent of the group lay heavy here, and the raiders would not second guess attacking the site. At the last decoy campsite, Soulo successfully set a trap for them. Jack hoped they would fall for this decoy again. Most military men would not use the same tactic twice in a row, and Jack was betting Voxx was a true military commander. But he also knew of his desperation to capture Westin and quickly deliver him to Gwilim.

Luka's wolves predicted, almost to the minute, the arrival of the raiders. Jack marveled at the accuracy of the animals as one of his own scouts ran down a hillside, waving his hat wildly over his head.

He double-checked the trenches dug around the campsite to make sure the thin layer covering of leaves and dirt were doing their job. The high winds they endured earlier had ended, and a still air filled the area around Needle Rock. "Probably Jep's work," he thought hopefully. The old wizard was using every ounce of magic he had left in him to assure their victory.

He ran low to the ground as he sought cover with the others. He prayed the demok kept their attention on the scent of Westin's group and not pick up theirs. There had not been enough of Jetta's spices to hide their own.

They waited no more than half an hour. The raiders did not even bother to hide their arrival since they expected to find only an old man and few of his companions. They would surely pose no threat to them.

The demok howled in victory and anticipation of fresh food as they made their way toward the crude camp set up beneath the tall rocks. The raiders held their weapons at ease, not expecting a fight from the small group.

"Come out, Westin!" yelled Voxx in a dangerous voice. "We have traveled a long way to take you home! Come out now, and we will not harm your people!"

He waited for a moment, then sent a few raiders to check inside the cave and tents around the site. When they returned without Westin, Voxx gave out an enraged cry that filled the air. "OLD MAN! You will watch your friends die at the hands of these demok if you do not show yourself, now!"

Jack gave a shrill whistle, giving the signal to attack.

The air around the raiders was filled with a hail of fiery arrows, some making their marks in nearby bushes, setting them ablaze. The ones that found their mark in man and demok made a sickening thud, followed by screams as the flames spread over their bodies. This was a sure defense against the demok. They feared fire.

Voxx yelled for the raiders to arm themselves and return fire. Jack saw the look of confusion on his face, as he tried to comprehend how Westin and his group were capable of putting up such an attack.

"How can this be happening again!!!" he screamed in frustration. "How could they know what we were planning?"

As the raiders prepared to protect themselves, Jack gave the order to set the trench ablaze. Zi, who was particularly accurate with a long bow, sent several blazing arrows into the leaf-filled ditch, setting it on fire. The trench had been filled with a black oil Jep had forced from the surrounding earth, and soon a fiery wall surrounded the raider army.

The demok were quick to panic, just as animals do. Luka had given Jack the valuable strategy. "They fear fire more than anything else, and it always panics them," he explained. "Use it to your advantage."

They ran wildly around the area, stampeding anyone who happened in their way. Their trainers did not bother trying to control them. It was pointless. Their size and weight were triple that of the normal man, and with panic overtaking them, they were impossible to keep under control.

The raiders slowly began to realize there was no escape from the ring of fire. Instead of lifting their weapons to fight, they ran in all directions, looking for ways to cross over the fiery trench. Even the bravest soldiers fear being burned alive.

Some jumped and missed, falling into the inferno. Others made the jump, but with their eyes blinded by the oily smoke, they found themselves impaled on a wall of spears waiting on the other side.

The arrows continued to rain down on the men in a hail of death and pain. Jack saw Voxx rushing to the caves to avoid being hit. Heavy black smoke filled the area, stinging everyone's eyes, raiders' and Homelanders' alike.

A slow and deliberate breeze began to blow, and suddenly, Jack found the acrid smoke drifting their way. "They must have their own wizards at work, no doubt," realized Jack. With Jep already heading for the waiting dragons, he yelled for the rest of his men to call off the attack and make their way toward their escape.

Just as Jack was preparing to follow, he spotted a familiar face emerging from behind a scrag tree. "Quoto," he hissed as he watched the man scurrying from his hiding place.

Jack grabbed one of the long spears they used to make the impaling wall and made a run for the trench. When he reached the flames, he jammed the spear into the center of the trench and propelled himself over, landing in the center of the enemy camp.

Quoto's back was turned, but as Jack's feet hit the ground, he turned to face him.

His face was filled with shock, recognizing his one-time leader and comrade standing before him. Jack saw fear creep over Quoto as he steeled himself for the death blow from the spear Jack still held in his hands.

Over his shoulder, Jack saw the still confused and burned men trying to get their bearings and their enraged commander emerging from a cave.

He looked back into Quoto's eyes, then stepped forward. Quoto flinched as Jack's hand reached out, grabbed a leather cord, and snapped it from his neck.

"This belongs to a friend of mine!" he growled, his face looming in on Quoto's as he held the gold-tipped bear tooth in front of his face.

Then, to Quoto's surprise, Jack put his hands on his shoulders and gave them a friendly slap.

Quoto was in total confusion. What was Jack doing? He should be running me through with that spear instead of greeting me as a friend!

Jack's friendly smile spread across his face as he gave Quoto another friendly slap. He pulled him close to him in a bear hug then whispered, "I hope you have a slow and painful death. For Owyn and Bragos."

The next minute, Jack was sailing over the trench again and running to join the others, mounting huge, winged dragons.

Quoto stood dazed, looking at Jack as he sped away. He still could not believe Jack did not kill him. He rubbed his hands over his body to make sure there was no blood. Surely, Jack had stabbed him, and he just did not know it yet.

As the dragons lifted into the sky, Jack gave Quoto a final look, a look of triumph.

Quoto stood dumbly, staring at the dragons carrying the men away. He turned slowly, with a look of confusion still on his face, when his eyes locked onto Voxx.

It took him a moment to understand the rage he saw was meant for him. He suddenly realized his plight.

"No!! No!!" he cried as he furiously motioned to Voxx. "This is a trick!! He wants you to believe I betrayed you!! Don't you see? I swear to you, I had nothing to do with these ambushes!"

Voxx' eyes never left Quoto's as he motioned for the guards to take him. "So, this explains why they always knew what our next move was going to be. This is why they were always ready for us. US! US, the mightiest army this, or any other land has ever known, and these. . . farmers outwitted us! Now I understand."

Quoto could see, full well, Jack's plan. "He wants you to believe that!!" he begged. "This is a trick, I tell you!!"

Voxx put his face close to Quoto. It was red with fury, and spittle sprayed as he spoke. "And I suppose you are going to tell me you could not possibly betray a comrade."

Quoto knew his betrayal of Bragos and Owyn had become his downfall.

"The demok will have their fill tonight!"

The surrounding rocks shook with the sounds of his screams as Quoto was pulled away to his waiting justice.

Chapter Seventeen

The trip back to camp on the backs of the great dragons was not as frightening as the first trip had been. Jack let himself relax for the first time in months. Westin was safe at last.

It took the dragons only a brief time to reach the others. They landed as gracefully as a leaf falling lazily to the earth. Perhaps they decided humans were not so bad after all. Jack wondered why they were condemned to Exiled as he walked over and gave Scala a friendly rub on her neck. She purred like a kitten now at his touch and rubbed her great head against him.

Jep and Zi had already dismounted their dragons, and Jack saw Zi had not fared any better this trip than the last. He pushed Jep aside, hurriedly ran for a nearby bush, and lost what little food he had in his stomach.

Jep helped Owyn off his dragon, and Jack could see his friend was still not fully recovered from his injuries at the hands of Voxx and his men. Owyn walked painfully toward the waiting troopers and Westin when Jack caught up with him.

"Here," he said, and he shoved something into Owyn's hand. "And take better care of it next time."

Owyn looked down and saw the sparkle of the shiny gold on the bear's tooth twinkling in his hand. He looked up in surprise. Jack smiled and gave his friend a pat on the arm.

"No one hurts my friend and gets away with it!" he smiled at Owyn.

Owyn stood, holding the bear tooth in his hands as Zi walked up to him. "Hey, where did ya get that, little frog?"

Owyn smiled at Jack's departing back, "A friend gave it to me," was all he answered, and he followed Jack to the waiting group.

"I gotta get one of those!" whispered Zi, shaking his head and following close behind.

Westin was waiting anxiously when they arrived. Blue was standing beside him, holding his arm, supporting him.

"I was so worried!" he called out as they approached. "You don't know how barbaric those men can be."

Jack just nodded as they walked over and sat wearily beneath the trees. They smelled of heavy smoke, and their faces were black with oily smudges. They wiped the oil from their faces with their clothes, trying to clear their burning eyes.

"Do you think we are far enough away from them to rest a while?" Jack asked Luka, who was sitting on a nearby log.

"They would not be able to get to us for a full day at a hard march, even if they were in good condition. It will take them several days to catch us now that we have crippled them. I think we are safe for a while."

Jack was relieved to hear it. His men had ridden hard to reach Westin before the raiders and then had to make a stand and fight. They all needed to rest and have a delicious meal before they set out again.

Luka, always the man of the woods, had a meal cooking for them when they returned. He found meat, root potatoes, berries, and some other vegetables, which Jack did not recognize, cooking over a slow fire.

"Well, it appears Luka thought we would be successful," he grinned, looking over the feast.

As weary as his men were, Westin looked worse. Jack realized the old doctor had been running from these raiders non-stop since his escape. The old man looked as if he could sleep for a week.

Jep was giving him a guarded, worried look.

"Dr. Westin, do you feel up to travel again?" he asked.

"Oh, do not worry about me, Jack, I will be fine. I think, for the first time in years, I can let someone else take care of us. I am more than ready for that!"

Jack was reminded it had been a full year since Westin had escaped Exiled. He felt a deep sympathy for the old doctor and his group.

"Doctor Westin, if you're not too tired, there are a few things we would like to know about Balak and his plans and where we need to go to stop him," Jack asked.

"How can I be too tired, my dear boy. You and your men did all the hard work," smiled Westin.

Jep began, "Just how advanced is Balak in making the opening of the Barrier? Is it possible he can proceed without your aid?"

Westin shook his head, "He is *very* advanced as he was my most promising pupil. He taught me a thing or two of his own. But, as far as entering the Barrier alone, his hands are tied without me. He made several attempts, with limited success, and allowed many of Gwilim's army passage, but also caused the deaths of many when his openings failed."

"That is good to know. I was afraid in the year you have been gone, he might have found a way around the process," sighed Jep in relief.

"There are no shortcuts when it comes to the Barrier. Elidor and the other wizards of his time combined their magic to weave a strong spell, binding the wall. Balak's attempts eventually caused the Barrier to protect itself, making it even harder than before to penetrate it again. I believe there have only been four exits in a hundred years, mine being one of them."

"Whew," said Zi as he stretched out his legs, "why would anyone think it possible. It seems to me each try would make the wall stronger."

"That is exactly what happens. Balak knows better than to try to make any more faulty openings. It could seal them in Exiled tighter than ever before."

Owyn looked at the old doctor, "What in heaven's name did you and Balak ever hope to accomplish with Exiled. It seems to me we would all be better off if they had been left alone."

Zi gave Owyn a hit on the arm, which Owyn briskly rubbed. He returned Zi's look with a sour look of his own. "Well, look at what has happened since they began talking with those people. If Balak and Gwilim had never communicated, he would never have joined him."

Westin looked at his hands as if the weight of the world had fallen into them. The shoulders of the old man slumped as weariness settled on him like a heavy blanket.

"I just believed," he continued, "if there was a way to save those poor souls, we had a duty to try. Not everyone in Exiled is evil. Most are common families with children, just like in the Homeland. Their only reason for being there is that they were born of people who were sent. Nonetheless, they are all condemned victims of Gwilim.

"I really believed Balak felt the same way. We talked together for hours into the night about their plight. He seemed as devoted as I was to rescue them. I was so wrong about him. When at last I discovered his true heart, it was too late." Again, he sadly shook his head.

Jack hated to push him too hard, and he felt the old man should rest, but information was important. They had so few answers to their questions.

Finally, the old man continued his story on his own.

"As our discussions with Exiled continued, I became increasingly suspicious about Gwilim's intentions. We began to argue over the opening. He insisted it should be a permanent one, but of course, I had no authority to do so. Troubling things were brought to my attention, such as the treatment of his people and the creation of the demok, and I began to see the real horror that was Gwilim. I most certainly did not want to allow him the chance to enter helpless lands to start his madness all over again."

Jep interrupted, "So you and Balak had already been working on an opening without approval for the Council?"

"We monitored both the Barrier and the Veil for years to make sure their integrity was never compromised. Gwilim had, of course, tried to break through several times, but the Barrier had always protected itself.

"One day, while studying in the Halls of Confine, I stumbled upon a secret room. It was quite by accident. In that room, I discovered the writings of Elidor. Among them were the symbols needed for making an opening in the Barrier. Runes of protection engraved over the surface of a golden tunnel.

"Gwilim and I began to argue at every turn, so it was my greatest mistake not to watch Balak more closely. Of course, the rest of the story you know. Gwilim wooed him to the dark, with little effort, it seems.

"While I worked late one night, Balak entered my chambers and began asking me questions about the scrolls I found to allow access through the Barrier. We argued over the consequences of such actions, and for the first time, I saw the true heart of the man. Before I realized what had happened, he struck me, knocking me unconscious. He must have given me a powerful potion to keep me unconscious, and when I awoke several days later, I was already in the Grand."

Jep put a hand on Westin's shoulder to comfort him. "You know, until recently, everyone thought you had been killed when Balak left. When we first began this journey, we believed we would only have the expertise of Jetta, Blue, and myself," said Jep.

"Yes, Stevien was very surprised when I was finally able to reach him. I had no way of contacting him to let him know I was alive and finally free of Balak." Westin motioned to the smiling man sitting across from him, "Jonas here, and his families were originally traders who traveled the Grand, and he knew his way around very well, so we were able to evade Gwilim's men for quite a while."

"One day, we found the body of a raider who had been attacked and killed by a large animal in the forests to the South. Luckily, for us, he had a communicator on him. Since I had developed our own communicators to Exiled, I was able to make the changes I needed to contact the Homeland and Stevien. Of course, now, it seems, it also allowed Gwilim's men to trace our location."

Jack listened to Westin and asked, "Was that while you were staying in the Tourashon Village?"

Westin sadly nodded his head. "I suppose they were able to locate us by my communication with the Homeland. They knew we carried the plague with us and could not afford to let us kill off the people of the Grand." Westin rubbed his forehead wearily. "The sickness was another of the blights of Exiled. They suffered with many types of plagues due to the conditions of the land and the horrible living conditions of the people. Too late I understood we still carried it with us. I truly believed we left those poor people protected. I am afraid I made quite a mistake with them as well. I owe them more than I can ever repay."

"It was not your fault," interceded Blue, breaking his quiet mourning since Jetta's death. "You did your best to assure their safety. Gwilim is the one who killed those people, not you."

Westin nodded, patting Blue's hand, "Yes, he gave the order, but it was me who lead him there to destroy them. I was the one who drew his eyes to the little village."

Owyn squirmed nervously on the log he was sitting before clearing his throat and asking, "So, this plague is gone now, is it?"

The old doctor raised his hands in assurance, "It is quite gone now. You are all safe."

Everyone around the fire seemed to relax when their unspoken question was answered.

Blue hung his head as he thought of the proud people of the Tourashon village. He looked older than Westin and Jep both, and Jack wished again he would have made his last transformation into someone youthful. He hated to see the sad effects of life showing on Blue's face.

"How long were you in Exiled, Doctor?" asked Luka as he whittled a long tree limb into a walking stick. The end of the walking stick was beginning to take the form of the head of a large wolf.

"Almost 2 years," he said sadly.

"Two years!" exclaimed Owyn.

Jep seemed a bit taken back as well, "I must admit, doctor. I cannot imagine why the Palace of Ages did not alert us to your absence before now."

"I suppose if they thought I was dead, their only option was to wait and see what Balak's intentions were."

"It seems to me he made his intentions pretty, bloody clear from the beginning," snorted Zi.

"So," asked Jep, "you and Balak were in Exiled for two years while Gwilim was getting ready for this invasion?"

"I was sent straight away through the Northern Portal into Exiled. Gwilim, himself, met me on the other side of the Barrier. Balak stayed in the Grand for many months, setting up alliances with the villages and arranging camps for the troops he would send to stay in the Grand until the fall of the Veil. He completed many light cannons during that time as well."

Jack sighed heavily, "That would explain why the people of Serenity held him in such high regard. They thought he was a friendly wizard sent to help them."

"Yes, well, with the help of the light cannon, the plans of which he took from the Homeland when we left, he was able to transfer much of the resources and water we they were collecting to this land. It became a garden of paradise. The people were, no doubt, overwhelmed by his gifts. Unfortunately, the lands he robbed became withered and desolate."

"Most of the land was rich farming land at one time. Even the Wilds was once a rich, fertile land. That is until Elidor and Gwilim met there for their last battle. It was almost destroyed then. Amazing what man can do to the world around him.

"The light cannon was originally designed to restore the Wilds. Another thing I found while examining Elidor's secret rooms were the designs for the cannon. Elidor had always regretted the effect his battle with Gwilim had on the Outlands, turning them into the useless Wilds. He planned to restore the land to its former beauty. Balak, of course, knew the same cannon could be used to 'take' resources from the land instead of reviving them. He used the information to prove his worth to Gwilim. Gwilim was overjoyed when Balak promised to make many cannons to begin draining the Homeland and replenishing the Grand. When Balak finally entered Exiled, he left the cannons with the army in the Grand. Soon, he planned to send more troops to help use the cannons against our home. It appears he was successful."

Jack marveled at the power of the light cannon. He recalled seeing fields emptied of fertile resources and shuddered to think how often it was happening in the Homeland.

Jep watched everyone's faces as they comprehended the atrocity to their land. He, too, was appalled at Westin and Balak's actions but understood Westin had been trying to help innocent people break free from Gwilim.

"So, how many troops were left in the Grand?" asked Jep, trying to get the conversation moving again.

"Hundreds of troops were stationed there already. Gwilim left quite a large, dedicated army behind before being condemned to Exiled; demok too."

Jack and his friends nodded, knowing all too well the hoard of violent men and animals raiding Homeland. That is why they became border rangers.

Westin continued, "Once Balak entered Exiled, he made his own attempts at making cracks in the Barrier. He was somewhat successful. And in those few times, many troops had access into the Grand.

"It was also extremely dangerous, and some of those men died trying to make their way through. The openings were weak and collapsed, crushing the men and animals making their way.

The men who were able to pass through joined the others already waiting here and in the Homeland."

Soulo looked around, then asked, "Homeland? Did Gwilim have men living among us in Homeland?"

Westin nodded, "I believe the Northern Region areas were set aside as a sanctuary for them. They hid their troops there and here in the Grand. I doubt anyone knew how large their armies really were since they were hidden in two places. Those troops somehow adapted to the land and did not need to rush back into the protection behind the Veil."

Several of the troopers sitting around listening began to move around uncomfortably. Jack knew many of them were from that region. He looked at the men and saw on their faces the look of men who had been deceived; first, Quoto, now their leaders.

One of the men stepped forward, "Sir, on my honor, my bond is to you and this mission. I have no knowledge of any allegiance between my region and Gwilim. I swear my life on it!"

Several of the other troopers stepped beside him and swore with him. Jack knew these men well and had never seen any type of treachery from them. He smiled and saluted them back. "It is alright, men, I think you have proved your loyalty more than once. It is my hope your leaders back home have realized their mistakes. If not, well, there are enough of you here to make sure your countrymen know the truth of it. It only takes a few to start a revolution."

The men relaxed a bit, but Jack could see they were deeply hurt by the betrayal of their leaders. They lived the truth of Gwilim's treachery. They could not understand how their leaders could fall for his lies.

Westin looked around, uncertain. "I am sorry," he offered, "I did not realize you had men from that region. I would have tried to be more delicate."

"We have been become a faithful group since this journey began. We know who our friends are now," Jack said as he offered the group of Northern Region men a smile.

Westin glanced at Jep, who gave a nod of assurance before he continued. "Anyway, after months in the Grand, making the arrangements for sending through more troops and training the men to build the light cannons, Balak finally entered the Portal himself and became part of Exiled. He was welcomed as a prince. There were great celebrations as Gwilim whirled him around his palace like a long-lost son. He was placed in a position of high power immediately and set about fulfilling Gwilim's dreams of conquest.

"He brought with him one of the light cannons he made while in the Grand and had spread the precious resources across Exiled. Once a horrid and desolate place, it soon began to live again. I will have to admit, the cannon made their life so much easier, as the land became fertile and able to grow crops once again.

"Immediately Gwilim directed Balak to start work on his most important project, the Barrier wall. I was held in Gwilim's Palace, so Balak had access to me anytime he wished. Gwilim made it obvious my comfort in his Palace was contingent on my willingness to help with Balak's work.

"Balak soon realized he could easily trigger the wall's protective magic, causing it to re-design its magic and seal up even tighter. The slightest pinhole could cause an alarm. He knew he was jeopardizing the integrity of the Barrier wall every time he tried to make an opening. So he began to 'persuade' me a bit harder for Elidor's inscriptions. It was a very hard time for me."

Blue waited for the doctor to finish, then finally spoke, "Doctor Salto gave me the knowledge of the work you and Doctor Balak were doing on the Barrier Project. She cautioned me it was only partial knowledge, and only you had the final information needed. Why does Gwilim want to just make an 'opening' in the wall? Why doesn't he destroy the entire wall? Then everyone in Exiled would be freed."

"Balak's instructions are not to destroy the wall. Gwilim intends to use it for his own. It is Gwilim's intent to make the opening to free himself, his most trusted followers, and the huge army of creatures he needs to overcome the rest of the world. He will have the power to choose who goes and who remains."

Jep asked, "Why wouldn't he want to free all his people? Instead of allowing only a select few go?"

Westin smiled a knowing smile, then answered, "They are not all his devoted people. In fact, most of the populace hates Gwilim. They have suffered his tortures for years confined in Exiled, their only crime being born into a family where parents or grandparents were once condemned. It may have even been a great-grandparent. They are innocents who want nothing more than to be free and live their lives without the threat of Gwilim."

Luka nodded. "He is right. I would say most people have never committed a crime, yet they live in a prison because of the crimes of others. I knew many people like that. I wish I could have taken some of them with me when I left, but I was too afraid news of my attempt would get out and warn Gwilim."

"What must it be like, to be a total innocent, sentenced to a life of fear, always knowing your life and that of your wee ones was never your own, but at the whim of a madman," wondered Zi.

Owyn stirred the dusty ground with his boot. "What does he intend to do with those poor souls?" he asked. "If he will not take them with him, what good are they to him? Why not just destroy the wall and let everyone go?"

Jack answered, having already put the pieces together. "Because he _wants_ a place like Exiled. He wants the keys to the prison. Instead of being a prisoner, he will be the warden. Am I right, Dr. Westin?"

Westin nodded. "Yes, Exiled will belong to him. He will be able to control who is sent in and who can leave. He can condemn people at his folly."

Blue again questioned Westin. "Was Balak able to get any knowledge from you to open the Barrier"?

Westin sat sadly, looking out into the distance. Finally, Jonah, his companion spoke, "The Doctor was forced to reveal some of the information he wanted. Balak has the cold heart of an executioner. He used terrible means to extract the information from the doctor. Torture was nearly the death of him. Balak, almost too late, realized any physical means of forcing the information was dangerous and could cost Dr. Westin his life. He was forced to look for other ways to make him cooperate. So, he began taking the lives of the people the doctor had come to call friends. Dr. Westin spent most of his time in isolation to protect anyone else from being used by Balak."

Zi stole a look at the old doctor and muttered, "It sounds more like the work of a real coward than a man of learning."

Jonas nodded, "He assigned someone to help the doctor with his work. Bodecia had powerful magic when she lived in the Homeland, and she seemed a capable assistant. But, of course, we knew from the beginning she was one of Gwilim's spies. Many worked with Doctor Westin also, but we always kept our distance so Balak would not be able to use us against him. We plotted in secret to one another to plan our escape through the Barrier. It was good fortune for us to make our escape when we did."

"Four of those who escaped with us died, and the rest of us became gravely ill from the plague. Even with the use of the herbs we found, we only barely were able to survive ourselves."

Dr. Westin continued, "When we found the Tourashon village, they helped nurse us back to health. We stayed with them several weeks to regain our strength. I tried to protect them from any of the effects of the sickness. There were large deposits of silver in the hills around their village, and with a little work, we were able to extract enough to make the protective bracelets. I made a protection spell to keep them strong against the sickness. It never occurred to me they might be able to transfer the sickness to another village or that if they did not wear the bracelets, it would ultimately end up killing them. Oh, I have made so many foolish mistakes."

"A man on the run does not have time to fully think out his actions. You did the best you could, and no one can blame you." Jep comforted the old man.

Westin put his head in his hands and shook his head. Jack thought it was a suitable time to end the conversation for a while and eat. The venison Luka was cooking filled the area with the delicious aroma, and he knew his stomach was growling with hunger.

Luka sliced thick pieces of meat and laid them on tree leaves shaped like big green platters. The vegetables were all simmering in their pots, and everyone was more than happy to take their share.

Blue took a tin plate and filled it with hot food and gave it to Westin. He smiled at the old Blue and thanked him. Blue took a small share for himself and sat quietly, eating next to Westin. He seemed determined not to leave his side. This was, after all, what he had been sent for, to be an aid for the old doctor.

Jack watched Jep join them and shook his head at the three old men sharing a log. He knew Blue was a baby compared to the other two, but sitting with them, he looked older than both. He wished to have the old Blue back, curious and excited.

The meat and vegetables was ample dinner for the group. There was a time when one deer would not have fed the group, but now, with less than sixty left, there was plenty.

Luka took the bones and spread them out for his wolves, who snarled and growled among themselves for their share. Turi, the lead wolf, was the first to eat, and finally, when he had his fill, trotted over to sit with Luka, allowing the rest of the pack to fight over the remainder.

One of the dragons circled overhead before finally landing nearby. Luka stood and joined Scala for several minutes.

"I wonder what they eat?" wondered Owyn, observing Scala rub her huge, scaled head against Luka.

"Anything they want, I imagine!" laughed Zi. "And I doubt anyone would ever try to color her head yellow for leaving scraps!"

"A Familiar, I take it," asked Westin, pointing toward Luka with his head.

"Yes, he and the animals have a unique way of communication. They are very loyal to him, and I know we would have never made it this far without his and his friends help," explained Jep. "He was once in Exiled. He escaped by flying over the Barrier wall with the aid of the dragons."

"Incredible! I never considered flying over the wall. I knew we could send communications over the wall, but to fly over it!" Westin seemed awed by such a simple escape plan.

Luka finished his conversation with Scala and returned to the group. He grabbed the walking stick and began his work carving on the wolf head handle.

"Well!" growled Zi. "Are you going to make us wait all day until you tell us what the lady had to say?"

Luka raised his eyes toward Zi in a mock surprise manner. "Didn't know you were interested, Zi," he teased. "She sends her regards to you as well."

Zi gave an irritated 'humph' and rolled his eyes.

"Actually, Scala says the raiders have not made a move yet. They seemed to have suffered quite a lot of damage from the fires. They have taken up camp to lick their wounds."

"Sounds good to me!" said Owyn, wiping his greasy hands on his pants. "I think I could use a little time myself." He stood and began to scout the area for a friendly bush. He looked back at Blue and pointed his finger, "Find your own bush, Blue," he told the old man.

Chapter Eighteen

When their meal was finished, the men pulled out their pipes and offered the aromatic tobac to Dr. Westin and his group. Westin happily took the flavorful blend, stuffed his pipe, and puffed great clouds into the air.

As usual, Blue was still confused about the strange human habit, but with a harsh look from Zi, sat quietly beside Jep and the doctor.

Luka lit his own pipe, made from the wood of some old tree and carved with the head of a wolf, much like the one he was carving on the walking stick, and reopened the conversation. "You know, it seems a shame to leave all those poor people in Exiled. They have suffered enough under Gwilim."

Westin smiled at the man and answered, "There are those among them who are willing to give their lives to free the others. While working on numerous projects, I also met secretly with a group of men and women intent on freeing their people. We decided the time had come to put an end to Gwilim and Balak. We devised a plan to utterly destroy the Barrier, allowing everyone the right to leave Exiled once and for all. No more would Gwilim have control over their lives. My escape was to get me to the Homeland and arrange our own army to fight Gwilim's army when they crossed over. We would end him once and for all! Unfortunately, he was able to contact his raiders here in the Grand to track me. We have been on the run and hiding ever since."

"What of your comrades now?" asked Jep.

Westin shrugged his shoulders. "I cannot say. They may even think I am dead. It is my hope they go on with their plans to destroy Gwilim. Even if they never leave Exiled, they will be free of him."

"Can they live off the land as it is?" asked Owyn. "Luka described it as desolate and harsh. How can anyone make a life in that kind of land?"

"These people have learned to live like desert people; they have lived for centuries on very little. They can survive. Besides, with the help of the light cannon, they have a better chance than ever. At least Balak helped in that way."

Soulo, who had been sitting quietly for the conversation, looked at Jack questioningly. "So then, does this change our mission? We were told to seal the wall. Are we still to seal it, with all those innocent people still behind it?"

Jack looked at Westin and then at Jep. This was a dilemma. Of course, they could not let Gwilim go free into the Homeland, yet sealing those people away forever was not right either. He did not want to be the one to make the decision. Which was more important, confining evil or releasing the innocent?

"Dr. Westin, did you speak with Stevien about the imminent revolt in Exiled? Was he aware of the people preparing to fight Gwilim?"

"No," he replied. "I never had the opportunity to talk with him about it. He was more concerned about getting me back safely to Homeland. My communicator long ago stopped transmitting to Baka Ton. I was barely able to reach you. Stevien knows nothing of the plight of the people in Exiled."

Jack looked at Blue, who was smiling a knowing smile. "Blue, I think we need to reach Stevien."

"I am ready when you are, Jack," Blue answered, the old familiar twinkle in his eye.

Jack walked over and sat on the ground in front of Blue. Blue soon had the hazy, filmy orb dancing between his hands. At first, nothing could be seen, but slowly, the small face of a young boy appeared. The boy's eyes widened in surprise, and then he began shouting for Stevien. "It is them! Lord Stevien, it is them!"

Within a few seconds the relieved face of Stevien appeared in the flickering orb. "Thank the Creator! I have been so worried about you. Is everyone safe? Do you have Westin?" Stevien's questions kept pouring out as relief over the safety of his friends finally settled in on him.

Jack quickly answered his questions as best he could, inviting Dr. Westin to join the conversation with Stevien. They gave him an account of their journey since their last communication and of the news of the death of Jetta.

Stevien was grieved at the news but was relieved at finding Westin safe with them. Soon Westin was explaining the latest dilemma, with the people of Exiled.

"What should we do?" asked Jack. "Our mission was to seal the wall, but it would most certainly trap those people forever. Can we do that, Stevien? Could we live with ourselves?"

Stevien pondered for several minutes, obviously distressed over the situation. He had to decide which was better, to condemn all to contain evil or to free all and suffer the consequences.

Finally, he admitted, "I dare not make this decision myself. I need the approval of the Council. We have a meeting here within the hour. I will advise them of the problems and ask for their opinion. We must have a vote."

Stevien bit at his lower lip, then continued. "Jack, could we speak for a moment in private?"

Jack and Blue exchanged looks and then nodded. The others took the hint and walked a distance away so they could have a private conversation. Owyn and Zi gave a deep scowl at Jack, disliking being left out of the conversation.

"We are alone now, Stevien. Is there another problem we need to discuss?"

Stevien nodded, then told Jack of the treachery of the Northern Region. "I know you are traveling with troopers from that region. I felt you needed to know they may be traveling under different orders."

"We are aware, Stevien. We found treachery here as well." Jack relayed the story of Quoto and his traitorous acts."

Stevien's face revealed his pain. "I am sorry, Jack. I truly felt I was sending you off with the best our land had to offer. It seems I did you a disservice."

"You could not have known the Northern Region made their own alliance with Gwilim. What are the conditions in the Homeland now with the Veil down and the Northern Region compromised?"

"Grim. With free access to our lands from the west and the north, they are assaulting our land mercilessly. We are constantly battered with violent storms which have destroyed many of our villages. The attacks from the raiders are daily now, and they approach the larger cities. I am told Baka Ton is only a few days from attack. We have hidden as many of our people as we can in the far regions to the south and east, but even if the raiders do not advance, the storms are enough to destroy us."

"It sounds as if we cannot expect more troopers from the Homeland to help fight Gwilim's followers if Barrier falls."

Stevien shook his head. "If we could spare them, you would have them. We have been able to push the raiders back in several areas, so we are not without our victories, but the storms make it very difficult. Jack, give me a chance to meet with the Council. Contact me in a couple of hours and I will give you my decision on the Barrier and the people of Exiled."

Jack agreed, and they said a hasty good-bye.

The others returned to the fire, and Jack gave them the report from the Homeland.

Soulo's face turned dark and angry as the thought of raiders crossing his land. "Those troopers are good men. I know they will fight hard. But those storms! Who can fight the wind?"

"It is the light cannons," confirmed Westin. They have turned the full force of energy on them. Stevien is correct. The storms alone could be the death of them."

"Doctor, you helped design those things, is there anything you can tell them that might be of help?" asked Jep anxiously.

Westin thought for a minute, then stood and walked away. "I must think," he muttered, distracted. Jonas, always at his side, left with him.

Owyn stuffed his pipe again and watched Westin depart. "What kind of mission is this? One minute, we are told to seal the wall, the next, we are thinking of taking it down. For me, I cannot see allowing Gwilim and Balak freedom to invade our lands."

Zi puffed a huge cloud of smoke and let it billow into the air, "Not to mention those horrid creatures Gwilim has created. Our people would not stand a chance against a hoard like that. When I think back of the devastation of the villages and people, my blood chills. And that was only from the few of those demons who were left in Homeland. I shudder to think of an army of them free to roam or home."

"I can't begin to sort it myself," confessed Jack. "It seems one solution is as heartless as the other."

Jep and Blue, still sitting next to one another on the ground, had been talking quietly to one another. Jack noticed Blue was attempting to explain something in detail to Jep, which the old wizard found quite confusing. Blue picked up a stick and began to draw on the ground. Before long, his face was close to the ground, making notations around the edge of his drawings.

"What's he up to now?" frowned Owyn.

Jep, still looking a bit confused, answered, "Blue thinks there is a way to stop the storms in the Homeland. His orbs contain information from Elidor's notes when he designed the cannon. He says there is a way to alter the flow of energy causing the storms. Just leave the boy alone and let him work. I will ask Westin to work with him."

Blue's butt was high in the air as his face hovered close to the ground, writing feverishly. He whispered and argued with himself as he worked. Much like any old man would.

Zi watched with a skeptical look on his face. Finally he grinned and remarked, "Elidor's knowledge inside the head of Blue. I will bet that is one thing ol' Balak never considered."

Soulo's troopers were finishing their care of the injured. Jep helped in whatever way he could with magic healing, but many soldiers would not be able to continue with them.

Luka summoned his dragons and helped the injured troopers on their backs to be flown back to his compound to join the other troopers there, who were also healing from their injuries.

Their numbers continued to dwindle. Jack was concerned that no matter which decision the Council decided, he might not have the men to complete the mission. There were bound to be other confrontations with the enemy, and they were in no condition to fight. They had lost so many, and they had not endured a full-on attack. So far, they had been able to initiate the battles.

When Westin joined Blue, they moved to an area farther away from the others to continue their work. They argued from time to time, then there would be a sudden agreement on Westin's part. Blue did indeed seem to have vital information stored inside his head.

When it was time to contact Stevien, the two seemed anxious to deliver their solutions. Blue sat nervously, waiting for the sphere to clear and to see Stevien's face. It was unusual to see him unnerved.

Again, the young squire was waiting for their contact. "I'll get him right away," he shouted and ran out of the room.

Stevien hurried in and sat before the sphere. "We had a rough meeting at the Council, but eventually, it was decided we cannot allow more of Gwilim's raiders to enter our land. We have our hands full now. More raiders would seal our fate. We must secure our own land before we can worry about freeing those behind the Barrier. Perhaps, someday, we will find a way to free them."

Westin's face fell as he listened to Stevien. Of course, he understood the decision, but the thought of his friends doomed behind the Barrier was crushing. "Stevien, have you considered the people in Exiled would *add* to our number of people fighting Gwilim? We may be releasing thousands of raiders, but we would also be releasing tens of thousands of men and women willing to fight for their freedom."

"Doctor Westin, if they have not fought for their freedom before, why should we expect them to fight now? We cannot open our lands to certain invasion and 'hope' these people will, at last, make a stand against Gwilim. What if they decide to run?"

"I assure you they will fight!" Westin argued. "Even as we speak, their revolution has begun. We cannot abandon them now!"

"And I cannot abandon our people!" snapped Stevien. Noting the harsh tone of his voice, Stevien gathered himself and continued. "This is not a decision made easily. You, of all people, understand the true source of this mission. None of us in the Council want to leave the people in Exiled to the whim of a madman. We must fight the battles at hand before we can take on any new ones. As it is, our troopers are spread all along the borders of the Homeland, fighting to keep the raiders away. We have lost more ground than I care to think, but if we send those men to aid the people of Exiled, our own people will be lost. Then there will be no 'free' land left for anyone."

Of course, Westin understood. He sat numbly on the ground. "I know Stevien. I'm sorry for arguing with you. It is just....," he paused, "You and I both know just how unjust this is on those people. It is not only unkind but also unfair. They are no different than we are. Stevien, we have been given this chance to make things right once and for all."

"I do understand, believe me, and I promise you if there is a way to rescue them later, we will try." Stevien and Westin stared at one another, harboring a secret they shared.

Blue pulled Stevien's attention away from Westin, "Lord Stevien, Doctor Westin, and I think we may have found a way to stop the storms destroying the Homeland."

Stevien's eyes widened, "Tell me!" he urged. "Every day here could be our last."

Westin began, "We will need the help of the Palace of Ages. They should have the materials we need to complete a light cannon similar to the one the enemy is using. If we can pinpoint the cannons they are using, we can trigger a 'ripple' effect which will send the storms energy back on top of them."

Stevien shook with excitement. "I will have them ready. If this works, we will all owe you our lives. Contact me within the hour."

"Perhaps, then, you would be able to rethink your decision on Exiled?" said Westin as he lifted an eyebrow in question.

Stevien smiled back at the old Doctor. "If you can help us with these storms, I think we might be able to see ourselves clear to send some help your way. You lead quite a bargain, Doctor."

After the connection faded, Jack and the others looked warily at Westin. The old doctor seemed very aware of the stares but kept his eyes focused on the fire before him.

Finally, Zi grunted a great "Hummfff" and added, "Well, if no one else is going to ask, I will! What is this great secret you and Stevien have about the Exiled people? If we are all asked to give up our lives for it, we certainly should know the truth of it!"

A grunt of agreement was sounded by everyone around the fire, and Westin looked into their curious faces. "Yes, my friends, you are entitled. If anyone should know the truth of it, it should be you."

Owyn winced and groaned, "Awww, I do not think this is going to be good."

"Please know, there has never been an attempt to deceive you. That much, I promise. We were afraid too much information would cause further confusion."

Jack gritted his teeth at the possible deception. "Get on with it, Doctor."

"Many years ago, we were visited by a group of beings from another land. They appeared quite suddenly in the Palace of Ages during one of our meetings regarding the supervision of the Barrier. Without warning, the great doors of the meeting hall flew open, and three beings entered.

"They explained they had been monitoring our lands for many years. Watching to see us evolve and progress. They had come to warn us of the danger Gwilim posed to our lands."

"It was the first time we knew of the atrocities Gwilim was performing. We had no idea since communication behind the Barrier was impossible. They described in detail what Gwilim was doing to his own people. How he was taking the very life source of man and placing it in the body of a beast to serve him. It was only one of many of his horrid deeds. They told us of the empty shells of bodies he left behind, constantly hungering for the lives stolen from them. They were little more than walking dead.

"They explained it was time for us to intercede on behalf of those people behind the wall. We argued that the people behind the wall were lawfully condemned, and we had no right to intercede."

Westin closed his eyes and shook his head. "They told us of a tale from their own land. The evil and condemned men and women from their land were also sent away to keep the people safe. They sent their evil ones to a land surrounded by water, so it was impossible for them to escape. For hundreds of years, they used the land as their holding area for anyone condemned of crimes or the wrongful use of magic.

"They watched over the land and the people constantly and finally began to see the people progress into a peaceful society. A society that, itself, hated evil. They saw the land cultured and made into a garden because of their hard work. Any sign of the old 'evil' was gone. The people lived as normally and peacefully as the people in the old land.

"These people also made a place where their evil ones could be sent far away from the others. They were sealed away in an area guarded by a great wall to protect the innocent people who wanted to live a peaceful life."

The camp became deadly quiet as everyone listened. Realization began to dawn on them one at a time.

"_**We**_ are the people?" asked Jep. "_**We**_ were the ones originally confined here to rid them of their evil?"

"Yes, our ancestors were the evil ones sent away to protect the people of their lands."

Soulo, ever the proud soldier, paced in front of the old doctor. "Are you telling me we are no better than those people behind the Barrier?"

"That is what I am telling you," answered Westin. "You see, this place, the Grand, is the garden of peace of our land. On either side, a wall was erected for <u>their</u> protection. We are as exiled as those beyond the Barrier. But it does not mean the people who live there are all evil, just as all people in the Homeland are not all men of peace."

Jack could hardly believe his ears. "So, we were also exiled!"

Westin nodded. "To a degree. We were blessed to have compassionate leaders, unlike those in Exiled. You see, that is why we must help those poor souls beyond the Barrier. They are no different than we are! We cannot just leave them to die in the hands of that creature Gwilim!"

Jack looked at Westin, "And Stevien knew?"

"Yes, of course. He met the Visitors. They stayed with us for many months and taught us many things."

Jack looked over at Jep, "And you, did you know any of this?"

Jep held his hands out and shook his head, "Not me! This is the first I have heard of it."

"What about Jetta? he asked of the Doctor. "Did she know?"

"Yes, Jetta knew. You must understand, she could not tell you. In these times, it would be terribly disarming for our people to find out their origin was no better than the people we fight. I knew Jetta well. It was probably tearing at her heart."

"So, we have done the same thing as those visitors. Sent people away and abandoned them." Jep shook his head in disgust. "So why didn't these men go to Exiled themselves and free those people?"

"When this land was set aside, many of their great ones were sent here to help lead and guide us. It was their presence that eventually caused the dividing of the land. They were powerful wizards, and they helped to create our villages and set our laws. They did their best to help with a new life for the people of this land. Unfortunately, evil can woo even the greatest of people, even powerful wizards. Soon, a war of magic was waged, and our land became a battleground."

Jep stared at Westin in realization, "You mean Elidor and Gwilim? They were from that faraway land? They were the ones sent here to help us begin new lives?"

"Yes. They were originally sent to guard and protect us, to help us. You see what wickedness was born in Gwilim. The Visitors were remorseful over his turn to evil and felt responsible for the division in this land. Elidor and his wizards felt so responsible they gave their powers to make sure Gwilim was contained."

Jep nodded, "I was a young wizard at the time of the great war, but I was honored to add my powers to the wall. I was also one of the fortunate ones able to retain a small portion of mine. Many did not. Elidor eventually was so weakened it cost him his life."

"Well, if those Visitors can't help how can we be expected to do so?" huffed Owyn. "It seems to me they are the source of this chaos, why is it left for us to clean it up?"

"This is **our** land, Owyn. We made the decision to exile those people, never considering eventually, their descendants would be suffering for the crimes of their ancestors. Where there is good, there will always be evil. But evil cannot be allowed to win over good. We have allowed that to happen in Exiled." A sad smile spread across the face of the old doctor.

Zi looked long at Westin, "And what if we do not help them? What if we just leave them as they are and go our own way?"

Westin looked around at the faces at the campfire. "Gwilim will not be denied. He is planning to take our lands for his own. Evil is like wildfire; it will not be denied the fuel it needs, and if left untended, it will cover the land and demolish everything in its path. The Visitors warned us if Gwilim escapes, this land and everyone in it, will be destroyed. They cannot risk his evil spreading to their lands. He would eventually get his revenge against them."

Soulo slapped the side of his leg with his hand whip, "So they sent the few of us to face this impossible task alone to try to save the people of our land!"

"Not exactly," Westin answered. "They knew the difficulty of the task, so they left us a weapon to aid us."

"A weapon!" said Soulo excitedly, "Well, that's more like it!"

Jack frowned as he looked from Soulo to Westin, "So, where is this weapon?"

Westin began again, "During the time with us, they gave us a wonderful gift. It took many months of learning, and our brightest people worked with them. Jetta was the best of them all. Luckily for us, Balak was not aware of what was happening at the time. He was already in deep conversations with Gwilim. We kept this project well hidden.

"It is the perfect weapon, with understanding, capabilities, and a knowledgeable purpose; a weapon that learns the good of mankind and well as the danger of the evils."

Suddenly, everyone knew. Every face turned to Blue, who had been sitting quietly listening.

"What?" he asked as he returned their looks.

"Blue is the weapon?" asked Zi. "Awhhh, we are doomed indeed! He gets confused when he must lace his boots!"

"I assure you," Westin continued, "he is quite capable. More information is stored in his orbs than all our minds combined."

With his mouth hanging ajar, Owyn gaped at Blue. "Why didn't you tell us, Blue?"

Blue frowned as he looked back at the group. "I am afraid I do not know what he is talking about. I am here to help seal the Barrier. That is all I know."

"And you will, and much more, Blue," assured Westin, as he smiled at the old man Blue had become, "and in doing so, we will help the people of Exiled."

Soulo rolled his eyes at the thought of Blue as a weapon. "Well, beyond that, we are sorely outnumbered. Gwilim's troops are two steps behind us, and we have no help from the Homeland. I doubt Blue can do it all by himself."

"You are quite correct," a loud voice announced, and two men stepped from the darkness, followed by a group of hulking demok.

CHAPTER NINETEEN

Andro walked slowly through the great golden tunnel, touching the smooth sides as if touching something sacred. He looked closely at every inch of the shiny gold. There could be no flaws.

His hands swept across the surface, feeling the warmth of the gold. The tunnel tall enough for a considerable size man to stand and wide enough to allow supply wagons to pass and many people at one time. He still worried about their exit from Exiled. So many lives depended on him, and so many things could still go wrong.

The other men in the tunnel also examined the walls, each one double-checking the other. Without Westin here to supervise, Andro could only pray the notes left for him were enough. It had to be!

For long months, he worked beside the foundry workers, pouring and finishing the tunnel pieces. When connected, it would be one solid unit with no visible seams to allow the powerful magic a crack to seep in. It had taken several tries to get it perfect. The first two tries had been dismal failures, and their hope had almost been lost.

But it certainly seemed perfect now. He had even crawled along the top of the structures to examine the outside walls. His heavy body sliding along the smooth surface.

The outer shells were etched with markings foreign to him, but Westin had insisted it was necessary to re-direct the flow of the magic coursing through the Barrier. Many wizards had used their magic to build the wall, intertwining one with one another. They had given their magic and their lives to make the Great Wall. These strange inscriptions were the missing piece Balak had so desperately desired.

There were six sections in all and they would have to be transported a few miles to the Southern Portal. They were massive heavy pieces, and huge wagons were designed to carry their weight. Each wagon had twelve bull-ox to pull the sections. It should take two days and nights to get to the Portal and set the sections together. Then, they would wait for the Southern Portal to make its move across the golden tube.

His fingers outlined the ancient inscriptions, and he again wondered why it had been so important to keep the people of Exiled away from the others in the land. He knew there was much evil here, but how could anyone believe they were all evil? Many of these people were simple, hard-working peasants who only wanted a peaceful life for themselves and their families. They were innocent of committing crimes and did not deserve this fate. And no one deserved to live under the cruel reign of Gwilim.

Women and children buffed the surface of the gold feverishly to bring it to a bright shine. The constant touching by the workers caused to surface to dull, and the women worked hard to keep the gold gleaming.

Andro gave the workers a warm smile and nod as he turned to walk back to the foundry building. From here, the tunnel looked almost small. It would be quite long when assembled, yet such a small distance between them and the outside world.

He rubbed the back of his sore neck and moved his head gently from side to side. He was tired; so very tired. He had not been able to sleep in weeks. The responsibility was so great upon him, and he did not know if he could handle it another day.

More people poured in every day from every part of the countryside. He had taken great precautions to make sure Balak and Gwilim did not know of their plans, but so many people! He constantly feared a leak and their plan discovered. "Dear Creator, just a few more days! Let us have just a few more days!"

Gwilim's escape plan included only his select few, his army, and his demok, of course. He cared little if the others were to die. If Gwilim succeeded, everything would be lost.

He had most of the people sent to the nearby hillside to wait for his call. He could not afford to have too many strangers around, attracting attention. Most of the people were members of the underground movement, just as he was. They had been meeting for years with great hopes of overthrowing Gwilim and ridding their land of his madness. But then Balak came, and the madness increased. Gwilim found his trusted confidant, and they finally realized they could never defeat Gwilim in an all-out war.

Then he met Westin. They were both assigned to work in Gwilim's labs for a time. Andro and Westin made a strong friendship immediately. In this land, you had to be careful of new friends, but Andro felt an instant kinship with the old doctor.

Westin also seemed to trust and respect his friendship. Andro helped nurse him back to health when Balak had been particularly cruel in his interrogations, and the old doctor never forgot his kindness.

It was Westin who gave them back their dream of freedom.

Westin was constantly under surveillance, so he and Andro established a secret means of communication.

The simple servants, who were almost invisible in the house of Gwilim, were the sons and daughters of Andro. He had sixteen in all, and they were his eyes and ears. Westin even had one of Andro's cousins assigned to him. A cheerful lad named Jonas who kept them in constant communication with one another.

The day was beginning to cool a bit, and that was good. The precious gold became hot enough to blister their hands under the hot sun.

He called out for one of the men to give the order to cover the tunnel for the night.

Several men scrambled about, pulling great sheets of cloth over the tunnel. The cloth had been coated with sticky glue then covered with hay, so when they finished, it looked like nothing more than huge rows of hay for the animals.

Andro's wife, Helen, and several of his children were at the palace, readying for a moment's departure. He looked into the waning sky, wondering if he had done everything he could. If only Westin were here. He had never been good at the finer details of making a plan work. Westin had placed much trust in his hands.

Westin was in a weakened state when Andro arranged for his escape. They were only able to find enough gold to make a tiny tunnel, barely small enough for the group to crawl through, and it collapsed as soon as they left it.

For days, he worried, not knowing if they had made it, till finally, a carrier pigeon they had taken with them returned with a white ribbon tied to his leg. Success! Freedom!

He witnessed firsthand Balak's limited success in making his own tunnels many times. He was able to send thousands of troops and their demok through only twice, that he recalled. Of course, his tunnels were much larger, but they always collapsed quickly, the precious gold swallowed by the great wall. The Barrier would not be denied.

His last attempt was a horrible failure. The men and demok were still inside the tunnel when it failed, entombing them. The screams of those men still haunted him.

It was the inscriptions. They did not have the protective script covering the tunnel. Westin had promised them it was the only thing to hold back the magic.

He gave a heavy sigh just as a strong hand grasped his shoulder. "Father, if you do not cease your fretting, you will never live to use the tunnel!"

Andro rolled his eyes and smiled at his eldest son, "Calais, you would not recognize me if I did not worry. We must go and eat before your mother has us both strapped."

Calais grinned and began to pack the tools he used to engrave the carvings in the soft gold. He spent months studying the inscriptions Westin left and carefully carved the symbols on the surface of the tunnel.

Andro knew Calais also felt the strain of responsibility on his shoulders. He was the only one allowed to carve, and he worked day and night to etch the tunnel. When a section was completed, he began again, making sure the symbols on the new section joined perfectly with the ones on the old section, so not even a joint, where the sections connected, was visible.

Andro took one last look at the tunnel and put his hand on his son's shoulder. "Just a few more days, just give us a few more days." he prayed.

CHAPTER TWENTY

Bodecia's heart pounded inside her chest, as she thought about finally leaving this land. Her long months of work at the mines had been brutal, and had cost her much, but they had made her strong. Now she was wanted her reward.

Her mind wandered back to the land she had once called home. She remembered the green trees and snowcapped mountains, the air, clean and crisp, with the smell of spring flowers. Yes, she would soon be home.

She took precious little when she left the mines. There was nothing there she wanted. In fact, she never wanted to be reminded of it again.

She smiled as she felt the softness of the fine silk of her new gown. She had it specially made for her. She had delighted in taking the time to pamper herself and oil her sun-ravaged skin. She did not look like any of the pampered, porcelain-skinned ladies in the palace any longer. She appeared more like the field workers. She did not care. Her reward would be to finally be rid of this horrid place.

She glanced about the streets as she made her way to the palace. "Where in the world is everyone?" she wondered. "Is this a holiday?"

She passed several shops who had closed their doors and continued to wonder. Oh, there were a few people in the streets, but not on a typical workday.

Most probably, Gwilim has frightened them again, and everyone is in hiding. It happened many times before, and since Balak joined him, even more frequently. Gwilim had an unquenchable appetite, and everyone knew it.

The palace guards did not bother to question her. Of course, they knew who she was, and she was sure word had been given to allow her entrance.

She fully expected to be treated as a queen after the tortures she had endured to get that cursed gold. She recalled how eager Andro had been for every nugget, always pushing for more.

She climbed the steep ramp leading to the upper chambers of the lords and ladies. The men and women bowed and smiled at her as she passed. Now, this was more like it. It felt good to be back among the favored and well-bred.

She continued down the hall to the chamber where she knew he would be waiting. She could hardly wait! Her breath quickened as she pushed open the heavy doors.

"My dear! It is so good to see you again," purred Gwilim through his sharp, pointed teeth. "I understand you have some information for me?"

Chapter Twenty-One

"Do you have it yet?" yelled Stevien, pushing his way into the courtyard. Men were crowded around the large cannon, working feverishly to finish in time.

High winds pounded against the walls of the palace, blowing tiles and pieces of trees in every direction. Baka Ton itself was almost gone, the harsh winds tearing it apart more each day.

One of the men looked over his shoulder and answered, "We are working as fast as we can, Lord Stevien, but every time we get close, the wind and lightning threaten us. It is like trying to work inside of a windstorm."

Stevien knew they were doing their best. Every minute was closing in on them. The last of the Homeland troops surrounded the city while raiders covered the hillside. They waited, like vultures, until the storms broke them like withered sticks. Then, they would descend and wipe them out.

Most of the people fled weeks ago to where he could not imagine. The raiders seemed everywhere. All four regions had reported similar weather catastrophes just as Baka Ton was experiencing.

The Southland was covered with flood waters, leaving much of that land dead. The Eastland also had flooding, as well as horrible hailstorms, while the Northland had been in a deep freeze for months. Even their alliance with Gwilim did not protect them. There did not seem to be a safe place for the people to go for protection.

Stevien stood beside the strange cannon. "Do you think this will work, Hedges?" he asked the young wizard, finishing the last bit of work to be done.

Hedges looked solemnly at Stevien. "It had better work! It may be our last hope! If Westin helped Balak design those things, let us hope he knows how to counter them! According to him, our cannon will seek out the greatest source of power, which should be their cannon. Once it connects with their cannon it will seek another, then another. Hopefully, connecting to all the cursed machines. It should hunt all their demon cannons." He made one quick look into the housing of the giant machine and gave a nod. "Anyway, we will know soon enough. Let us give it a try!"

Hedges grabbed Stevien by the arm and yelled for everyone to retreat behind a nearby wall.

"We can't be sure what this thing is going to do, so it's best to be shielded as much as possible," he yelled, trying to make himself heard above the wind. "Westin said to make sure we do not look directly at the light. It will blind us."

Stevien nodded as Hedges picked up the rope tied to the trigger housing of the great cannon.

"Dear Creator, let your face shine on us today, and forgive us for what we are about to do," he prayed. Hedges gave the rope a pull.

At first, they did not see the light, but they felt the rush of heat as it leaped from the cannon. The air around them vibrated from the sheer force of its mighty charge. A great whooshing sound surrounded them, causing them to hold their heads in pain and felling them to the ground.

The earth trembled and shook, and stones began to fall from the walls of the castle. Men cried out for fear of being crushed.

Hedges grabbed Stevien and pushed him against the outside wall just as the wall began to sway. Stevien soon found himself lying on the ground outside of the palace walls, covered in dirt and fallen rock. Beside him lay Hedges, crushed by the falling wall.

Stevien shook his head, trying to regain his senses. The air still shimmered as if they were under water, but the wind had ceased. He could hear men pushing their way from the rubble and tried his own feet. He had a badly sprained ankle and cried out in pain when he tried to put weight on it.

He realized he could hear the voiced of the men around him. The harsh wind was gone, and except for their voices, silence had fallen on the palace courtyard.

"Help me, help me," he shouted at a man passing nearby, "take me to the front gate!"

The man took Stevien by the arm, and together they made their way across the courtyard to the gate.

Soldiers were still picking themselves up from the ground. Many sat dazed, looking about in confusion.

Stevien looked up at the hillside, where the raiders had been camped with their cannon. The top of the mountain was completely gone! It was as if a great hammer had sheared it away. Stevien could not believe his eyes. No one moved there.

"Soldier," he shouted at a nearby soldier, "get some troops and find out how many of those raiders made it out of that blast alive."

The man stared dumbly at Stevien for a minute until Stevien repeated his order. Finally, he turned and barked orders to his men, gathering a troop together.

"What kind of power have we unleashed?" he wondered in horror and awe. "How can mankind be capable of such destruction?"

The young man holding him replied, "Better them than us!"

Stevien thought for a minute, then answered back, "Who said it wasn't us?"

He asked the young soldier to help him to what was left of his rooms in the palace. He wanted to contact Westin and let him know the cannon was a success. As they passed the great cannon, Stevien stopped and looked up at the crystal barrel shining dully against the gray smoky sky.

He realized he was shivering at the destruction it unleashed. He wondered how many times the enemy had used them on his own people. It frightened him to think such power was now a part of his peaceful world.

Chapter Twenty-Two

Andro watched Calais move along the top of the tunnel. His face and arms were burned from where the hot sun had reflected off the bright gold. His hair, once a sandy brown, had turned as golden as the metal he worked, lightened by the sun.

Calais' face was almost touching the gold as he concentrated on the carvings. They were so close now. Only a few inches to complete!

Andro's heart was leaping in his chest as he mentally began the checklist of things to do before their plan was finally complete. The timing must be exact, and there were still so many things that could go wrong!

He ran his hands on the carved walls of the tunnel, praying again he made all the right decisions and prayed everyone had played their parts as planned.

"Well, it seems you have been a very busy boy," a mocking voice remarked from behind him.

Andro turned, stunned, as he recognized the callous voice.

Gwilim, his long black robes shrouding him like a shadow, stared back at him, his red eyes blazing in amusement. Balak stood close beside him, smiling with equal amusement.

Stepping from behind the two men, Bodecia sheepishly gave Andro a sorrowful look.

"Girl, what have you done?" he hissed in horror.

Bodecia stared at Andro for a minute, then answered, "I had to pick a side, Andro, I thought I should pick the winning one."

Calais stopped his work, as did all the men and women. Everyone stared in shock and horror as demok filled the area around the tunnel.

"I do appreciate all of your hard work," smiled Gwilim. "Now, come and tell me how we will transport this great hall to the Portal." His long nails bit into Andro's shoulder as he led him back into the work tent.

Chapter Twenty-Three

The people sitting around the fire did not even have time to reach for their weapons as the group stepped out of the darkness.

The scouts who had been stationed around the camp were being held between the massive bodies of demok. The men shook with terror as they stared back at their friends.

Owyn squinted his eyes for a moment, then took a step forward. "Chambers?" he asked. "Is that you?"

The soldier looked at Owyn in a kind of amusement. "Well, it appears you are either a ghost or you are more durable than we imagined."

"Where are the rest of your killer friends," snapped Zed as he took Owyn's arm protectively. "If you think we are going to give up this easy, you obviously haven't learned anything yet!"

Chambers held his hands out in front of him. "Hold on, big man, we are not here to harm any of you. We could have taken you at any time if that were the case."

Jack looked at the demok holding his men and motioned, "If you wish us no harm, let those men go free."

Chambers turned and nodded to the demok, and the men rushed behind their comrades.

"What do you want?" asked Jack, still watching every move closely.

"We are not part of Voxx's raiders. We were sent here under different orders to find Dr. Westin."

Blue stepped in front of Westin to block any attempt to take him. "You will not leave with Dr. Westin." Blue's fists were clenched at his sides, and Jack knew he would fight to the death to protect the old doctor.

"We are not here to fight; I told you that. I understand why you are suspicious, but please hear me out before you make any decisions. If it will make you feel safer, go ahead and arm yourselves," Chambers motioned to the stack of weapons stacked to the side of the camp.

With a nod from Jack, the men scurried and grabbed their swords and spears, and stood in a tight ring around Jack and the others.

Once the men were armed, Jack continued, "So if you're not part of the others, then who are you?"

Owyn stepped forward and pointed an angry finger in Chambers' face, "I will tell you who he is! He is one of the men that almost killed me. He stood by and watched Voxx beat and torture me. I did not see any concern from you then! Do not trust him, Jack!"

Chambers closed his eyes and sighed, "Owyn, I could do nothing to help you. You walked right into the middle of a bee's nest. Quoto saw you the first day you entered the village and warned Voxx. All they had to do was to search the taverns until they found you. Had I helped you then, I would not have been able to help my people in Exiled. I am sorry for what happened to you, but if I had to sacrifice your life to help thousands, then I am afraid it is what I would have done. I would have gladly made that sacrifice myself if it would help my family.

"Voxx is a cruel man completely dedicated to Gwilim. He would have been Gwilim's heir apparent if not for Balak's timely arrival. But even so, he would do anything for that evil Lord. He was given the assignment to care for these lands until Gwilim's escape from Exiled. When Dr. Westin escaped, Voxx was given the duty of returning him to Exiled. He would rather die himself than to fail Gwilim."

Zi spat on the ground at the foot of Chambers. "And what does that have to do with your appearance at our camp."

The demok clawed the ground and gave a fierce growl as Zi stood facing Chambers. Zi was a hulk of a man, but next to these creatures, he looked like a small child.

Chambers looked at Zi for a moment, then turned to the demok. He spoke in a quiet voice, and the creatures sat on the ground, their heads lowered as if they had been scolded.

Even Zi raised his eyebrows at seeing such a sight.

Chambers looked around at the men in the center of the camp. "Which one of you is Jack?" he asked.

Jack stepped forward, "That would be me."

Jonas pushed his way through the men, "Keno? Dear Creator, is that you?"

Jack grabbed Jonas before he could reach Chambers and held him back. "Hold on! Do you know this man?"

Jonas looked at Chambers and the demok with him, confused. "He is my cousin. What are you doing here, Keno?"

"Andro asked me to join these men years ago," said Chambers, obviously surprised to see Jonas. "I have been mapping the area for him so when the time came for escape from Exiled, we would have information on areas to live. When Westin escaped, Andro knew Gwilim would have Voxx track him. It was my best way to locate Westin.

"Voxx has been aware of your mission from the beginning. Gwilim had a spy from the Northern Region placed in your party. He has been reporting to Voxx."

Jack nodded, "Yes, we found out some time ago. We were able to use his treachery to lure your Commander Voxx into a trap. Voxx decided he was also a traitor to his raider army and executed him after our attack on Needle Rock."

Owyn and Zi both looked at Jack. It was the first they had heard of Quoto's death. Owyn smiled, knowing his friend had taken retribution for him.

"You will have to tell me, "Chambers said. "My troops and I set out two days ago to make our way to the Southern Portal. Voxx held us back in Harmony to wait his orders. When men came back to gather more of the troops, we took the opportunity to make our way here. We hoped we would run across you on the way."

Jep eyed the demok warily. They sat quietly, but their huge muscular bodies shook from time to time as if they were in some sort of pain.

"Why did you bring those beasts along?" he asked. "I didn't think they could easily be controlled by anyone but Gwilim."

"That was true at one time," answered Dr. Westin as he stepped from behind the protective Blue. "Son, are you working with Andro?"

A relieved smile spread on Chambers' face. "Dr. Westin! Thank the Creator you are still alive. I was afraid Voxx had succeeded in capturing you. Yes, Andro sent us to make sure you reach the portal and to keep Voxx from harming you."

Owyn pushed Zi, trying to get closer to Chambers, "You seemed ready to do whatever you could to deliver Westin to Voxx when we last met!"

"It was never my intent to deliver Westin to Voxx but rather to find Westin first. Voxx would not share any information on his whereabouts, and I could not afford to let him get to Westin first."

Jack put his hand on Owyn's shoulder and could feel him shaking. He knew the beatings he had endured at Voxx's hands were all becoming very real to him again. He needed to calm Owyn and to get to the truth of this Chambers and his group.

Jack sent a look to Zi to indicate he needed to help Owyn.

Zi took Owyn's arm and led him back to the fire.

Soulo took Zi's place between Chambers and Jack, his massive hands holding a heavy mace, ready to spring at a moment's notice.

"You must be Soulo, the military commander. It is my honor, Sir. I must say I am more than a little surprised we were able to surprise you and your men so easily. I would have thought there would have been at least a bit of a fight."

Soulo raised his eyebrows and turned his head, "Who said we weren't ready to fight? You have been under constant watch since you entered our camp."

Chambers looked around at the ragged men, a confused look crossing his face.

"We would have torn you limb from limb had you made a move against us!" a voice boomed from the darkness, and Luka and his wolves stepped into the light.

Chambers and his men stared at the massive wolves and the large mountain man with them.

"Well, it seems you have resources even we didn't know of."

Luka smiled dangerously and lifted a thumb toward the sky. The whoosh of a huge dragon wing dipped down toward the group, fanning the flames of the fire to the ground.

Chambers, his men, and demok scrambled to the ground for cover as the wings missed their heads by inches.

Looking up from the sooty ash, Chambers checked to be sure the danger had passed. "Impressive!" he whispered. "I would never have guessed."

While Chambers and his men picked themselves up from the ground, Dr. Westin talked quietly with Blue, assuring and explaining the sudden appearance of Chambers and his men. Blue still looked more than a little suspicious. In his short life span, he had experienced more than enough treachery, and the presence of the creatures on the ground made him cautious.

Jep looked over, annoyed, "Doctor, if you have anything you would like to share with us concerning this matter, I am sure we would all be interested."

Westin looked up, a little embarrassed, "I am sorry, my friends. Of course, of course!"

"I told you the story of my friend Andro and how we were working on a plan to free the people of Exiled. Andro was a resourceful man and had many resources at his disposal to aid us. He was also part of a very large family. Jonas, as I explained, is part of that family. It seems Commander Chambers is also family to Andro."

Chambers, still brushing soot from his clothes, nodded. "It has been our goal for many years to free our family and friends from Gwilim and Balak. I would do anything for my family. Even give my own life to save them from his abominations." Chamber's voice shook with anger and conviction. His face was twisted in hate, and his eyes filled with hot tears.

Jep watched the man closely, and for the first time, Jack noticed the old wizard was holding a glowing ball of swirling light behind his back. He had seen Jep use the balls of fire before and knew between Jep and Luka, they had been better protected than he imagined.

Jep pulled his hand from behind his back and let the glowing orb flicker out. "I think I would like to hear a little more from you, Chambers. But mind you, if even one of those creatures makes a move, I will roast every one of you!"

Chambers looked at Jep and nodded. Again, he motioned for the animals to sit quietly along the side of the camp, his men attending.

They sat around the fire as Chambers approached them. Jonas threw both arms around him and gave him a hearty slap on the back. "It is good to be with family again!" he exclaimed.

Keno smiled and hugged him back. "Same here, Jonas. You cannot imagine the horrors I have witnessed while with Voxx and his raiders. They are true savages."

"Yes, savages, we have been fighting for years as they killed our people and destroyed our lands," said Jack. "Were you also a part of that?"

Keno watched Jack's face closely. "I was part of several raids. It is nothing I am proud of, but if I had not taken part, Voxx would have been on his guard against me. I was able to smuggle some of the captives to small villages here in the Grand. Those people stand ready to help us fight for the freedom of our people in Exiled. I have spent much time with them, helping them secure their safety from Voxx. The destruction of your land, however, I was helpless to stop. I could not jeopardize my position any further with Voxx."

Owyn sat quietly next to Zi, listening to Keno. From time to time, he rubbed the area where his ribs had been broken.

"Keno, I have tried to explain to them what life in Exiled is like. The horrors Gwilim has dealt to the people there. Perhaps if you could explain to them how Gwilim commands his people and the fear they must endure each day, they will see why it is necessary to take such risks as you have taken." Urged Westin.

Keno nodded and began, "I don't know how much the doctor has told you, but for many years Gwilim has taken our people to build his army of creatures." He motioned toward the demok.

Their minds, or at least the part of them that was human, is removed, and only the primal instinct of the wild animal is left. There is little humanity left to them. You can see even the wolves are wary of them. Only through pain are their handlers able to control them; except for Gwilim. He can cower one with the touch of his hand. I have seen it many times. Once, I witnessed a demok attack its trainer, ripping away his arms as if they were chicken bones. Gwilim was in the courtyard and watched the whole incident. The demok was wild with fury, clawing at the body of its trainer while other trainers tried to approach to subdue it. Gwilim simply walked up to the creature and put his hand out, touching its head. Like a father would his own child. I swear the animal whimpered and fell to the ground, crying and moaning for more of its master's touch."

Zi pointed to the demok sitting at the edge of the camp. "And what keeps them so tame?"

"After many years of handling and training demok, some of our men discovered that a small disk, inserted at the base of the brain, would allow the creature to keep the memory of its human side. They found those creatures were not the same as the others, untamable. They looked the same but kept the knowledge of what Gwilim had done to them."

Luka's eyes stared openly at the demok, "Stars! That must be worse than losing your life altogether. To know what you once were and what you had become!"

"Yes, many had to be destroyed. They simply could not accept their fate. You see, while their minds had been restored to them, Gwilim still has hold of their souls. He holds all the souls of the people he has devoured. Even in death, they are not free."

Chambers looked in sympathy at the creatures, whose eyes lifted one by one to look at the men around the fire. For the first time, Jack saw the human locked behind the creature and shuddered at the unspeakable act against them.

"How many were able to keep their minds?" asked Soulo, also staring back at the unfortunate creatures.

"We have a couple hundred or so. Sometimes, for no reason, they die. While on our morning march, they fall dead. We think their human bodies, which are sent away to roam the desert, have finally been destroyed, so the link was broken. We have no way of knowing what has happened to those 'walking dead.'"

Blue, who had been quietly listening to Chambers, asked. "So, these creatures are linked to Gwilim, to the body of the animal they were enclosed, and to the body they once were?"

"That is correct."

"It seems to me these creatures would be better off dead then," offered Soulo. "I know I would."

Chambers stood, walked over to the group of demok, and stood before one of them. "We have often considered it, of course. But it is difficult to condemn those you love to a death without hope. I would like for you to meet my brother, Nile."

The dirty, hulky creature stood beside Keno, dwarfing him. His face had mighty horns protruding from the sides and thick, wiry hair that covered his head. His ears were thick and pointed, his fingers tipped with long, thick, vicious claws. He had seen a lot of battle, and his fur-coated body was matted with scars.

A gasp left Jonas as he stared at his cousin. "NO! Oh Nile, NO! Dear Creator!" He walked over and slowly placed his hand on the arm of the smelly creature. At his touch, the demok winced as if in pain.

Keno explained, "Gwilim still has a strong hold on them, even though they have some of their free will returned to them. They feel his power always. It is with constant pain they join us to fight him. I dare say I would not be able to withstand such a torment."

Tears streamed down Jonas' cheeks as he looked at his cousin, "We are the same age. We spent most of our lives living just a few houses apart. I knew he was away with the armies, but not this. Why would Gwilim do this to his own men?"

"Nile spoke out against the atrocities Gwilim embraced. That was all it took. Once Gwilim's glare falls on you, there is no hope of escape. He needs no explanation for his actions. The smallest of transgressions was excuse enough to bring the innocent before him. You know how he works, Jonas."

Dr. Westin walked over to comfort his comrade. Jonas was completely overtaken with grief at the harm done to Nile.

Blue approached the creature also and looked questioningly into its' eyes, trying to identify whether it was human or animal.

"I cannot understand how man can dishonor another man so," he wondered out loud. "Are there no limits on the evil one man can give another?"

Jep rubbed his eyes wearily and answered, "I suppose it is the duty of all men to stop such actions against others. I think that is what Doctor Westin has been trying to explain to us."

Jep looked at Luka. "What do your instincts tell you about these creatures?"

"They seek release," said Luka sadly. "They. . . . .are. . . hurting."

Owyn had not said a word during the revelation of the identity of the demok. He simply looked numbly at them as if he did not believe what his eyes were seeing.

"Doctor, is there any release for these men?" asked Blue.

Doctor Westin answered, "The death of Gwilim. His demise would release the souls of these men and women. If Gwilim were dead, his hold on them would end, and they would at last have their souls returned to them."

"Would they return to their former selves?"

Doctor Westin shook his head sadly, "They no longer have a body to return to. Those shells have been thrown away like scraps of garbage. No, most likely, they will perish. But they will at last be free and will die human."

Blue turned and walked back to the fire, and sat next to Owyn. Jack was as unsettled as everyone else at the news of the demok, but he sensed a heavy despondence settle in on Blue.

He and Jep looked at one another in alarm.

At last, they made their way back to the fire, and the demok, that was, Nile, sat next to the other demok.

"I think we can finally understand the people of Exiled need our help," said Jack. "Now, tell me what you and your friend Andro have planned."

"I thought you would never ask!" smiled Westin as he began to reveal the details of a plan set into action so many years ago.

Chapter Twenty-Four

"I miss Dr. Salto," said Blue.

"Yes, Blue, we all miss our dear Jetta," consoled Jep. He worried about Blue's reaction to the demok, and he whispered to Jack that Blue should be watched closely. Blue still had a limited understanding of many things, and this situation was by far one of the strangest yet. His confusion was cause for worry. And it could have deadly consequences.

It was hard to decide who needed more attention, Blue or Owyn. Both seemed withdrawn and out of sorts. Neither cared about eating nor hearing the plans being laid out by Dr. Westin.

Jack, busy with preparations for their arrival at the Barrier, looked up from time to time at Jep with great concern in his eyes. Jep was not sure if it was due to Westin's plan or his concern for Blue and Owyn.

"Dr. Salto helped me understand many things. My understanding is not advanced enough to comprehend what has happened to those demok." Blue said quietly.

Jep could understand why Blue was confused. He did not understand such an atrocity himself. Looking at the beasts sent waves of compassion over him. He thought of the thousands of other demok who had no memory of their former self and would never get even a small piece of their humanity back. He felt such sorrow for all of them that his heart felt as if it would explode.

Owyn's voice brought Jep back to reality, and he realized Owyn and Blue must have been talking for some time while his mind had wandered over the injustice of the demok.

"But why would any man want to destroy the part of a being that is human and turn them into a creature. Why could not Gwilim have just made them a loyal army?" Blue's forehead was drawn in a wrinkle of confusion. He looked even older than before, the stress of understanding mankind weighed on him heavily.

"I suppose Gwilim is not quite a man himself. I think part of him must be monster, too, if he is able to communicate with them so easily. I doubt he would trust anyone who was not completely under his power," said Owyn. "He gets a feeling of immortality by taking their souls hostage and commanding their every action. That is not the way the Creator planned for men to treat each other."

Blue studied Owyn's face closely then asked, "Why would your Creator allow such a man to exist? Is it not within his power to destroy such an evil person and rid the land of his evil? I find this hard to understand."

"So have men always," replied Jep, joining back in the conversation. "I have seen many horrible deeds against mankind in my time, against men, women, and even children. I always ask the same question. Why? There must be a greater plan, even if we do not see or understand it."

"When the souls of the demok are released, what will happen to them?" Blue seemed stubbornly intent for answers.

Jep searched for ways to explain the situation to Blue, for he could see he was determined to get answers to his questions. He silently wished in his own heart Jetta was still here to help dear Blue.

He drew a deep breath and began, "The Creator lives in a place where there is no evil, only good. The people help and love one another. There is no sickness, hate, or death. It is a beautiful and abundant land where no one is ever without. It is Paradise."

"Why can you not go there and live with him now? Why do you live in a land where there is little food and always filled with sickness and death? Does your Creator not want you to have these wonderful things?

"I suppose if we entered Paradise as we are today, we would only contaminate it. We are naturally vile to Him, yet he has said that, upon our death, we will be purified and will be allowed to enter his Kingdom."

"Will Gwilim be allowed in Paradise when he dies?"

"That, my dear friend, is doubtful. He has much to answer for. No, it is my belief Gwilim will kiss the face of the Dreaded One."

Blue looked between Owyn and Jep in surprise. "Where is this Dreaded One? Is he the king of Gwilim?"

Owyn had to chuckle a bit before he answered, "Out of the mouth of babes! Yes, I suppose you could say that. Gwilim has chosen to follow the evil ways."

"Where exactly does this 'soul' reside in a person?"

Jep had to scratch his head for a minute, then looked at Owyn. Owyn shrugged his shoulders and shook his own head.

Blue saw he was not likely to get an answer, so he moved on to his next question. "Does everyone have one of those souls?"

Now, the intent of the conversation was revealed. Jep looked closely at Blue and could see a spark of fear in his eyes.

Owyn also finally understood why Blue had been so upset over the demok.

Blue looked at Jep, then asked, "Jep, do I have a soul?"

Chills ran up Jep's spine as he realized they had no answer for Blue. They had come to love this funny creature, but in truth, he was no different from the demok. His body had been formed for a specific duty, just as theirs had been, and his mind filled with knowledge from the Palace of Ages. Were their actions as misguided as Gwilim's? Jep suddenly felt very ashamed.

It was Owyn who came up with the answer; crazy, care-free Owyn who never took any situation seriously.

"Blue, the Creator knows the difference between good and evil. You came to us to help fight the evil that He hates so much. He will reward you for that."

"But will I go to Paradise too?"

Owyn nodded his head. "We will all be there together, my good friend. We will conquer this wickedness Gwilim used to poison this land, and we will make up for the evil he has caused.

"You will be there, Blue."

Jep did not know if Owyn was right or not, but Blue seemed much happier. He supposed Blue feared departing this life into nothingness. He said a silent prayer to the Creator on Blue's behalf.

Jack and the others talked for hours, sometimes arguing. Jep, Owyn, and Blue finally joined them and listened as Westin explained his plan over and over.

"I just don't see how you can be sure it will work!" argued Soulo. "We need more men for backup. He waved his arms around him, motioning to the men.

"We barely have a hundred and fifty men here, including your men, Chambers. What if something goes wrong, we will have no way to stop them."

Chambers explained, "We have men coming in from every corner of the Grand to fight with us. We cannot ask for more. They may not be soldiers, but they are fierce with determination to protect the Grand. You said the Homeland is under attack, and I am here to tell you they will have their hands full. Gwilim sent the bulk of his army to hammer the Homeland with the light cannon. I doubt we will be able to expect help from them."

"We can only hope Stevien was able to build his own light cannon and destroy Balak's. If not, then I fear the Homeland has already fallen," said Westin.

Jack looked at Westin, "We should try to reach Stevien."

Chambers shook his head, "I would not advise that. Voxx has been able to intercept many of your messages. I do not think we can afford to let him know what is going on. There are problems with his communication in this area, but I still think we would be taking a chance."

Jep nodded, "Yes, we have had our problems communicating also. The mountains, I suppose. However, I would like to know if Stevien had any success with the cannon."

"I, too, would like to know if our plans for the cannon were successful," urged Blue.

Jack thought it over, then decided to give it a try. They desperately needed the extra troops to help guard the Portal, and he hoped Voxx was still licking his wounds from their last battle.

Stevien's face was filled with relief when it appeared in the sphere. He was pale and drawn. The man had lost a great deal of weight, and his hair was completely white.

Westin and Jep were also concerned. "Stevien, has the Homeland fallen?" Jep asked in alarm.

"No, my friends, the Homeland is safe. The cannon was a success. It stopped the horrific storms on the Homeland. We have had much damage, and Baka Ton was almost destroyed, but at least we survived. There have been no attacks for two days."

"What about the other regions? Are they free of attack also?" asked Soulo, worried over his own region.

"As far as I can tell, all the enemy cannons have been destroyed. Our cannon caused severe damage not only to the enemy's camp but to Baka Ton as well. The death toll of the enemy was complete, everyone in the area was destroyed. Their bodies were burned to ashes; there were no remains to be buried. We suffered casualties also. The power of the cannon does not discriminate between enemy and friend."

Westin and Blue both looked saddened by Stevien's news. Neither had guessed the power they had unleashed.

"Are you nearing the Southern Portal?" Stevien asked.

"Yes," replied Jack, "We are within two days travel. We have new information for you. A member of Gwilim's army has joined us with more information on Gwilim and Exiled." Jack told Stevien of the information Chambers had given them, stopping from time to time for Westin and Jep to add their thoughts.

Stevien sat quietly listening, then shook his head in sorrow. "We knew of some of the horrors there. I am sorry, Jack we did not tell you of the Visitors, but I did not see any reason to go into detail where they were concerned. They gave us as much help as possible, but I suppose it is up to us now to see that things are set straight in this land; not just in the Homeland and the Grand, but for those in Exiled also."

Stevien turned to speak with someone in his room for several minutes and then returned his attention to Jack and his group. "We will send troops as soon as possible. With the Veil down, our army's travel should not be impeded. The Wilds have tamed considerably since the fall of the Veil, so travel should be easier than before. If they leave within the hour and ride non-stop, they can meet you at the Southern Portal in three days. I cannot say how many we can spare, but you will have the bulk of our surviving army."

Westin breathed a deep sigh of relief. "Stevien, you do not know how this news blesses my heart! Now, if only the rest of our plan works."

"Yes, it is in the hands of the Creator now. I will pray for you, my friends. Now, I must attend to restoring this land so you will have a place to come home to."

Everyone was hopeful after the conversation with Stevien. But not Luka. He seemed perturbed and restless. Jack was surprised, as the rough old mountain man never seemed unnerved by anything.

"Luka, what are your thoughts on these plans." Asked Jack.

"There are too many things out of our control, Jack," he argued. "We do not know what is waiting behind the Barrier. What if this 'Andro' is not successful? What if the Portal opens, and Gwilim's army comes pouring out like locusts? Even with Homeland's help, we would be overrun. If we were able to communicate with them, to find out what was happening there, we could be better prepared. But this is insane. We could be opening the door to our own destruction."

The group sat quietly as Luka paced back and forth, ranting. They knew of course, he was right. There was no way of knowing if Andro had been successful at his end. Gwilim had many resources at his disposal and was more than determined to penetrate the Barrier. Luka knew firsthand the horrors waiting on the other side to be released. They were operating on the hope the people on the other side were still able and determined to escape, but no one could say if Andro was even still alive to carry out his part of the plan.

"Commander Soulo," asked Blue, "is there another option but to go forward with the plan we have?"

Soulo's frustration was also obvious, and for the first time, he and Luka were thinking the same thing, but he finally shook his head in grim acceptance, "No, Blue, I am afraid we are out of options. I would rather be in control of the battle and have ten times the men, but of course, that is not the case. My military training, I suppose." He smiled an apologetic smile at the group. "I will set up a strong perimeter around the portal, so if Gwilim's army streams through, we will be waiting."

Jep warned them, "Another caution; if Gwilim sets foot in this land, his powers will increase tenfold, back to what they were before he was sent to Exiled, and that is a force we really don't want to reckon with!"

Luka huffed again and stared up at the sky in frustration. "We cannot let that portal open! We will condemn this land, as well as yours. If we lose our lives here, what good are we to our country then?"

Zi came to his feet, his face twisted and angry, "I have never run from a fight in all my days, and I will not be running from this one. I will die before I let those people in Exiled live another day under that evil rule!"

Luka and Zi stared back at one another like two angry bears ready to attack. Finally, Luka shook his head and looked at the men sitting around the fire.

"You're gonna need more than your good hearts to win this one, boys," he said and looked back at Zi. He gave him a small smile and gave his shoulder a pat.

Everyone breathed a sigh of relief. There was no need to start a fight among themselves, and certainly, no one wanted to step between those two. They needed to save all that rage for the enemy.

Luka walked over to join Chambers and his men, grumbling quietly to himself as he made his way.

Jack was a little surprised by Luka's outburst. It was not like him to show such emotion.

Soulo also left them to go back to his tent and work out other potential strategies with his officers. Being a military man, he always wanted a backup plan.

Jep's eyes followed Soulo, "Poor fellow, I have had to live most of my life not knowing what would happen in the next minute. Can't imagine how it must be to have a plan ready for every possibility!" He gave a chuckle and stood. "Maybe I can at least give him some information on the lay of the land; might be useful." Jep straightened his weary back with a loud 'creak' and shuffled after Soulo.

Zi rolled his eyes and shook his head, "When those two agree on anything, that alone will be enough to bring that wall down!"

Everyone shared a laugh at the thought of Soulo and Jep working together, but in fact, Jack was relieved when Jep offered his help.

Everyone was dead on their feet. Jack could not remember the last time he slept, and after today's battle, every muscle in his body ached.

Owyn handed Jack and Zi a cup of hot brew he had perked on the fire and sat down with his own.

"Are you alright with Chambers joining us, Owyn?" asked Jack. He hated Owyn feeling threatened by their presence.

Owyn looked to where Chambers and Luka were talking. "I suppose if it helps us stop Gwilim. The truth be known; if there was any kindness shown to me during my 'questioning,' it was by Chambers. I think, even then, I could tell there was something different about him. Voxx knew it, too. Once, I swear Voxx threatened to take his life when he tried to stop him from torturing me. Any help, I suppose, is good help."

Zi's jaw hardened at the thought of Owyn's torture. It made Jack's stomach knot too.

This mission had been so consuming that the three friends had spent very little time alone together. For years, they had been the only confidants and companions the other had. Their close friendships had strengthened each of them, and now, at the face of battle, they needed to draw on that strength again.

"I suppose we either stop him or we die trying," said Jack softly.

"Well, there is a nice thought! I do not know if I should have a good night's sleep or live it up, being my last and all," huffed Zi.

"You know what I mean," said Jack. "We faced many battles together, and many times, we have wondered if we would wake up to another day. But this is the first time the future of everyone in the land has depended on our success. It is quite a responsibility."

They sat quietly for several minutes until Owyn finally spoke, "Yeah, but just think what an exceptional story this will be for Master Lir! And the ladies, oh, but the ladies will love it!"

They laughed hard at the thought of Lir sitting before them, wide-eyed, barely breathing. How he loved their tales.

When the laughter had died out, Jack continued, "It has been a long time since I had a family. I just want you both to know you two are like family to me, brothers, really. I cannot imagine anyone I would rather stand beside me. I believe the Creator planned for us to be here together at this dark time, where all things will be decided."

Zi and Owyn looked at Jack, then one another, and smiled. They knew it was true. Brothers.

Blue left the others and walked alone through the thick fir trees. He liked the smell of the needles on the trees and pulled some of the fragrant branches down to get a good sniff. His senses were sharper than ever, and he relished using them.

He bent and picked up scoops of earth and breathed in its' fragrance. It smelled musky and sweet. "That must be the smell of life," he thought, "since everything seems to have a touch of that scent."

Stars were beginning to dot the sky, and Blue watched them sparkle to life. There was no moon tonight, and he wished he could see the golden glow across the land.

As he made his way through the trees, Turi loped over to keep him company. Blue rubbed the big wolf behind her ears and enjoyed a rub against his leg. The animal had become quite friendly with Blue after its first hesitation at meeting a non-human.

He watched Jack, Zi, and Owyn sitting at the campfire and smiled as they laughed and talked quietly. He enjoyed watching the three of them together. "So that is friendship," he thought. "I wonder if I am a friend?" He turned his head to one side, thinking it over. "Perhaps Owyn thinks of me that way now." He decided to ask Owyn later.

Of course, Jetta was a friend; more really. He missed her terribly and wondered if she would approve of him now. She had worked so hard to prepare him for his part in this mission. He did not want to disappoint her. He did not understand the entire spectrum of people who would be influenced by his actions, but he wanted to succeed for Jetta.

Westin and Jep were talking with Soulo, and Luka finally stretched out on his sleeping mat, accepting the inevitable.

As they neared the sleeping area where Chambers and his men were camped,

Turi gave a low growl and trotted away to set up a protective watch near his sleeping master.

Blue did not like the smell of those creatures either, but knowing the injustice and cruelty heaped on them, he felt sorrow for them.

He was still confused as to what his part should be in the battle, but he supposed when the time came, he would be ready. Jetta explained once he "linked" with the Barrier, he would become aware. It felt strange to know secret information was locked away inside his orbs.

A night owl sat on a tree limb close by, and Blue watched, fascinated, as the bird twisted and turned his head every which way. It stared at Blue, blinking his bright eyes, then deciding he was no threat, began looking for his nightly prey.

"Blue, come and join us," shouted Owyn from the campfire.

Blue was happy to be included and hurried over. He had been in a deep sorrow since Jetta's death, but tonight, he wanted to be his happy self again and to be with his friends.

For hours, they sat and talked about their many adventures on this trip. He was glad he remembered them also and even had his own memories to include. They talked of Towak and the Rogel people, of the Tourashon, of their trip across the vast desert and crossing the frozen mountains. They recalled the wild animals, as well as the breathtaking scenery.

Blue wondered how much those orbs inside his head could hold. He had already lived more life than most humans ever would.

Chapter Twenty-Five

Calais watched in fascination as the sections of the tunnels were loaded onto the large wagons. The heavy-duty springs squeaked with objection as the sections were lowered down. Deep ruts bore into the ground from the weight of the gold.

They were heavy, there was no denying that. Each golden section was two feet thick and covered with a woven thick cloth to protect it from being scratched. To mar the symbols would compromise the integrity of the tunnel. That would be costly; very costly.

Balak stood nearby, watching closely. His face was twisted in a snarl as he watched the peasants positioning the sections in their braces on the wagons. Calais saw Balak was unnerved by Gwilim's attention to Bodecia. She seemed to have become the new favorite of the evil lord. Of course, she was the one to deliver him his precious golden opening that would bring his release from Exiled.

Balak found the fact very bitter indeed.

The first wagon began to pull away with its heavy load. The ten oxen strained and pulled to get the wagon moving, but once it began, the huge wheels made the burden a little easier. Four brakemen rode on the wagon to slow the cargo when they had to travel down slopes. Thankfully, the Southern Portal was only a short distance from here. He knew that is why his father had picked this place to be their meeting spot.

Andro stood on the other side of Gwilim. He was not allowed to leave Gwilim's sight. Calais wanted to be with his father but was afraid to anger Gwilim. Gwilim was unpredictable and violent, so he decided to just continue his assignments as if his father were still in command.

Bodecia watched the first section on its path that would take it to the portal. The heavy cloth covered most of the section, but from time to time, she could see the shiny gold sparkle through the wrapping. It made her feel good to know she was responsible for the gold needed to build the golden pathway to the Grand.

She felt Andro looking her way from time to time, but she never diverted her eyes to meet his. Gwilim was a jealous master and demanded her total attention, and she planned to make sure he got it.

Her skin crawled whenever his scaly hands touched her arm when they walked, and she prayed he could not feel her revulsion. Soon, she would not have to endure his attention. Soon, it would all be over.

Her greatest enjoyment was Balak's discomfort. For so long he had been the chosen of Gwilim. He brought the knowledge of the cannons with him, as well as the promise to penetrate the Barrier and allow Gwilim's army to enter the Grand. It had been his abilities, with the help of the cannons, which brought down the Veil.

But she had been the one to deliver Gwilim's ultimate dream of escape. It was always his utmost desire, and she knew she had finally beaten Balak at his own game. He promised to bring Westin back to complete the work on his golden tunnel, but in the end, had also failed in that promise. If not for her, Gwilim would be waiting at the Northern Portal, as Balak had planned, for Westin to be delivered to them to supply the precious inscriptions to make the tunnel safe for travel.

But she was far from through with that loathsome snake. He had defiled her, and he would pay. But for the death of her best friend, Gilee, he would die; horribly! She knew Gwilim would give her Balak's head if she asked, but this was one reward she wanted to take on her own.

Gwilim chatted constantly; almost giddy with the anticipation he would soon be free from Exiled. She knew she should be listening closely, so she trained her attention to him once again.

"So, of course, everything has been prepared. I have been prepared for weeks for this departure. Balak promised me it would be soon, but of course, now, you are the one to bring me my deliverance! You will have your pick of any kingdom. You will be worshipped as the Queen of the Land!"

She enjoyed the idea of being a queen. She had lived the life of a mine worker and the pampered life of a lady and much preferred the latter.

Ando's family had been grouped into an area near one of the sections. Helen, his wife, was holding her children close and weeping softly. Bodecia knew if Gwilim's plans were complete, these people would be dead before morning. All the people of the Exiled would be left to whatever would befall them. Gwilim cared little about what happened here and intended to use it as his own prison for those who opposed him in the Grand and Homeland. Once he had the power to control the portal, he would banish his enemy here; it would be a slow, deliberate death sentence.

Any luxuries he had been afforded here would not be offered to his enemy. And as for the people here, well, they were only fodder for Gwilim's whims. After all, he still needed to feed from time to time, as did his precious demok.

As Bodecia stared at the group surrounding Andro's wife, she spotted two young girls she thought she recognized. She looked hard, trying to place their faces.

The breath left her body as if she had been struck. Suddenly, she knew! They were her young maids she had given Balak in place of herself. Her eyes went wide when she saw their mangled arms and scarred faces. Most of the hair on their heads had been clawed away, the remainder turned completely white. Empty eyes stared out into the nothingness their minds revealed. They clung to one another like frightened little rabbits.

She felt suddenly sick, and her stomach lurched as she quickly turned away.

"My dear, the hot sun must be too much for you, go and sit in the shade and take a cool drink. This work will take several more hours," cooed Gwilim, stroking her face with a sharp talon.

She was glad to take her leave of him and quickly made her way to a nearby cooling tent.

Wet pieces of cloth hang throughout the large tent, and young children turned long cranks, which moved a huge paddle fan above, cooling the air. She idly wondered how many of these children must be the family of Ando. He had an unusually large number of relatives.

A cool cloth was brought to her, along with a cool drink. She sat heavily in a chair, wishing today was done. Every minute seemed like an eternity, and she had never been a patient woman.

She watched Calais giving orders for the second section to be lowered into the brace inside the wagon. Again, the groan from the springs squealed as the full weight of the section hit the wagon. After it was strapped down, it was on its way.

It was amazing how large each section was! She marveled at the engineering to put such a project together. True, she had helped mine the gold, but this was a feat of brilliance.

Andro and Calais had been only two of the people involved in the tunnel, but still, she knew it was Andro and Westin's design. Westin had been a clever sort to leave the inscriptions with Andro. He looked so unassuming, but he had the mind of a genius.

Balak, even with his magic, could never match Westin's skill. She supposed Balak knew that by now. He still had an important part to play in Gwilim's escape, but she wondered if Balak realized he might be expendable after that time. She hoped he was terrified.

She fanned herself and looked again at the two girls who had once been her maids. By their actions, she could see at least one of them seemed to have lost her mind completely and was being helped by the others.

She had done this! She had delivered them to Balak in her place. She had never even thought to ask what had become of them. They had been so young and innocent. She had become the same monster as Gwilim!

The second wagon moved on its way, and the third was now being loaded. The men looked weary from handling the heavy sections, but of course, Gwilim was not concerned. Time was precious; the portal was to open in two days, and the tunnel must be in place at that time. These men could drop dead in their tracks for all he cared. He could almost taste his freedom.

CHAPTER TWENTY-SIX

When morning dawned, it brought two surprises. The first was the weather, dark and threatening.

The second surprise was that Luka had left during the night.

Jack was stunned by his departure. He knew Luka felt their plan was not a secure one, but he never would have guessed he would have just abandoned them.

The others were equally surprised as they recalled his reservations from the night before. It seemed so out of character for him, but Jack understood Luka's fear of facing the Lord of Exiled again. Once was enough, he supposed; but to run away and leave them to fight alone? It did not sound like Luka.

Zi was enraged that Luka should leave them. "A man's true colors show in times of trial!" he growled, kicking the dirt stirring up clouds of dust around the camp.

They rode the remainder of the way with dark skies closing in around them. It felt as if the land knew of the evil which threatened to enter and was trying to hide from it.

After riding late into the night, Jep grunted as he slid from his saddle, his feet slipping on the wet grass. As usual, the chilly rain pelted them, causing the ache in his old joints to scream with pain. "This cursed weather seems to be following us!" he groaned.

"I do not see Stevien's men anywhere. Soulo, have any of our scouts reported in?" Jack called.

"Not yet, but this weather cannot be a help to us. When is the portal to be opened, Jep?" he called back.

"We should have a full day and night, I would say. It only opens once in a year's time to accept new prisoners, usually at first light, so it gives us a little time," Jep stretched his old back and rubbed his backside, trying to get circulation going again. He wished for his old colorful coat that always kept him warm.

Rising before them like an ominous gray rock wall, they had their first glimpse of the Barrier. It moved slowly, in a hypnotic rolling motion. Sparks of lightning snapped and sparked, warning death to any who ventured too close. The surface of the great wall seemed to move in and out as if it were breathing. It was impossible to see how thick the wall was, but it ran in either direction as far as the eye could see. Jep said it ran from one sea, across the snowy mountains, to the other sea without a single break, except for the two portals.

At the far end of the valley, near to the Barrier, a high stone platform stood. Tall poles laden with heavy shackles hung at the center. Here, the condemned were left to be swallowed up by the Barrier as it blossomed to encase the portal. Only then were the guards of Exiled able to access its new citizens.

Jack shuddered to think of the people left on that stone platform waiting their doom. Knowing the wall would swallow them into a world of nightmares.

He strained his neck to see how high up the Barrier went, but it was lost in the low clouds.

He looked over at Owyn, who was also straining to see the top. His hands were placed on his hips as he stared into the gray drizzle. "It is a long way up. That's all I can tell you." He offered.

Jack remembered Luka's story of flying over the great wall with his dragon friends. Once again, he was disheartened by the rough mountain man's sudden departure.

Zi let out a soft whistle, "Whew, and we thought the Veil was an eyeful. Now, that is what I call a wall!"

Owyn glanced over to Zi, "I wouldn't try touching this one!"

Zi sheepishly returned Owyn's look, recalling touching the Veil and its shocking effect on him.

Jep, Westin, and Blue spent the rest of the day with Soulo and Chambers. They worked on the positions of the troops, to maximize their efficiency of attack when Gwilim's army broke through. They were pitifully few; no more than two hundred men in all.

Jack, Zi, Owyn and the troopers spent their day shaping long spears from tree limbs from the trees which surrounded the area, supplying them with extra weapons.

Demok were set busy digging a wide trench in hopes of slowing the progress of the horde passing through the portal. Their muscular arms rippled as they pulled mounds of dirt from the earth, digging the great trench in half the time the soldiers could have. They never seemed to tire and only occasionally stopped for water.

By the end of the day, everyone was physically and emotionally exhausted. The rain dwindled to a slow drizzle, then, thankfully, stopped completely. When a welcomed fire could be lit a quick meal was quickly eaten, then everyone curled up to get as much rest as possible. Tomorrow, the battle!

As the others slept, Jack sat on the hilltop looking down on the Barrier. Even in the dark, he could still see the gray, misty wall slowly rolling and moving into itself, crackling with tiny veins of lightning.

He felt completely helpless when he thought about what lay ahead for him and his men. The burden seemed so monumental he felt as if he were suffocating. He felt his heart hammering in his chest, and fear began to sweep over him. "Too much at stake. What if we fail?" his thoughts whispered to him.

He heard a shuffle of feet behind him, and Owyn sat down next to him.

"Man, that thing looks pretty scary," he observed, kicking a rock down the side of the hill.

Jack nodded, never taking his eyes off the wall.

"Seems like we are forever finding ourselves in a scary spot," Owyn chuckled. "Remember the time we had to cross that big, raging river near the Chipokole village. Phew, now that was scary! We were chasing bandits who raided a farm and killed that family. Remember?"

Jack just sat, staring numbly out over the Barrier.

"The river was high and rolling, impossible to cross. We found a little raft and decided to try for the other side. Halfway across, we flipped over. Man, I was so terrified. Those waves were rushing over me, pushing me under, and holding me down so I could not get a good breath of air. I thought I was done for when I heard your voice yelling to me. I could not tell which way was up or down. You just kept yelling, "Owyn, stop fighting and let yourself float away from the rapids. Slow down and think. You can do this!'"

Owyn stopped and looked over to Jack. "Jack, you can do this. You just need to take it one step at a time. If you try to take it all on yourself, you are going to take in too much and drown."

A slow smile moved across Jack's lips as he listened to Owyn. "Thanks, Owyn. I guess I am feeling a little overwhelmed. It has been a long trip, and a lot has happened. And now, well, this is what we were sent to do, and I just want to make sure we get it done."

"You have a lot of people here to help you, do not forget that. We are in this fight together. No one has all the answers, friend, except, hopefully, Blue."

Owyn gave Jack a crooked smile and wink, then stood again, looking down at the boiling gray wall. "It doesn't look as bad as that river!"

Owyn left Jack sitting on the hill and walked back to his bedroll. He snuggled in for the night and took a deep breath, waiting for sleep to fall on him.

"How is he doing?" asked Zi in a deep, sleepy voice.

"He's fine, Jack will be just fine," answered Owyn as he began to fade into sleep.

Chapter Twenty-Seven

The golden tunnel gleamed dully in the gray morning light. It stretched out like a huge yellow worm toward the place in the Barrier that would soon become the Southern Portal.

Gwilim was giddy with excitement, saliva drooling from the sides of his mouth. It was nearing time for him to feed again, shown by the gray pallor which had returned to his face. His eyes were the eyes of a man long dead, sunken and dark but burning in anticipation. The evil he possessed still reeked from him.

His usual black robes had been exchanged for the robes of a king. His tailors worked for weeks preparing robes which would declare him royalty; with threads of gold flowing through the purple and red silk. He would not enter his new kingdom looking like a peasant. He would look like a king!

When he reached the other side, he would feast on the mighty powers of the Barrier and be whole again. His youth and vigor would be returned to him, and no one would ever look at him with loathing. Not that anyone ever let him see that reaction on their faces. If they had, they never lived long enough to regret it.

Bodecia stood in shocked awe, looking at the tunnel. So, it had finally happened! The golden tunnel was complete! She could hardly believe her eyes. She had tried many times to imagine this day, but never had she pictured it so.

She glanced over at Andro. He had joined Calais, and they were examining the symbols which covered every inch of the tunnel. She knew it was an important detail, and Balak stood nearby, looking over their shoulders. This was the vital part Westin had not shared with Balak, and the anger over the loss of that information radiated from him like heat rising.

Calais finally straightened and took his father's arm. "It is complete," he confirmed. They stood looking into each other's eyes for a moment, then turned to face Gwilim.

"Well, let's hope so," snarled Gwilim, since your family will be the first through. He motioned for the guards to bring Andro's family to the opening of the tunnel. "A test of its continuity is always a good idea. I would imagine you would not be inclined to harm your family."

Andro and his wife looked at one another. Their children stood by, clutching or holding each other. He gave her a reassuring, sad smile.

Balak kept himself busy barking orders to the army. The smell of the demok was overwhelming as the excitement of the day overtook them. Their mood seemed to reflect that of their master. Their trainers were forced to take them to their knees several times to control them.

Balak stood at the head of the army. He and his men would follow Andro's family after they made it safely through. Gwilim and his followers would be last. Balak fully expected a battle on the other side, and his army was primed and ready. He had over ten thousand men and demok ready for battle.

Bodecia closed her eyes to keep from taking it all in. "Only a short run to freedom!" she whispered in her mind.

Just beyond the far end of the tunnel, a section of the Barrier began to shimmer brightly and move outward.

"PUSH!!!!" yelled Balak, "Push, or your lives will end this day!" The logs under the tunnel rumbled and groaned as the men and women pushed the tunnel down the slope. Soon, the long, heavy tunnel was moving slowly toward the Great Wall.

Chapter Twenty-Eight

Jep stood before the Barrier and lifted his arms to touch it. Threads of lightning quickly crept over his body, covering him like a spider's web.

The old wizard grimaced in pain as the web covered him. He warned them to keep far away until the wall began to glow. "It will first begin to glow, then the Portal will expand to fill the valley and cover the stone platform. Do not touch the Portal, or you will most certainly die."

Jack and his men were stationed as close as possible. From where he stood, he could see Jep wincing in terrible pain and wondered again at the power it had taken to erect such a wall.

The old wizard's body shook with tremors as the magic surged through his body. He cried out several times as the pain overtook him. His knees threatened to buckle under him, but still, he worked to control the magic.

Blue sat on the stone platform. It was necessary to have a victim to invoke the Portal. He sat staring straight ahead, unafraid.

He had not hesitated when Dr. Westin asked him to take the place of the Portal sentinel. "This is the part I am to play," he declared, resigned at the prospect of completing their mission.

They watched closely as the glowing section of the wall grew in height and width. Soon, it began to 'bow' and moved slowly into the valley, toward the stone platform and Blue.

As the Portal began to expand, Jep removed his hands and hurriedly joined Jack and the others a safe distance away from the rapidly moving wall.

Jack motioned for Soulo to be prepared and received confirmation that all was ready. Chambers and his men and demok stood close by also, readying themselves for the first of the Exiled invaders.

The Portal moved along the valley floor like a mammoth gray curtain, lightening flickering furiously over its skin. It rolled steadily forward until it reached the stone platform, then came to a stop. The Portal turned from gray to a shimmering web of light to consume the platform and its doomed captives.

Suddenly, the Portal convulsed as something inside began to move. The thin web of light covering the end exploded into a mass of sparks as the end of a golden tube pierced through the wall.

Blue stood on the platform, a look of confusion on his face, just feet from the tunnel. He looked back at the men and quickly yelled, "Do not shoot, it is women and children!"

Blue jumped from the platform and ran into the tunnel. Jack and the other stood numbly, looking at one another. Could it be true? Had Andro succeeded in his plan, and Balak and Gwilim had been defeated?

Blue came rushing from the tunnel with a child under each arm. Close behind him, other children followed, along with several women.

Owyn and Zi, along with Dr. Westin, ran to help the new refugees to safety.

An older woman yelled out as soon as they cleared the opening, "They are right behind us! The army and Gwilim are right behind us!"

Their group was herded into the trees as they waited for the enemy to appear.

They poured through the opening like a black swarm of bees. The demok were the first, howling and screaming in their hideous voices. The sound was deafening. Jack was astounded by the sheer number of them. How was it possible there were so many?

Chambers and his men waited on the other side of a covered trench. The sight of other demok confused the wild beasts entering the Grand. They stood in confusion, looking at the other demok. But, when Chambers' men began to rain a hail of arrows at them, they regained their senses and attacked with all their fury.

In their rage, the hapless creatures stumbled into the covered trench, where sharp spikes Jack and his men had placed awaited. Their bodies hit like rocks, thudding against the spears and impaling the beasts. Howls of pain cried out from the death pit as the animals kept coming, falling in on one another. Soon, the trench was filled with the bodies of their fallen comrades, and yet they came.

The raiders then began to pour through. Men marked with the red fists of Gwilim's army. Their faces were painted with ferocious markings, much like the faces of the demok, intending to further frighten their enemy.

Soulo and his men descended on them. Arrows whistled through the air and found their marks in the soft flesh of a human body. Men stumbled and fell, causing the men charging closely behind to trip and fall in the tunnels exit.

Gwilim's men never wavered. They raised their swords and trampled their comrades under their feet. Some even slashed away the arms and legs of their own men to make room for their attack.

On the right, the demok began to cross over the trench, now full of dead or dying. Chambers and his group charged them as they made the crossing, cutting down even more. Demok fighting demok was a fearful thing to see.

A loud horn sounded, signaling Balak and his guards were making their way through the Portal opening.

At once, Westin and Balak locked eyes.

A look of sheer hate and rage covered Balak's scarred face. His lip curled in disgust. From his fingertips, balls of white fire flew toward the old doctor.

Jep, seeing the white-hot flow, leaped before the old doctor and sent a shimmer of blue air between them, scattering the fire to either side enveloping many of Gwilim's men.

Balak screamed in frustration and again sent flames of fire toward the group.

Jep continued to throw up a protective wall while sending rippling blue flames back toward Balak.

Balak easily tossed the fire to the side, never a sign of remorse for the men he was killing. The anger inside him was driving him to a fury. But quickly the impact of his power was taking its toll on Jep.

The old wizard used his waning magic to block Balak's attacks, giving Westin the opportunity to find a place of better protection.

Jack slashed and fought with all his might. His old trusty sword had saved him from many a battle, and he prayed it would again. He hoped his friends Owyn and Zi were having good luck in their fight but knew if he concentrated on anything more than killing the man standing in front of him, he would be dead.

The only thing in their favor was the opening itself. It only let a few of the enemy through at one time, so they were not completely overwhelmed. Inside the tunnel, they heard the voices of the Gwilim's army, in a fever pitch to get out of the tunnel and into the battle.

He was not sure how long the battle lasted before the rain began again, pelting them with fat raindrops, blurring their vision. The heat of battle began to create a fog which soon filled the little valley, and the stench of blood choked the breath in them.

Jack could no longer see his feet as they moved among the dead. He was in a mindless dance of death now. He cut, clashed, and stabbed, not looking at the faces of the men he was killing. They would all be ghosts to him.

Balak's barrage of fire had ended when the rain began, and Jack saw him hovering near the opening of the tunnel, calling out orders to the men around him.

Jack tried to force his way to him, but at every turn, another of Gwilim's army was there, waiting to die.

It was impossible to tell how many of his men had been killed or injured. The bodies were mingled together like a lover's embrace, but he knew everyone was a precious sacrifice. Every man was needed to stop this madness from reaching their land.

Jack stumbled and fell to his knees just as he heard the loud horn blow again.

The enemy began to retreat back into the tunnel. The demok, in a blood thirst, were twisted in agony as their trainers forced them back into the tunnel.

Jack kneeled on the ground, watching the army retreat into the tunnel. He wiped his hair from his face and discovered his hand was covered with blood. He assumed it was his.

He stood shakily and looked around him. In the distance, he saw Soulo gathering his men and Jep with Dr. Westin. His eyes swept the area until, at last, he spotted a ragged Owyn and Zi stumbling toward him. He closed his eyes in relief, even if it was short-lived.

Blue stayed with the families, fighting to protect them. He had a fondness for children, and Jack saw him fighting with the fervor of a mother lion.

They gathered their forces together to count their losses.

Chambers and Jonas ran to the little family group and wept as they grabbed for them and held them close.

When Chambers finally returned to the others, they began to evaluate the forces they still had available to them. No one knew how much time they had to prepare for the next attack, so quickly they set about their next strategy plan. Their plight was not good, and Gwilim's army seemed endless.

"Ho....Jepthya!" a voice shouted from beyond the ridge.

Jep turned and shielded his eyes from the rain to get a better look.

"Dear Creator!" he whispered. "Brennak! My friend! Are we ever glad to see you!" he called out.

Wizard Brennak waved to the men below and descended the hill, followed by a large group of men.

The troopers cheered and whooped at the sight of reinforcements. Many ran up the hill to meet up with the men, clapping them on the back.

Jep and Brennak warmly embraced, and Jep wiped away a bit of moisture from his eyes.

"Now," urged Brennak, "how about getting us up to speed on what is going on. We heard quite a ruckus a bit ago."

Jep quickly explained to Brennak and his men the situation of the people behind the Barrier, and of Gwilim's plans once he entered the Grand.

Although some of the new recruits were frightened by the sight of demok, their fears soon turned to sympathy when Jack explained their plight.

"How did you know where to find us?" asked Jack, still in shock at the fortunate timing of the men.

"It was that wild man, Luka. He flew into the village yesterday morning and told us what was happening. I gathered together as many men and women as possible to join the fight. This is our land. We cannot allow you to sacrifice your lives for us. It is our fight, too."

"Luka!" whispered Zi in disbelief, "That explains his sudden disappearance." He slapped his legs and gave a loud laugh. "That old dog!"

Brennak smiled, "He also said Stevien's troop should be right behind us. That should make a better fight!"

Soulo completely lost his military composure and began dancing a jig, laughing and shaking his fist the Portal opening. "We will have something for you to think about now, you demons!"

His men, accustomed to his solemn demeanor, stared, then began to laugh and clap each other on the back.

This was the encouragement they needed. Now, they could almost taste the victory.

While the wizards were caring for the injured, Stevien's men arrived. They were also happily greeted, but Jack was anxious how few had been sent.

Upon talking with the young lieutenant Davo, he began to understand just how badly Homeland had suffered. Stevien still had his hands full, pulling injured and dead from the rubble across the land. These men were the better part of the army left to him. Jack felt a new grief for his homeland.

Soulo and his officers took a head count and began to position the new men in areas of strategic defense. After he finished, he motioned for Jack and his men to join him.

"It is better," he advised. "We have been joined by almost seven hundred more men. Thank the Creator, Brennak also brought women who could care for the injured and help keep our men properly armed. He also assures me they can fight as hard as the men."

"But Jack," he paused, "we lost over seventy-five of our own and ten demok. We are still badly outnumbered. If the next battle goes as the first, all they will have to do is simply attack and wait. Their sheer numbers will outlast us. If only we had one of those light cannons!"

Jack knew he was right. Gwilim had tens of thousands of troops, according to Chambers, ready to come through the Portal, and there were still troops stationed in the Grand who could come to his aid and ambush them where they fought.

Their true advantage was the location of the portal. The little valley was carved into the hillside, and the entrance to it was small. Much like the Portal itself, it would only allow a few hundred through at a time.

And, with Voxx and his army mistakenly waiting at the Northern Portal, their odds were improving.

Jack and Soulo watched the men cleaning and sharpening their weapons. Their spirits had been greatly raised by the addition of the new men, and of course, it was always a help with moral.

But, while their numbers had increased, the probability of success had not.

A shout from the lookouts posted at the portal opening announced the next wave of attack by Gwilim's army. Again, they came pouring out like oil from a pitcher, almost immediately falling from the hail of arrows by the Homeland force.

Yet still they came.

Chapter Twenty-Nine

Andro and his son, Calais, clutched one another as the army again poured into the portal opening. Waiting around the opening, men, and demok stood shouting, working themselves into a heated frenzy, waiting their turn to join the fight.

"There are so many, father," whispered Calais. "How can we possible be victorious over so many?"

Andro whispered, "Freedom can be a great motivator, my son. Love of family and freedom."

"What is Gwilim doing now?" asked Calais, watching the fearsome emperor with anticipation.

Andro looked at a small group of men surrounding Gwilim and Balak. Bodecia, standing near, glanced over to Andro and Calais in alarm as she listened.

The men, twenty in all, wore robes of white, tied at the waist with golden rope. Andro recalled a group of people in the Homeland who wore those strange robes but could not remember exactly who they were.

The twenty-robed men knelt before Gwilim, waiting. Andro and Calais watched curiously as Balak and Gwilim walked before each man.

Gwilim, at last, raised his hands, and the air around the men rippled and shimmered with a bright green glow.

"What is he doing?" wondered Andro aloud.

"The men fell limply forward, their arms holding them from falling to the ground, and shivered violently as the green glow entered their bodies through their noses and mouths. Their heads snapped back in silent screams as Gwilim looked on with satisfaction.

After several minutes, the glow disappeared, and the men pulled themselves from the ground and stood erect and focused on Gwilim. Some of the men were crying.

Gwilim turned to Andro and smiled a sharp, ugly grin. "I think it is time to add a little spice to the cooking pot."

"Who are those men?" asked Andro, already fearing the answer.

"My wizards," bragged Gwilim in a sweeping bow. "They have wizards, so shall they meet mine."

Andro's stomach clenched at the thought of those twenty entering the Grand. They alone could slaughter the men on the other side.

"Calais," he whispered, "give the word; we dare not wait any longer!"

Calais turned and looked over his shoulder at the people huddled on the hillside, watching the army enter the portal.

He spied his brother, Neno, standing at the foot of the rocky hillside. Calais waited until Neno was focused on him and then nodded.

Neno lifted his hand in recognition, gave his brother a loving smile, then turned and ran into the rocks.

"It is done, Father," Calais whispered.

Andro nodded and again closed his eyes in a silent prayer for his people.

The attack took them completely by surprise. The first barrage of arrows took out the guard holding Andro and Calais, allowing them to scramble for safety in a nearby stable.

The sky had been darkening throughout the day with hard rain from time to time, but it suddenly turned black with the number of arrows descending on Gwilim's army waiting around the portal.

Men and demok fell in vast numbers, still confused as to what was happening. Gwilim roared with such rage it made the very ground beneath them shake.

Before the army could turn their attention to the new attackers, at least four of the new wizards lay dead. It seemed arrows could pierce the heart of even the fiercest wizard.

Balak was barking orders for the men to pull the mighty wagons used to haul the golden tunnel in a barricade to protect them from the onslaught.

Andro and Calais took advantage of the confusion to make their way further away from the portal and closer to their men.

Streaks of lightning raced across the dark sky and slammed into the rocks, protecting the new attackers. Rock exploded and flew into the air, falling on the men and women fighting nearby.

But this was their land, and they knew every cave, hill, and crevice that could afford them advantage. Soon, the arrows, tipped in oils and set ablaze, raced to the wooden wagons protecting Gwilim's men and ignited them into flaming infernos.

Gwilim was frantic with anger. He could scarcely believe these meek, worthless people would dare put up a fight against him. They knew his wrath was fearsome, now, he fully intended to destroy this land and everyone in it.

Bodecia crouched behind a wheelbarrow to avoid the arrows. Several bounced against her, but none found their mark. She strained to look over the top to see if she could see the people firing at them, but the rocky landscape had become a strong fortress for them.

Balak continued to send troops through the portal while barking orders for those still waiting to return fire at the new attackers. His scarred face was twisted in hate, and Bodecia was pleased to see a look she had never seen on his face, fear.

She noticed Gwilim and his personal demok guards made their way to a small stone structure to take cover there. This was her chance!

Bodecia crawled on her stomach to the next safe spot, always keeping Balak in her sight. The mud from the rain covered her, even getting into her eyes, but still, she kept her eyes on Balak. She ripped at the beautiful gown Gwilim had provided her, tearing away the cumbersome cloth.

A vicious jolt of hot, searing pain suddenly caused her to cry out. She reached down and felt an arrow protruding from her upper thigh. She felt the tip of the arrow scraping the bone as she grasp it's shaft. She gritted her teeth and gave it a quick yank, pulling the arrow free. Blood began to flow heavily, and she pressed against the wound as hard as possible. The pain was unbearable. If only she had some of her healing powers! But Gwilim had made sure he was the only one to hold magic in Exiled and had taken hers many years ago.

She tore a long piece from her gown and wrapped it around her leg, twisting until the blood flow began to slow down. She grabbed huge chunks of mud and forced it into the open wound, continuing to slow blood flow.

She glanced over her shoulder to where Balak had been standing and saw he was gone. "NOOO!" she wailed. "You are mine!"

Lightning continued to race across the sky, delivering blows to the people hiding behind the boulders. Andro and Calais at last reached their group and joined the fight. All around them, men and women lay wounded or dying, dying for their freedom.

Andro hoped the battle on the other side was delivering a heavier blow. They had so little to work with and most certainly had never planned to battle powerful wizards.

Balak returned to the portal and shouted for the wizards to join the fight on the other side. Half of them quickly ran into the golden protective tunnel, making their way to the other side.

"That should help us," said Calais hopefully.

"When you're talking about wizards, one is too many!" replied Neno.

Chapter Thirty

Jep and Brennak gasped as the eight men poured from the portal opening. "Wizards!" Brennak shouted.

Soldiers nearby stopped and looked back curiously at the opening. Their hesitation proved to be a fatal mistake, as a massive ball of fire rolled over them, leaving nothing more than a pile of ash.

Jep and Brennak returned fire, but the eight were able to thwart their attacks by throwing a protective shield in front of them, disarming their magic.

"They will take us out in no time at this rate," yelled Jack to Soulo.

Dr. Westin, holding Blue back with both hands, yelled, "Jep, can you do anything?"

Jep looked back at the doctor and yelled, "We are trying, doctor, one wizard would be plenty to worry about, but eight is going to be a challenge."

Dr. Westin looked at the men standing around the opening firing huge balls of fire, allowing more of Gwilim's men to enter.

Blue tugged and pulled, itching to help his friends. "No, Blue!" Westin hissed. "We cannot afford to lose you now. Your time will come to help. But right now, you must be kept safe."

Blue huffed and moaned as he watched his friends Owyn and Zi battling just a few yards away.

Both men had wounds and needed medical help, but both seemed lost in a trance. They moved like dancers, even assisting one another from time to time. Blue was amazed at how fluidly they moved. Especially Zi, who was a hulk of a man, and proven clumsy on more than one occasion. But not today. His feet moved with the grace of a dancer; a skill that comes from much practice and training.

Owyn had always been light of foot, but today, his feet barely touched the ground. It was as if he floated from one stance to another, confusing the men he was fighting.

He looked for Jack, who was, of course, in the center of the fight. Jack's strong arms wield his swords to either side, slashing men down before they even had time to reach him. Bodies were mounded around him, and he stepped over them to reach other enemy attackers. His face was set in grim determination. Beads of rainwater streamed down his face.

Blue marveled at the three. What kind of men were these? Where did they find the passion; the soldiers from the Homeland, fighting an evil they had never heard of before a few months ago, these villagers who lead a quiet, peaceful life, and these old wizards, stripped of most of their magic, where did they find the spirit to fight so hard?

Jep and Brennak continued their attack against the wizards with no luck. Each time they sent a barrage of fire, a quick barrier was set up for protection.

Owyn, in a brief lull, took notice of the battle between the wizards. Jep and Brennak were tiring, and each new attack weakened them more. Soon, their strength would be gone, and the wizards would destroy them.

As Owyn watched the eight at the Portal, he observed their use of the protective shield. He smiled and notched an arrow.

As Brennak threw another barrage at one of the men, Owyn waited. When the man thrust his hands to return fire, Owyn freed his arrow. It found its mark easily, passing through the man's upper torso. The wizard looked down, confused, and then fell in a lump to the ground.

Those around him looked at his body in alarm and then at one another.

Without warning, a pair of giant talons reached out of the gray, rainy sky, grabbing another of the men. His screams were cut short as his body was ripped into pieces.

Another of the wizards, moving back toward the portal opening, was attacked by three large wolves who made little work of ending his life.

Jack looked up to see another great dragon grasp one of the wizards and toss him into the jagged rocky hillside.

Luka waved down to Jack, "Couldn't let you have all the fun, boy!" he shouted as Scala banked her leathery wings and headed back into the battle zone. Her wings swept men and demok to the side like fallen leaves.

Luka's wolves filled the battle area, ripping and tearing at the demok until the creatures howled in pain and, in a panic, began to turn against their own men.

Blue jumped up and down like a child, clapping his hands and laughing. When he looked beside him, he noticed the old doctor doing the same.

Soulo's deep, rumbling voice was howling in laughter as the wolves and dragons made attack after attack until the enemy retreated into the opening once again.

"Should we follow them, Jack?" shouted Zi. "We've got them on the run!"

Jack shook his head. "We do not want to make the same mistakes they have. We'll collect ourselves and wait."

Luka landed his dragons nearby and whistled for his dogs. He gave each one a loving pat and hug and praised them. The big wolves jumped and clamored in celebration.

"I should have known!" said Jack, shaking his hand. "You're a crafty one, Luka."

"I knew you were going to need more help. I've met this enemy, you know. Chambers had already prepared some of the villagers for what was to come, so I just needed to get word to them. It is their land, Jack, and they are willing to fight for it."

Jack put his hand on Luka's shoulder and smiled, "Did anyone ever tell you that you are a beautiful man?"

Luka threw back his head and bellowed a hearty laugh. "Not since me mum."

Zi made his way over to the two, "Jack, you had better come! It is Chambers. He is badly hurt."

Luka and Jack ran to find Jep and Brennak, trying to heal the young man. Three arrows protruded from his chest. His eyes blinked away tears streaming down his face. His men crowded around him, and his demok brother sat near, rocking back and forth.

Jep looked up and shook his head, then moved aside so Jack could talk with the man.

"Jack," he whispered hoarsely, "do not think Gwilim is finished. He is very clever. He would want you to think you are winning to throw you off guard. You have not seen the half of his army yet."

His family rushed from the safety of the trees to be at his side. The women cried and touched his face lovingly.

Owyn was standing silently behind the group when Chambers locked eyes with him, "Owyn, I hope you will someday find it in your heart to forgive me."

Owyn gave the man a slow nod, "You did what you had to do to free you family. I understand now. There are no hard feelings between us."

Chambers smiled and took his last breath, finally tasting freedom for himself.

Jack and the others left the family to mourn Chambers.

"He said we have not seen half of their army!" moaned Soulo. "Jack, we have no other choice but to seal that opening. We cannot fight them forever! They will win by sheer numbers alone."

Westin and Blue stood near the opening, listening. "He is right, Jack," agreed Westin. "You cannot fight forever. It is time to end this war."

Jack stared at the old man, not understanding what he meant.

"The wall must come down, we have all agreed on that, but the evil must not be allowed to escape," said Westin.

"And how can we accomplish that without defeating Gwilim's army first?" asked Jack.

"Andro and his people have built the weapon that will work that miracle," said Westin, waving his hand toward the golden tunnel.

"I don't understand," said Jack. "Why destroy the tunnel and bring down the Barrier? Gwilim will have the freedom to walk out of Exiled then."

Westin smiled, "I trust my friend Andro has worked his magic, and we have brought ours with us." He took a step and placed his hand on Blue's shoulder.

"So, Blue has something to do with this?" he asked.

"Blue has everything to do with this. He will be the one who will destroy Gwilim and bring down the Barrier."

Blue stood motionless as if trying to take it all in. Everyone was staring at Blue, waiting for some sort of confirmation that he knew what had to be done.

Westin continued. "The gold on that tunnel has been inscribed with a series of symbols, deferring the magic of the wall. As I explained before, the Barrier magic consists of the mingled magic of many wizards and is impossible to untangle. That pure gold tunnel has interrupted the webbing of the magic, allowing the army to cross through the portal. That is about to end."

"Blue has the knowledge to reconnect the magic and cause it to crash into itself. It will destroy the Barrier wall by using its own magic."

"You know how to do this?" asked Owyn in disbelief.

Blue was silently glancing about as if reading some written text inscribed in the air around them.

Soulo added, "Then, if the Barrier is to fall, we must be ready to fight all of the army at one time. How is that possible?"

Andro's wife, standing to the side of the group, spoke. "It is possible because my people, on the other side, are also in battle as we speak. Gwilim's army is under attack on two fronts."

"But what about all along the Barrier? What about the army further north?" questioned Soulo.

"Gwilim's army is concentrated here, at this entrance. Andro took great pains to make sure this was the portal chosen by Gwilim for his escape. Since he means to overthrow the leaders of the Grand and the Homeland, he will need his entire army with him. He could not risk sealing them behind the Barrier again."

Zi looked back and forth between Jack and Soulo, "Even so, there still remains a vast number of raiders and demok. Can we fight so many?"

"I do not believe many will carry on the fight without their leader," said Westin. "Gwilim must die."

"And just how does one kill the Lord of Evil?" asked Owyn.

CHAPTER THIRTY-ONE

The blood finally slowed its heavy flow, and Bodecia pulled and tugged on a nearby watering trough until she was able to stand. She noticed a pitchfork leaning against the stable wall and tucked it under her arm to use as a crutch.

Gwilim and his protectors looked out from the little stone shed but quickly moved behind the closed door for safety. It seemed even Gwilim was not willing to risk injury or death at this point of the battle. He exhausted a great deal of his magic on the wizards he sent through the portal and had not yet regained his strength. His magic would not be much help in this battle until he fed again.

While peering out at the battle, he saw Bodecia limping along the far side of the portal. "Come, girl," he called out for her to join him.

She waved back and called out, "Stay safe, I will find shelter here. I will come for your when it is safe."

She wanted to be near the portal opening. Balak would surely return soon. He was by no means a hero and would not put himself in any more jeopardy than necessary. She leaned heavily against the side of a building and checked her leg again. With all the movement, it had begun to bleed again. If she crossed the yard, Gwilim would be able to heal her, but she did not want to lose her chance at Balak. She would have to endure the pain.

The rain slowed to a fine drizzle, and she wiped the mud from her face. She knew she must look a fright, her face covered in muck and her hair dripping certainly not like a lady from the house of the emperor.

Her head was swimming with the loss of blood, and she feared she might faint at any moment. She knelt again and picked up another handful of mud, pressing it against her wound to slow the bleeding one more time.

When she stood again, she saw him standing in front of the portal like a prince at his throne. The barrage from the attackers had ended for the time, and Balak was barking new orders to his officers.

Once left alone, he began stripping his wet battle uniform. She choked as she looked upon his hideous body, shivering at the memory of him ever touching her.

She had taken several steps before she realized she was moving toward him. His back was turned from her as he donned a dry tunic. He heard her approach and turned to face her. When he saw her, he sneered and laughed.

"Well, the pig will always find its' pen! Go and find a place to hide. You make me sick to look at you."

When she was an arms length away, she snapped the pitchfork upright and thrust it into Balak's chest. A look of total surprise filled his face as he looked down at the sharp prongs pushing their way through his body.

Bodecia pushed with all her might until Balak lost his balance and fell against the golden tunnel. He slapped at his chest as if he could toss away the sharp prongs like an annoying fly.

He raised his eyes to meet hers in total disbelief.

"You have a lot to learn about how to treat a lady," she snarled and made a final push, sending the prongs through his body and making the tiniest scratch on the golden tunnel.

She was thrown back against the ground as the magic of the Barrier tore through his body. He twisted and turned in agony as a web of lightning covered him. Smoke poured from his mouth and nose, and his eyes exploded in a sickening pop. Tighter and tighter, the threads wove around him until the flesh began to melt away, then, finally, muscle and bone were crushed into a bloody goo. The powerful magic sizzled and burned until only a heap of ashes was left of the mighty Balak.

Bodecia stared at the last remains of the man she had hated for so long. Her vengeance was almost complete. Retribution time!

She looked quickly over to the stone house where Gwilim and his men were hiding and saw no clue they had witnessed her attack on Balak. Indeed, his men had all been sent off by his command to prepare for their next attack on the Grand.

An arm grabbed her by the waist and pulled her through the mud into a nearby stable. She tried to fight, but her loss of blood had made her weak.

"That was quite an execution!" a voice declared as the mud was wiped from her face.

Andro and Calais were holding her up on either side, Andro wiping away the filth.

"It was a long time coming for many," she sighed.

"You have done enough, Bodecia," said Andro, concern filling his eyes. "You are wounded. Let us take it from here. We cannot ask you to do more. You have done us all a great service."

She smiled at his pudgy face and remembered a time she thought he was disgusting. He seemed the dearest man she had ever known now.

"We have worked this plan so far with much success. We dare not stop. Gwilim trusts me now, so it must be me."

She reached up and snapped away the diamond and ruby necklace given to her as a gift of appreciation by Gwilim. Few people in Exiled owned or had even seen such a treasure.

"Please, for your nieces. See, they are well taken care of. It is my deepest shame that I caused their misfortune. Tell them I am so sorry."

Andro's eyes were filled with sorrow as he took the necklace. He shook his head sadly, "Our people will sing of your bravery forever."

Returning his smile, she answered, "No need for that. Besides, not much rhymes with Bodecia. Now help me up and both of you and be prepared. It is time for the final act to begin."

The men helped her to the door of the stable, careful to avoid being seen. Andro gave her hand one last squeeze, and she limped out of the barn. She clenched her teeth to ignore the pain shooting up her leg, threatening to take her to her knees.

She glanced at the place where Balak died and could still see the sparks of magic dancing from the tunnel wall. Perfect.

When she neared Gwilim's door, she called out to him, "Lord Gwilim, we must hurry! Before the attack on us begins again! The tunnel, we must make our way through the tunnel!"

Gwilim slammed the door open and looked toward the rocky hillside. Already, arrows were flying again.

"Let me heal you first, girl!" he commanded as he looked at her bloody leg.

"No! Sire, there is no time. We must go now while Balak is protecting the other side. Once there, your full power will be restored to you, and we will be safe. Then you can attend to my healing."

Gwilim took one last look and then rushed past her toward the tunnel. He grabbed her waist as they hurried. As they neared the opening to the tunnel, Gwilim looked at the mound of smoking ash lying against it.

His eyes narrowed as he saw the flash of the magic flickering.

"I don't know how much longer the tunnel will hold," said Bodecia, trying hard to convince him to move quickly.

"What is this?" he demanded.

"An arrow pierced one of the men and nicked the wall of the tunnel. It scratched the carved symbols which hold back the magic. Sire, we must hurry! The tunnel may be compromised!"

Gwilim took another look at the lump beside the tunnel, then at Bodecia. "After you, my dear," he said, his eyes narrowed in suspicion.

"As you wish," she answered, and she stepped into the sparkling tunnel she had worked so hard to make.

Chapter Thirty-Two

Blue stood facing the opening of the portal. He finally knew why he had been created, his true destination. He put his arms out as far as they could reach, measuring.

No rain was falling now, and the clouds were pulling their curtain back to reveal a soft blue sky. Blue smiled. It was going to be a wonderful day, after all.

Jack, Owyn, and Zi joined Blue at the opening.

"Blue, more troops could be coming out of there any time now. You can take measurements later," said Owyn, stuffing his hands in his pockets.

Blue looked at Owyn and smiled.

Zi, concerned over Blue's attention to the portal, added, "Come now, Blue, the good doctor will need your help. You must not keep him waiting. Let us move away from this thing."

"The doctor is aware I am doing what I must, Zi." Blue looked at the burly man, smiling at him.

Jack, also curious asked, "Blue, what exactly are you doing? Are you sure you know?"

"Yes, Jack, it is clear to me. There is much to comprehend, and I must learn the pattern of these etchings on the tunnel before it is too late."

Jep looked at his friends, "Boys, let us leave Blue to his work. Come now."

Blue sat on the stone platform, looking down at Jack.

Jack read something in Blue's soft brown eyes. "You <u>are</u> coming back to the Homeland with us, aren't you Blue?"

Blue hesitated a moment, smiled sadly at Jack, then answered, "I finally found the reason I was created. This is my purpose."

Jack's heart caught in his chest as he understood. He stared at Blue, then at the sparkling golden tunnel. "There must be another way, Blue! You cannot give up like this!"

"It is not giving up when you help save your friends. You and the others fought today, ready to die for people you never met, in this land and in Exiled. Chambers gave his life to make sure his family would be free. And Jetta," Blue stopped as he thought of his creator and teacher, "and Jetta left her life of comfort and safety in the Palace to make sure the people of all lands could remain free. Even old Luka could have left and spared himself this battle, but he came back and stood with us. If you can fight for this cause, how can I not do the same? This is my purpose; the reason I was given life. I gladly give my life for you."

Jack realized tears were streaming down his face. This sweet Blue: this innocent child, born a man, was going to end this nightmare for all.

"She would have been so proud of you, Blue. Jetta would have been so proud."

A clamor came from inside the tunnel, and a horn of announcement began blowing, declaring the arrival of Gwilim.

Jack's men notched arrows and drew their swords, preparing for another attack.

Jep shouted, "Gwilim must not be allowed to enter the Grand! If he regains his full powers, we will not be able to stop him!" He and Brennak set up as first defense, preparing to die before they allowed Gwilim to enter.

Jack took the leather strap, holding the golden bear tooth from around his neck, and placed it over Blue's head.

Blue looked down in awe at the tooth, then back at Jack. "Jack, it is your lucky medallion. Why?"

"I only give them to the best of my friends."

Blue held the tooth tightly in his hand, then bowed his head. "Friend," he whispered softly.

He reached behind his head and clicked the panel which held the memory orbs. He pulled a small blue one out and held it in his hand. It glistened with tiny tendrils of green dancing over its surface.

He handed the orb to Jack, "Please see this gets back to the Palace of Ages. It holds all the information I have collected. They will know what to do with it."

The horns sounded again, and Jack moved from the stone platform. The voices of a man and woman could be heard inside, the women pleading for the man to follow her.

"And Jack," warned Blue, "move everyone as far away as possible behind the big rocks. This is going to be.... spectacular."

Jack nodded and rushed to evacuate his people. The group ran as if their lives depended on it, not even asking about Jack's orders. For once ever Soulo did not stop to ask why.

Jack was helped up a large ledge by Owyn, Zi, and Jep, pulling and pushing. When they reached the top, he looked back for one last glimpse at the small figure on the platform.

As the figure turned to look at them, the shining face of Jetta Salto smiled back. It seemed Blue had 'become' one last time. She smiled one of her sweetest smiles, then turned her head back to the task at hand.

"Will the saints preserve me," whispered Jep.

Blue stretched out her arms and released bolts of streaming white light, reaching out and attaching to either side of the golden tunnel. The gold began to crackle and pop as the protective symbols were melted away.

Blue continued channeling the magic of the Barrier, allowing it to flow through her. She had become the receptacle for all the mingled magic, absorbing it and redirecting it back into itself.

The opening began to melt like a huge piece of golden butter, closing off the entrance for those inside. Screams of rage and pain were heard as the golden tunnel melted and covered those inside. Gwilim's shrieks of rage rattled the bones in their bodies.

Still, Blue continued to melt the tunnel. The bright light surrounded the stone platform so that even her image was lost in the glare.

Owyn cried out for Blue, "NO, BLUE!! NO!!" trying in desperation to save his friend.

Jep yelled for them to hide behind the protection of the rock ledge as the light burned the surrounding area around the platform.

The screams of those inside the tunnel became more intense. Suddenly, a flash of green lightning raced from the tunnel, rushing down the length of the Barrier wall and was lost; Gwilim's last act of defiance. The melting gold sounded like a mighty mudslide as the golden walls finally gave way, entombing everyone inside.

The demok suddenly fell to the ground, their huge bodies crumbling like rags. Soft wisps of white smoke were released from each animal, swirling and dancing, as it made their way to paradise, finally free from the grasp of Gwilim's magic.

The earth began to shake, and people pressed themselves against the walls to avoid falling rock. A rumble began, at first low, like a peal of thunder far away, then it increased until the sound was so deafening it was useless to cover their ears.

A rush of hot wind rushed over them, knocking people to the ground and pinning them there.

Jack believed they would surely all be roasted alive when it quite suddenly ended.

The silence was deafening.

They slowly stood and looked down into the valley. The earth was scorched black as far as they could see in either direction. In the center was a long swipe of shiny gold where the tunnel once stood.

"The Barrier is gone!" shouted Luka. "It's gone!"

He was right. Jack was able to look across the valley floor to the hillside on the other side. People were beginning to leave their hiding spots there, standing dumbly looking where the Barrier had once stood.

Men and women fell to their knees, weeping with joy, holding one another.

The demok, on the other side of the wall, had also died with their master. Their ugly bodies littered the valley. Jack was appalled at how many there were. Westin had been right. There was no way they could have won this war without Blue.

Gwilim's army stood confused and beaten. They lay down their arms and looked around, dazed. There was no longer an evil master to direct them. They also were free at last.

A pudgy little man and a tall, curly-headed young man stumbled their way toward the new land, holding one another up.

"Andro!" shouted Helen, "My dear Andro." Her skirts flew around her feet until she reached her husband. They stood holding one another, crying. Their son swooped up several of the children who had tried in vain to keep up with their mom.

"I take it we won?" asked Zi.

Chapter Thirty-Four

The trip back across the Grand was slow. There were so many more people now to care for.

When the wall fell, people flooded over into the new land. Jack was ill-prepared to handle so many.

He assigned men from each region to route people. Some settled in the Grand, and others were to go to the Homeland Regions. He assigned eight men in all, but in truth, could have used a hundred.

The people were all cooperative and seemed to look to Andro for leadership. Chamber's maps of settlement locations were of immense help to them.

Andro and Westin re-established their friendship right away. Westin was more than happy to go with Andro and his people to an area Chambers had found for them to settle.

It was with mixed emotions they said their goodbye to the doctor they spent so many months trying to find. In some ways, they felt they still needed to protect him. Wizard Brennak agreed to go with the new group to aid them anyway he could to get their new lives started.

The masses began to dwindle more and more as they crossed the Grand. People saw an area they loved and decided to stay there and start new lives.

Jack was in no position to argue. Every place in the Grand seemed perfect. He was tempted himself.

When they reached the valley where they had first entered through the Veil, a friendly face came running through the tall grass toward them, hooping and yelling.

"What in blazes," wondered Zi.

"It's Towak!" yelled Owyn. "I can't believe it!"

Towak jumped and tumbled, yelping like a new pup, when he spied his friends.

Jep chuckled as the little man fell and kissed his feet. "Towak, we feared you perished with the Tourashon people."

Towak's face fell as he told his story. "When you left the village of my friends, I also left to return to my village. It was my desire to have them take the Tourashon people back to live with us. Our chief is very persuasive, and I knew they would not deny him our help."

I was no more than a thousand steps away when the fire reigned down upon them. The heat was so hot it burned my hair from my head, even though I was far away. I returned to the village, but there were no survivors. Our village held mourning for our friends for thirty days. And for you! We thought you had also perished, but I see we fasted in vain for your loss!"

Jep laughed and gave the little man a hug. "Well, thanks for the thought."

They spent the night in the village with Towak and his people. They were greeted as heroes. It felt like coming home.

The village held and vigil of mourning for Jetta and Blue and sang songs of their greatness. Jack knew they would never be forgotten in this place.

The next morning, they began the journey again with small gifts from the people. They were grateful for their gifts and reluctantly left.

Everyone dreaded the trip back across the Wilds. But to Jack's surprise, the fall of the Veil and Barrier had allowed clean air and moisture to fill the area. There were even signs of green growth in places and traces of water from recent rainfall. This was a true sign of new life in their land.

If anything took their breath away, it was the sight of Baka Ton. The walls of the city were completely gone, as well as most of the little shops. Roofs were missing from almost every structure, and the walls of many buildings had collapsed.

Graves outside the crumbled walls circled the city. They had seen so much death in their battles, yet the sight of First City left them numb with sadness.

They stumbled over fallen debris in the streets as they made their way to the Council Building. It was almost impossible to walk, and often, they were forced to stop and detour in another direction.

Soulo was especially distracted, and Jack realized the man had family there.

"Soldiers of Homeland, you have crossed many lands and endured many battles to protect your land. I now dismiss you from your service to this cause and allow you to go to your families. I pray good fortune to every one of you, and blessings."

The soldiers saluted Jack for one last time and quickly made their way to their homes.

Soulo stood before Jack and his group. The big man snapped his ragged body into full attention and smote his chest in salute. He looked at each one, his eyes tearing, then gave them a big smile and hurried off to see what was left of his life.

Stevien was sitting in the garden on the old fountain. It was not much of a garden anymore, and the fountain had been cracked and broken, leaking away the water.

He smiled broadly when he saw them lumbering down the cluttered street. "Thank the Creator! I prayed you would all make it."

He reached out and grasped Jack and Jep by the shoulders, and only by their strength did he keep from collapsing.

He led them into what was left of his Palace.

"There are few rooms left somewhat undamaged, and you shall each have your own. After you have settled, join me for dinner."

The smell of decent food was something they had not enjoyed for some time, and it was intoxicating. At least some of the surrounding farms had been spared by Gwilim's army. It seems they focused their full attention to the destruction of Baka Ton and left some of the outlying farms alone, for the most part. At least there was a little food for the people to eat.

From the kitchen came a huge roasted pig and fresh baked bread, spiced apples, and sweet corn. Cider and ale topped the meal and bread pudding for dessert.

As the men crammed the food into their mouths, they heard a chuckle from the kitchen doorway and turned to see Master Lir standing there.

"Ho! My favorite customers!" he chimed. "And I'll just bet you have some dandy tales to tell me!"

Owyn grinned through his mouthful of food, "That we do, good friend, and even you won't believe some."

Jack watched his two friends pushing food into their mouths as fast as they could. At least he was blessed they were not lost in the terrible battles they had endured. He sadly thought of those who were.

He reached inside his pack and pulled out a small blue ball with bright green lights dancing across it. He laid it gently on the table between them.

Stevien stared at it for several thoughtful seconds, then asked, "What is this?"

"The cost of freedom," answered Jack, then turned to his own plate of food.

EPILOGUE

Far Moon crouched on a stout limb of the tree and watched the big man on the hill. The man looked like an angry giant. His face was hard and worn, his jaw clinched tight. His fists clasp tightly at his sides. He stood as still as a statue, staring wildly down the long expanse of the Barrier wall.

His men stirred restlessly, some holding the reins of their nervous horses while others tried to soothe the horrid man-beasts who traveled with them. They seemed as unnerved as the big man howling in agony and clawed madly at the ground.

Far had been following the group for days, curious as to their intentions in his land. His duty was to make sure his people were safe and protected from such strangers. These had traveled their lands many times, and as always, he worried to have them so close to his kinsmen.

A dull rumble began to shake the ground beneath the tree where Far hid. The forest around him began to sway, and rocks tumbled down the hillside in front of him. He threw his arms around the rough tree trunk and held on tighter.

"What a shaking." he whispered to Soli, who traveled with him. "Can you feel that?"

Soli nodded her head, her large brown eyes shining with fear. "A storm or perhaps a quake?"

Far shook his head slowly, then he noticed the mighty Barrier wall begin to tremble. The shaking became stronger causing small cracks to appear on its surface, like dried earth which had baked in the sun. A bright blue glowed between the tiny cracks, growing ever brighter, making the cracks grow ever larger.

The great wall had stood there as long as he could remember, a strong and constant part of the land, like the surrounding mountains. Far's heart beat heavy with fear. What kind of power could make the Great Wall shake as if it were a leaf on a tree?

A loud crackling sound ripped the air, then a peel of thunder followed by a sudden, furious wind. The forest's trees buckled from the gale force, and the limb on which Far and Soli were sitting suddenly broke, sending them tumbling to the ground.

Far moaned softly as he tried to pick himself up. He found the heavy tree limb had fallen on him, and he pushed with all his strength to move it off his body. He rubbed his legs to make sure there were no injuries and then remembered his friend was also under the limb somewhere.

"Soli! Are you hurt? Can you stand?" he hurried to his feet and rushed to Soli's side to see if she was injured.

"I am not hurt, Far, but what is happening?"

The wind continued to pick up strength, making it hard for them to stand without holding on to a nearby tree trunk. They noticed the tiny cracks in the Barrier wall had grown larger, spewing the blue light in all directions.

Far looked back at the hilltop and saw the big man still standing, his face glaring into the wind as if he were challenging it. Dirt, leaves, and pieces of trees blew past him, but still, the big man stood firm.

The soldiers around him fell to their knees and covered their heads. The horses and man-beasts cowered and ran for cover in the crevices of the rocks.

The mighty Barrier wall began to heave in and out as if trying to catch its breath. From off in the distance, a bright green bolt of lightning came rushing, crackling and twisting along the wall. As the bolt of light grew closer, the great Barrier wall suddenly exploded in a hail of wind and rock. The trees surrounding the area were flattened by the sheer force of the explosion.

The big man on the hill was hit by the full force of the rushing green light. It slammed into his body, thrashing him as if he were a limp coil of rope whipped about by the wind. His mouth and eyes opened wide, streaming green light high into the air. Green fire shot from his fingertips, charring men who were cowering nearby. Even the boulders surrounding him melted into hot magma when the green fire touched them.

His men screamed and clamored for safety, fearing the same fate, while the fearsome man-beasts wrenched in pain, howled once, and then fell dead.

As the wind finally began to die down, the ruins of the Great Wall were heaped into crumpled-like piles of ash as far as the eye could see. The Barrier was gone! How could this be! He and Soli stared at each other in disbelief.

Far scrambled over the felled trees to see what was happening to the big man on the hill.

The man's chest was heaving in and out like a mighty furnace. His fists were clenched so tight that blood dripped to the scorched earth.

"FATHER, YOU WILL BE AVENGED!" screamed Voxx into the dying wind.

***

The End of BURDEN OF TRUTH

About the Author

Karen Lockridge has always believed the best stories aren't just about heroes—they're about the choices that define them. Raised in rural Texas, she spent her childhood getting lost in the pages of classic adventures, drawn to characters who struggled with right and wrong, friendship and sacrifice. From the wilds of Middle-earth to the depths of Foundation's galaxy, she found inspiration in tales of resilience and determination.

Her Distant Lands trilogy reflects that same spirit. In Burden of Truth, the second book of the series, the battle for survival grows more treacherous, and the weight of destiny rests heavier on those who dare to fight for their world. It's a story of loyalty, deception, and the fine line between hope and despair—crafted by an author who understands that the best adventures aren't just about where you go, but who you become along the way.

For queries and staying up-to-date with Karen,
visit her website by scanning the QR code below:

www.ingramcontent.com/pod-product-compliance
Lightning Source LLC
Chambersburg PA
CBHW060303310726
48976CB00007B/2187